tun

jude

tumbling jude

NICOLA LINDSAY

POOLBEG

Published 2004
Poolbeg Press Ltd.
123 Grange Hill, Baldoyle,
Dublin 13, Ireland
Email: poolbeg@poolbeg.com

13 5 7 9 10 8 6 4 2

A catalogue record for this book is available from the British Library.

ISBN 1-84223-181-2

Typeset by Patricia Hope in Goudy 11/15
Printed by
Cox & Wyman
Reading Berkshire

www.poolbeg.com

About the Author

Nicola Lindsay started writing seriously when she was in her fifties. Her published work includes a book of poetry, a children's story, magazine and newspaper articles, and novels. Some of her radio scripts and monologues have been broadcast and she has written and acted in revue. *Tumbling Jude* is her fourth novel. Formerly living in Wicklow, she now lives in County Kildare.

Also by Nicola Lindsay

Diving Through Clouds
A Place for Unicorns
Eden Fading

Acknowledgements

A big thank you to all at Poolbeg for their hard work and support.

Also to the poet, Clemency Emmet, for her patience and much valued friendship.

For my husband, Charles,
who was blessed in having
a very special father

Chapter One

She'd fled the house after breakfast, not able to take the atmosphere of critical gloom emanating from her mother-in-law a moment longer. Jude knew that hiding would not solve any problems but at least it would give her time to take a few deep breaths and try and regain her composure – and possibly stop her from plunging the bread knife into Geoffrey's mother's skinny torso.

It wasn't just Patricia Larchet who was getting to her. Jude's daughter Flora with her violent mood swings, and Oscar her son, who was so laid-back and relaxed Jude sometimes feared he might just start to unravel at the seams – they too were more than she could cope with just now with their individual foibles and expectations. In the past, she had more or less managed to aquaplane over and around most domestic dramas, emerging relatively undented. These days, the slightest thing induced an alarming sensation of her being in free fall – especially where her husband Geoffrey was concerned.

And then, there was her father . . .

* * *

Jude looked down at her bare feet in surprise. When had she taken off her shoes? She must have been daydreaming again. I've been doing rather a lot of that in the past few weeks, she thought. I really will have to pull myself together. Difficult though the other members of the family might be at the moment, she hadn't exactly been a little ray of sun herself. She sat on the low stone wall that overlooked the sea and held her legs straight out in front of her, surveying them absent-mindedly. They weren't bad really although her toenails needed cutting. There was a bruise and a fresh graze on the side of her left foot. When had *that* happened? she wondered briefly. She turned them to the left and then the right. Her feet were tanned, matching her brown hands, emerging bonily from frayed denim shirtsleeves. Wiggling her toes, Jude thought that they were possibly one of the least attractive parts of a person's body. She'd let herself go over the past couple of weeks and the experience had been a pleasant one, only faintly tinged by guilt. Good not to care if her eyebrows had started to meet like an untrimmed hedge over the bridge of her nose. No make-up, no bright lights, no impossible deadlines. That part had been wonderful.

If only she could have begun to sort out the chaos in her mind.

Approaching footsteps made her glance over her shoulder. A middle-aged couple strolled along the path behind her, arms comfortably linked. The woman gave her a curious look, pausing in mid-conversation, catching Jude's eye and smiling slightly before turning away. If she knew who Jude was, she didn't do anything about it. There was no surreptitious nudge in her companion's ribcage, no not-so-*sotto-voce* hiss out of the side of the mouth. That had started to happen when Jude's face began to be more familiar to the telly-watching public after her years spent in radio. But now, there was just that passing flicker of recognition. She watched them as they descended the curving path down to the beach below. They looked nice. Content to be walking together; leisurely, intimate, hip touching hip. Like young lovers, she thought, as the sound of their voices floated back to where she sat on the warm stone wall with the long grass brushing the soles of her bare feet. She wondered how old they were. Early sixties? How lovely to reach that age and still want to walk closely enough to touch your partner of years and years. *Ah, yes,* said a cynical little voice in her head, *but what if they've only just met and are being unfaithful to their respective partners of years and years?* Beat it! said Jude to the voice. I liked the first version better.

Every now and then, the sound of the bees' buzzing would increase in volume, changing key as they struggled to fit inside the dusty pink foxgloves bordering the path. She listened with pleasure to the mix of noises. She could hear the gravelly sighing made by small waves as they broke and then regrouped, ready for their next watery assault at the water's edge. The barely heard piping of unseen larks filled the air above her head and the sound of a small dog's staccato barks as it excitedly barrelled a ball along the sand.

Jude shut her eyes and lifted her face to the sun, breathing in the smell of salt seaweed. How good it was to be warm, to feel the heat soak into her skin, like having your face caressed by invisible hands. The weather in Wexford had been extraordinarily un-Irish. A whole fortnight of waking to hazy warm dawns and going for early morning swims in a cool sea that was flooded with a red-gold path of light leading to the rising sun. Whole days of lying hidden in the dunes gazing up at an unclouded blue sky or floating, arms and legs outstretched, rocked on the gently undulating water. How good too, not to be clock-watching all the time. Jude had taken off her wristwatch two weeks ago and there wasn't so much as a strap-mark to show she'd ever worn one now. With eyes still closed, she inhaled deeply. There was a smell of cooking. Someone must be having a barbecue on the beach, perhaps round the other side of the rocks at one end. She realised that she felt hungry but was just too sleepy to actually get up and do anything about it. And she was putting off the moment of going back to the house and having to face Geoffrey, the children and, above all, Geoffrey's mother.

When she'd got back from Wexford the night before, they'd all seemed to assume that she would have come to her senses and would be apologetic for having disrupted their lives. Jude hadn't told them that, in fact, she was going away again – for how long she didn't know. When she'd tried to explain how she felt to Geoffrey before breakfast this morning he had first been puzzled and then angry.

Jude opened her eyes and looked down at the wall beside her, searching for signs of a bag. There didn't seem to be one. She must have left it back at the house. She

4

shifted her weight, digging a hand into the pocket of her skirt. It only contained a handkerchief and the key to the front door. What the hell! It was too nice here to move just yet. She smiled ruefully to herself. The descent from reasonably tidy and organised to almost total disorder had really happened with appalling ease!

Climbing carefully down from the wall, she discovered her sandals, half hidden in the greenery. She lay down amongst the grass and wild flowers on a narrow ledge facing the sea so that she was invisible from the path above.

* * *

Angry voices woke her a little while later. The sun, lower now, hovered above the horizon but it still felt pleasantly warm on Jude's legs and face. She raised herself onto one elbow and squinted down to the water's edge. The small beach below her was almost empty.

"Why can't you be more supportive?"

The voice was male.

"I spend my whole bloody life being supportive. I'm knackered being supportive. Why can't *you* support *me* for a change, Sean?" retorted a woman. A slight quaver in her voice spoke of unshed tears.

There was silence for a few seconds. When the man next spoke, he sounded more distant.

"Jesus, woman! I don't know what's got into you these past few months. I work all the hours God sends, we live in a great house, the children are doing well at school. What more do you want?"

The woman sounded more stolidly defiant when she answered him this time.

"You wouldn't understand or even listen if I tried to tell you. You've decided everything's terrific – apart from me that is."

Jude couldn't catch the man's words. From their faintness, it appeared that he had walked ahead, not wanting to waste any more time on a futile argument.

She sat up, leaning against the wall and frowning. Eavesdropping on their unwelcome disagreement had brought back recent memories: snatches of ill-tempered conversations, banged doors and car tyres spraying gravel onto the flower beds as Geoffrey drove out of the gate, looking furious.

He had seemed so even-tempered when they first got married. But then, so had she probably. It just showed how twenty-odd years of living together and two children could damage your equilibrium.

Jude banged her fist against her forehead. She'd promised herself that she wouldn't do this. What was the point of going away in the first place if she hadn't learned something, arrived at some sort of decision about the direction she wanted her life to take? She had vowed not to sit on her backside and think negative thoughts. What was the use in mulling over all the things that had made her flee in the first place? But that man *had* sounded rather like Geoffrey on a bad day. Jude just hoped she had never sounded quite as miserably pissed-off as the man's wife had a few minutes earlier.

She'd always liked to think of herself as a calm and reasonably well-balanced sort of person. That is, until she'd upped and left them all to it, having first hurled the canteen of Geoffrey's mother's cutlery at her startled husband. At the time, his expression of panic, quickly followed by outrage, had made her want to laugh. Now she just felt guilty at such a ridiculously out-of-control act.

The argument that had sparked her action had been so trivial. Geoffrey's mother had been the catalyst – as was so often the case. A chance remark made by Jude, misinterpretation by the other woman, ill-advised intervention by Geoffrey, and Jude had suddenly had enough. The really infuriating thing from her point of view was that her irrational behaviour had given yet more ammunition to her mother-in-law.

The question that had refused to go away, that she'd woken up thinking about in the middle of the night on countless nights, picked away inside her skull like a persistent woodpecker. Had she been right to walk out – even if it had only been for a couple of weeks? Had her leaving them to cope without her for a while been justified? Had it really been so bad – or had she just foolishly overreacted? Was she, as her daughter Flora, with all the wisdom of her twenty-one years, had spat out, totally selfish? It seemed that Flora's father was in complete agreement with his daughter on that one. Perhaps her leaving had ironically had some sort of a harmonising effect. It was the first time the two of them had been in agreement about anything in years, she reflected ruefully afterwards. Her nineteen-year-old son, Oscar, had been more ambivalent, not wanting to take sides.

"If you feel a break would be good for you, Mum, then go for it," he'd said.

But she knew that he wasn't happy with the idea of her going off, leaving them to fend for themselves.

"It's only for a couple of weeks, for God's sake. It's not as if you're small children. You are quite capable of looking after yourselves and Catriona comes in a couple of times a week," Jude said.

"Don't worry, Mum. We'll manage OK," replied her son with a smile.

He hadn't sounded at all sure that he believed that.

Geoffrey, on the other hand, hadn't sounded one bit ambivalent.

"What do you mean, 'you need a break'? You can't just go walkabout because you feel your life is unsatisfactory. What about your job? I know you're between series but they won't be too impressed. You could find yourself in difficulties if you treat them so offhandedly."

Jude noticed that her husband hadn't sounded worried about her. If anything, he appeared more irritated than worried. It crossed her mind that perhaps he was really quite relieved that she was going. He wouldn't have to explain his increasingly long absences after work and sometimes at weekends from the family home.

"Where will you be and how long are you planning to put your life on hold?" he had asked.

"Fidelma's caravan at Silver Strand. As for how long I'll be there – I don't know."

"So, you're just going to take off and I've got to patiently wait until you feel like coming home again?"

Put like that, Jude silently agreed that it did sound somewhat unreasonable.

"I'm really sorry, Geoff, but I've been trying hard to hide the fact that I've felt so down for months. I haven't been sleeping properly. I don't like the new job. It's only just over a year since Mum died and I'm missing her dreadfully. I –"

"Why don't you go to the bloody GP and get an anti-depressant or a sleeping pill like everybody else does when they feel like that?"

"Because it's not just the job, the feeling of marking time – and not being valued," she'd snapped back.

"Well, what else is there?"

She took a deep breath.

"I want to try and find my father."

This was the point at which Geoffrey had looked at her in amazement.

"Your father! Hang on a moment! Are we talking about the man who was unfaithful to your mother from the honeymoon on, the bloke who was responsible for one of his mistresses committing suicide, the man who never paid one penny towards your education, the father you never remember seeing when you were a child? We *are* talking about the man who walked out of your life when you were four years old and who went on trying to wheedle money out of your mother when he'd made a hames of a second marriage?"

* * *

She realised now that it had all come to a head three months earlier, around the time of Flora's twenty-first birthday at the start of June. It was then that Jude started to feel that she was not in control of her life any more.

"Why can't I have it in Temple Bar like Jessica?" For the first time in weeks Flora had looked animated. "Oh, Mum, it was fantastic! The band, the laser show, the food and tequila flowing like –"

"I know! Tequila flowing like no one had to get up the following morning to go to work and like her dad had an inexhaustible amount of money to pay for it all," countered Jude quietly, with a smile. "But *we* don't have unlimited funds and I don't see why you can't have a party at home. You don't have to worry! Your father and I will disappear for the evening and leave you all to it, unmonitored and uncluttered by geriatric parents."

"And what about Gran? Where's *she* going to hike off to for the evening, Mum? You know what a snoop she is. She'll refuse to go anywhere. She'll just stick around, complaining that the music's too loud, that my clothes are outrageous and I'll catch a chill, that people keep banging doors instead of shutting them nice and gently and what will the fu . . . neighbours think?"

Jude gave her one of her looks. It was the sort of look that Oscar referred to as 'silent but deadly'.

The fact was that Flora was right. Jude had to admit to herself that Geoffrey's mother did pose a problem. The woman *was* a snoop and she thrived on controversy. Not outside the house, where she had perfected the art of behaving like a frail old lady who was rather badly treated by her family, especially Jude, but who made the best of things and who didn't like to complain. Behind her back, Flora and Oscar jeered at the way Mrs Larchet senior would say primly, "I don't like to complain . . ." The "but" was waited for with barely suppressed amusement. As Flora once remarked with a giggle, "Pity they don't have complaining as a sport in the Olympics. Gran could moan for Ireland."

"Horrible girl," Jude had replied, laughing, whilst secretly agreeing with her opinionated daughter.

Three years earlier, Geoffrey had organised, with Jude's reluctant agreement, to have a granny flat built adjoining the kitchen so that his mother could live out her final years in comfort with her one and only son close to hand. Mrs Larchet hadn't seemed particularly grateful – which came as no surprise to her daughter-in-law. It wasn't just the complaining that 'life with Gran' had inflicted on Jude that she found irritating. It was the presence of Plunkett, the woman's Irish setter who regularly dug up the garden looking for imaginary bones, leaving craters the size made by showers of not-so-small asteroids that added considerably to the strain of having Gran constantly around.

"That dog's a complete moron," Jude remarked to Geoffrey, a few weeks after the animal's arrival, as she surveyed the sad remains of half-chewed daffodil bulbs strewn over the lawn.

But Geoffrey didn't want to get into a discussion over his mother's dog.

"Come on, Jude! Plunkett's a very handsome beast. He just gets bored, that's all."

His wife couldn't help noticing that it never seemed to occur to him that the reason the dog was bored was that he had nothing to do. The only time he was taken for a walk was when Jude managed to squeeze in a dash down to the beach to give him a run – between work, producing meals and coping with the frequent demands for attention Flora and Oscar made. All that and Geoffrey's mother.

When she had suggested that, if Patricia Larchet was not up to walking the dog herself and Oscar and Flora weren't interested in making the time to do it, perhaps they should try and find a good home for him, her husband had looked at her in surprise.

"Do you know how mean that sounded? Why should you begrudge an elderly woman the right to have a dog for company?"

She'd bitten back the retort that sprang to her lips, wondering if he were right. Perhaps as she herself grew older, she was becoming mean-spirited. When she next looked out of the window, just in time to see Plunkett thoughtfully munching his way through one of the legs of the garden seat, Jude decided that no, she was not mean-spirited – just a little 'jaded with life', as her mother used to say with a wry smile.

Dead for fourteen months now. How she missed her! She'd been the perfect antidote to Patricia Larchet – everything that the woman was not: interested and interesting, involved, animated and generous. And it wasn't just those qualities that she missed so much. Jude would have given anything to hug her mother again, to breathe in the *Samsara* she wore in the last few years of her life. She wanted to rest her face against the amazingly soft skin of her mother's cheek – just for a few seconds – to hold and be held. Like a small child really. Jude had wondered if most people, if they were honest, felt the same about their mothers too – no matter that they were middle-aged themselves. She would catch herself enviously watching other women accompanying their mothers on shopping expeditions or chatting to them as they sauntered along the beach.

After some upsetting incident involving Patricia Larchet, Jude could still hear her mother saying, "Darling, ignore the woman. Come and meet me in town after work and we'll go and see a soppy film and then buy ourselves a large helping of fish and chips afterwards in that little place behind The Lord Edward."

Jude had felt cheerful and capable after a session with her mother. She'd always had the ability to make her daughter feel settled when she'd been frazzled and fed up. It was a great gift.

"I know I shouldn't mind her. I really do. One day I'll be old myself but she just brings out the worst in me," Jude had admitted one day to Fidelma, friend and confidante of many years, over a hastily snatched lunch in the RTVI canteen. "She puts on this ladylike act when there's anyone else around, as if her background were too refined for words. I know she grew up in a semi-det in Luton before she got her teeth into poor Geoffrey's dad and they moved to Rathgar. No wonder he keeled over ten years ago. He knew when he was dead he wouldn't have to pretend any more. The way she carries on! She's the one they made the original joke about – you know, the one about what is a crèche? – a car accident in Rathgar. It makes me want to blow raspberries and fart in front of her bridge-playing friends. Just to see if I can get a spontaneous reaction out of the old bat."

Fidelma had looked amused.

"You should try it some day! It probably wouldn't make her change her ways but it might make you feel good! From what I've seen of her, that sort of woman doesn't change for the better. Have you noticed that as people grow older, they seem to divide into two kinds? There's the person whose nice qualities grow more marked and then there's the sort whose not-so-pleasant characteristics become more and more noticeable. I fear your ma-in-law belongs to the latter category."

13

"Well, I resent her having the ability to make *me* into a not-nice person because of the way she is." Jude stared across the top of her coffee cup at her friend. "Do you know, I sometimes lie awake at night and wonder what life would be like if she got run over by a bus. That's not very nice, is it?"

"No!" replied Fidelma laughing. "But, from what you've told me about her antics, quite understandable. You could always put laburnum seeds into her favourite cake next time you're baking."

"You know perfectly well that I've never baked anything since we were at school and I made that dreadful sponge thing that went in the oven ten centimetres high and emerged some time later, still ten centimetres high but slightly rubberised. I might be able to give her a bad dose of indigestion but I don't think I could kill her off with my baking, I'm afraid. No, I'll just have to try and carry on with my life and not let her get to me. It's just been increasingly difficult to do that over the past few months."

Fidelma looked at her friend, head slightly tilted. She'd been noticing lately that Jude's already pale complexion had been looking paler and there were dark circles under her large blue eyes. The usually marvellously glossy red hair that Jude had a habit of wearing loose had recently been shoved into a careless twist on the back of her head. The thing that was most marked about her was how the ready smile of mouth and eyes seemed to be less easily given these days.

"Are you all right, Jude?" she asked quietly.

Just at that moment, a tall, untidy man dumped a loaded tray down on the table beside them, making them both jump. Fidelma recognised him as one of the producers with whom Jude had worked and whom she'd said she liked.

"Hi, girls! Is this a private conversation or can a humble bloke join in?"

Jude laughed.

"You're much too good at your job, Alan Carruth, to be humble." She introduced him to Fidelma.

He shook hands and smiled at Jude's friend.

"I've seen you around. You've just moved to the *Good Morning, Ireland* office haven't you?"

"Yes, I have."

Fidelma sounded unenthusiastic.

Jude added, "All part of the recent hiring, firing and sidelining operation taking place at the moment with the new management, I'm afraid. None of us is safe. It doesn't seem to matter how well you do your job or how much the result is enjoyed by the public – it's almost as though the bods on high see it as a challenge. Good Lord! The ratings are up. If she's making a success of that it must be too easy. We'll take her off that and give her something completely different to get her teeth into." She swallowed a mouthful of orange juice. "Sorry, but I'm getting tired of having to be discreet and *appropriate* all the time."

Fidelma was surprised at the sudden bitterness in Jude's voice. She'd known that her friend's previous job in the Radio Centre had suited her perfectly and she also knew how much Jude had resisted being moved from the programme: a programme which she'd fronted, interviewing interesting and less well-known people with interesting occupations but not glamorous lives. 'Real people', was how Jude had described them. But Jude could hardly complain that she'd been sidelined. The new job in the television centre was definitely a step further up the ladder – unlike Fidelma's own situation. She knew perfectly well that, on the other hand, she herself had most definitely been sidelined and was hanging on to her place in RTVI by the skin of her teeth.

"Come on, Jude!" she coaxed. "You can't say that having your own current affairs slot on a Friday night is something to moan about. You do it brilliantly."

"She does. I've heard a lot of compliments about your approach, Jude," said Alan. He looked at her, fork halfway to mouth. "They're calling you 'the thinking man's crumpet'. Don't knock it, girl! There are half a dozen I could name who would kill to be in your shoes."

"And might just succeed." Jude leaned towards him, her long-fingered hands pressing down on the tabletop. "Yes, I know but when I did the radio programme, I had more say in it and I was a voice – not a recognisable face on the telly. I liked that. I never wanted to be centre-stage. The important element about the interviews was the people being interviewed. I don't think telly suits me, that's all. I feel I have to put on an act and that I'm not being me while I project this snappy, nothing-gets-past-me, on-top-of-it-all image. I'm sick to death of interviewing crooked politicians who never give a straight answer to a question and publicity-hungry second-rate writers and ghastly would-be pop stars. And I most certainly don't want to be pointed at in the street."

It had happened again that morning when she stopped at the local newsagent's to buy a paper. As she'd come out of the shop, two women walked past, staring at her as if she'd forgotten to put on her clothes. As they went by, one woman turned to the other and said in a loud voice, "They never look as good as they do on the box, do they? It must be all that make-up they plaster themselves with." OK! Nothing there that should have upset her but since starting the new job six weeks earlier, Jude was discovering that she was a more private person than she'd previously realised.

Chapter Two

Flora had eventually given in and her twenty-first birthday bash was held in her parents' house. The post mortem the following morning was not very enlightening from her mother's point of view.

"Did you enjoy yourself?"

"Yeah, it was OK, I suppose." A pause, followed by a muttered, "Thanks, Mum."

At least she'd managed a 'thanks'. That was something – even if it was rather unenthusiastic!

"Only just OK? What about the food? Did they like the West African curry?"

"Yeah."

It wasn't just her mother-in-law that made Jude sometimes want to scream with frustration. She felt like reaching over and stuffing ice cubes down the back of her daughter's neck – if only to get a bit of animated reaction out of her. But she could see that Flora was a little the worse for wear. Her dark hair hung down over her eyes in limp strands. She was picking uninterestedly at the remains of last night's fruit salad. Jude could smell the rum from where she sat. An illicit addition of Oscar's more than likely.

She let out an involuntary sigh. If only Flora would be a little more forthcoming. After all, it was Jude who had stayed up half the night before the party preparing the food. Flora had to work at some project that simply *had* to be in to her tutor by the next day. Oscar, when asked if he could help, moved swiftly towards the door, scooping up his jacket as he went.

"Sorry, Ma! I've got a night out with the lads organised." Seeing his mother's look of frustration he added, "It's been arranged for weeks. I can hardly let them down at the last minute, can I? Anyway, this is all for Flo's benefit. She's the one to ask."

"I already have," said Jude.

"You're too soft, Mum. That's your trouble."

"I wonder what your reaction would be if I got tough all of a sudden?"

But he was gone, slamming the front door behind him so that Geoffrey's mother, who had just come into the kitchen to see what sort of a strange meal Jude was making for Flora's party, had jumped, winced and clutched her hand to the area over her heart. She had been hinting recently that the new pain in her chest was just the beginning of the end. Even Geoffrey hadn't taken much notice of that.

"Whatever is that strange smell, Judith?"

She never called her daughter-in-law Jude like everyone

19

else. She said that she thought it was vulgar to shorten people's names.

"Presumably your mother and father gave a lot of thought to what they would call you. I'm sure they would have been upset to hear that you would never be known by your given name," she'd said to Jude early on in their acquaintance.

Jude had smiled brightly and replied, "Oh, no, I don't think so. In fact it was my *mother* who first called me Tumbling Jude when I was small."

She knew that the other woman was perfectly aware that Jude hated any reference to her absent father – that she only ever mentioned her mother who had been the one true parent as far as she was concerned. It was she who'd called her Tumbling Jude because of the constant falling over when she was a small child. The world was full of interesting things that had to be investigated and from the start Jude had done just that – with enthusiasm. As a result she had spent months of her young life covered in cuts and bruises. Even now, Jude occasionally bumped into things or dropped plates because she was occupied with something other than just the routine clutter of life. Jude said it was because she was distracted by ideas. Geoffrey said that it was because she was just clumsy. But the curiosity she'd had as a child, and that had been nurtured by her mother, had never left her. Colleagues at work would sometimes tease her for daydreaming when, in fact, what Jude had been doing was trying to work out the background to why someone had just said what they had or to puzzle out why a thing was the way it was.

"Tumbling Jude!" Geoffrey's mother raised her eyes to

heaven with an expression of 'what else would you expect from someone brought up in Bray?'.

Her daughter-in-law had known right from the start that the chemistry between herself and Mrs Larchet was volatile and that they would never really like each other. Added to the classic scenario of vulnerable widow's only son being seduced by scheming vamp was the fact that Jude had always worked outside the home, juggling baby-sitters when Flora and Oscar were small in a manner that Mrs Larchet found scandalous.

When she'd suggested to Jude that perhaps it was not the best way of doing things, Jude told her gently and firmly that she was not chucking in her job and that she was quite able to manage, thank you. Her mother-in-law had not liked her tone one bit.

Now, Patricia Larchet lifted the lid off the large saucepan simmering on the Aga and peered doubtfully at the contents.

"This has a very strange smell."

"It's groundnut stew. You know, peanuts. Flora asked me if I would do a West African main course for tomorrow night," replied Jude evenly.

"I suppose you realise that some people are allergic to peanuts?" The woman's eyes gleamed. "They can die within a few hours."

Her tone implied that Jude's cooking could only lead to some sort of appalling disaster and her mother-in-law couldn't wait to say: 'I told you so!'

"Then I shall make sure that everyone is warned that there are peanuts in the stew and for anyone who is allergic, there is always the *coq au vin*."

Jude concentrated on chopping vegetables.

"And what are *those?*"

Geoffrey's mother pointed with distaste towards the food at the far end of the table. She made it sound as though she were referring to a pile of sheep's eyes or the unmentionable parts of some sacrificial animal, slaughtered specifically for the occasion.

"That's yam and that's okra – otherwise known as ladies' fingers. The stuff in the other dish is a special Nigerian rice dish called Jollof rice. It's delicious. You should try some. We used to eat it with our fingers when I was out there."

Jude had worked during the holidays for an aid agency when she'd been a student at Trinity. She'd fallen in love with Africa in just a few short weeks and had always meant to go back one day to visit the Nigerian friends she'd made.

Mrs Larchet looked at her in horror.

"Didn't the poor things have knives and forks?"

"Of course they did! It's just nice to eat with your fingers sometimes. It makes it more fun and when you're sitting on a beach you only have to wash your hands in the sea after eating rather than deal with a whole lot of messy cutlery. It's a splendid idea. We should do it here and save on the dishwasher," laughed Jude, knowing perfectly well that she was winding the woman up.

Mrs Larchet sniffed one of her sniffs.

"Well, just so as you know that this awful smell is coming through to my end of the house."

"I'll give you the spray from the loo then and you can squirt it around a bit, if you like."

"No, thank you very much. That won't be necessary, Judith."

Geoffrey's mother made for the back door with a martyred expression and another tale to tell her friend Joan Ryan in the house on the corner next time they met.

* * *

On the morning after the party, unsatisfactory breakfast over, Jude collected her things for work. Then she stood at the bottom of the stairs and called out to Flora, who had retired back to her bedroom a few minutes earlier, clutching yet another cup of coffee and a packet of Disprin.

"Please do a little clearing up before Catriona comes, Flo."

There was no response. She bloody well heard me. I know she did, thought Jude as she shut the door behind her. There was no point in 'grinding on', as her two offspring called being reminded about promises not kept and domestic tasks undone. Thank God for Catriona! She had come into their lives a couple of years earlier, the daughter of the woman who worked in the local newsagent's. Just a few years older than Flora, she was plump, energetic and above all – reliable. At first, Jude couldn't understand why the girl seemed content to do housework for her.

"Wouldn't you like to get a more interesting job?" she'd asked shortly after Catriona started to work for the Larchets.

"Jaysus! No! I like it here," she'd replied in her strong Dublin accent. "Anyway, when Mick and me get married, I won't need a job. We're going to have a clatter of kids and I'm going to be up to me eyes mindin' them. So, what's the point in learning to type or whatever and spending me time travellin' backwards and forwards to some poxy job in

Dublin and using all me money on the fares, like? I'd be driven demented – an' I'd be permanently broke."

There was no arguing with her and Jude didn't try. She was just thankful to have Catriona's cheerful help.

As she started the car, she couldn't help wishing that Flora had more of Catriona's good-natured pragmatism. It was a shame in a way that her daughter had chosen to do drama. In Jude's eyes, she was quite dramatic and neurotic enough without nurturing her weak points by surrounding herself with, as far as her mother could make out, a crowd of young ones who were not exactly prime candidates for serious, responsible adulthood. She tentatively backed out of the narrow driveway. No, hang on a moment. That wasn't fair. Hadn't Jude herself been a wild, unmanageable child and teenager? At least Flora had never been expelled from school like her mother had. And anyway, she liked a lot of Flora's friends – even if they did appear a little over the top sometimes. She smiled to herself, thinking of some of the clothes worn at the birthday party the night before. One or two of the girls had been wearing garments that obviously cost a lot of money but that hardly covered the wearer. Bare midriffs, pussy-pelmet skirts and plunging necklines. No wonder tender areas got singed by cigarette ends sometimes when they were dancing! God! If I'm not careful, I'll end up like Gran, wittering on about unsuitable clothing, Jude warned herself.

It was funny though, the way the boys seemed bent on going to the other extreme – with trousers that sagged over their shoes, with the crotches down to their knees. Some of them were so well camouflaged, it was difficult to tell what body-shape lurked under the voluminous clothing.

As she edged out into the traffic, Jude found herself wondering what exactly it was Flora and Oscar expected from life. What were their priorities? What, if anything, did they want to contribute? Take Oscar. Six A's in his Leaving – a year ago – after hardly any studying. What had he done in these last twelve months? He'd stayed firmly put in the family home, expecting to be fed and clothed and his opinions listened to when he should have been dying to move out and start climbing the first steps of an interesting-career ladder. When Geoffrey had suggested he find some sort of stopgap work while he made up his mind about what it was he really wanted to do, the boy had looked at his father in amazement.

"Surely it's not too much to ask to stay here for a while – until I know what I want to do?"

"Fine!" replied Geoffrey dryly. "Stay until you are sure but in the meantime get some sort of a job so that you can pay a little bit towards your keep."

"Ah, come on, Dad!" Oscar made a face. "It's not as though you and Mum are stony broke. You're both raking it in."

"Whatever money your mother and I make has got nothing to do with it. It's a matter of principle. You shouldn't want to be mollycoddled like a baby."

Stopping at the traffic-lights, Jude nearly laughed out loud, remembering how stuffy Geoffrey had sounded and the comic look of incomprehension on Oscar's face. When he'd left the room, she'd turned to her husband.

"Oh, dear," she said, "perhaps that was a little unwise, Geoff. He just hasn't got himself sorted out yet. He'll get there in the end. Your going on at him won't make any difference. He doesn't look at things the way we do. Now he'll shut himself away, feeling all offended and misunderstood, and not come out of his room for the rest of the day."

"Only if you let him. Ignore his sulks and he'll soon stop. He's like Flora. Just likes to have an audience."

But he wasn't like Flora, Jude thought to herself. Not at all. There was a gentleness in Oscar that was missing in his sister. Although she could sometimes be entertaining and funny, Flora was really quite tough, more streetwise. She was certainly more manipulative and was more likely to shout at you than to show affection. Jude couldn't remember the last time she'd allowed her mother to give her a hug. Whereas Oscar frequently delivered spontaneous, rather clumsy embraces that nearly knocked her off her feet. And he had, to give him his due, started work in the local supermarket a few days after the conversation with his father.

The new regime lasted for three fraught weeks with Jude having to wake him several times every morning to make sure he got out of bed in time to go to work. When he finally packed it in, saying that the pay was below the minimum wage and that he absolutely refused to be patronised any more by silly women running him down with their shopping trolleys or to be bossed about by young ones who were power-hungry and ruthless with mad plans of becoming area managers before they hit twenty-five, she wasn't all that surprised. In fact, Jude had been secretly relieved. He had been impossible for almost all of the three weeks, changing from lazily sunny to monosyllabic and worried-looking. Geoffrey was disappointed.

"I thought he'd have a little more sticking power," he confided in Jude that night in bed.

"Give him time. He doesn't know what he wants at the moment. It sounded deadly dreary anyway. I don't think you would have liked it much either at his age."

"I knew what I wanted to do by the time I was *fifteen*. He's already nineteen."

"Well, lucky you!"

Jude hated it when he sounded smug. He never used to. When they first met at university Geoffrey had seemed every bit as full of self-doubt as she was. The fact that he had an all-consuming passion for the theatre and television and knew that one day he would direct hadn't stopped him swerving from being driven and highly motivated one day to being deeply despondent the next. They had propped each other up, giving encouragement and praise and judicious criticism as and when required.

It suddenly hit her that they hadn't laughed, really laughed, together for a long time. When had the magic gone out of the relationship? It seemed to Jude that it had been a long, insidious process, making it impossible to mark the beginning of the decline of passion. She remembered how her heart used to skip a beat when she glimpsed him unexpectedly in the street. These days, the only thing that made that organ miss a beat was when Plunkett destroyed yet another carefully planted shrub, or shat on the front path. Or when her mother-in-law made one of her jibes in front of Geoffrey along the lines of, 'how sad it was these days that a poor, overworked man couldn't expect to come home to a good hot dinner, a blazing fire and someone who would welcome him with open arms and listen raptly while he detailed his fraught day at the office/factory/boardroom – or studios'.

"And with his slippers all toasty warm, no doubt," Jude had added unwisely one day.

To which Patricia Larchet had replied tartly, "And what would be so terrible about that?"

You couldn't win with that one. There seemed to be nothing that would bridge the generation gap. As she so often found herself doing as she drove, Jude wondered if they would ever achieve a meeting of minds on anything. Her own mother had been seventy-two when she died and they had never had a problem communicating or enjoying each other's company. Must be genetic and environmental. Perhaps Mrs Larchet's childhood had been hideously unhappy.

Jude glanced at her watch. She would be late if the bloody traffic didn't get a move on. The Dublin traffic jams seemed to get more dreadful by the week. There was talk of a tunnel, a metro and even a tram service. She could just imagine the hell on earth that would be for the long-suffering inhabitants of the almost permanently log-jammed capital. Perhaps she should buy a bike. That might be a good idea as long as she wore a crash helmet. She smiled to herself. Most inelegant. It would *really* annoy Geoffrey's mother too! The trouble is it would really annoy Bettina in make-up if she arrived into the studio with a pink nose and her hair squashed as flat as a pancake before the show.

As she waited, drumming her fingers on the steering wheel, Jude felt profoundly depressed. It wasn't just because of the unwanted career move or the fact that she couldn't seem to really relate to Flora and Oscar – and especially not to Geoffrey these days. She didn't even think it was because of the problems with Geoffrey's mother or the woman's lunatic dog. In a strange way, she felt that although she still loved her children and husband, she had grown almost detached. How many women felt like that? Was she unnatural? Was it a method of self-protection, of getting by without losing it completely? These days she felt more interest and sympathy in the local bag lady or the worn-out-looking young traveller mum who lived in one of the caravans at the end of the lane by the railway. Jude wondered briefly if it would do Oscar and Flora good to get involved in something like the Simon community. At least night-time soup kitchens would suit Oscar's body-clock better than him having to get up at a reasonable hour in the mornings. On the other hand, Flora in a bad mood might well convince people that sleeping rough wasn't such a great idea after all. Even Jude found her daughter a little daunting from time to time. She wondered how, when both children had been given equal amounts of love and attention when they were young, Flora could be so very different from her brother. Where did all that aggression come from?

A prolonged blast on a car horn made her jump. The traffic in front had moved on, leaving a large gap. Another loud honk. All right! I hear you, she muttered as she changed gear. Picking up speed, she looked in the rear-view mirror at the grim-faced woman in the large car on her tail. If I brake hard now she'll never stop in time. What is her problem? Worried that she won't reach the next traffic jam fast enough? Idiot woman!

It was June, the sun was shining and yet, on that warm bright morning after her daughter's twenty-first birthday, and for the first time in her life, Jude's appetite to go on functioning as she had in the past – to keep on doing all that needed to be done, to do the things that were expected of her – seemed to drain away, leaving her feeling strangely deflated and miserable.

Chapter Three

Now, three months later, when Jude finally summoned up the strength of mind to leave the deserted beach and go home, nobody was in the main part of the house. Although, looking out of the kitchen window, she could see Geoffrey's mother sitting in the sun-lounger on the terrace outside the doors into her flat. She was daintily sipping a small glass of sherry with what looked like the *Irish Tatler* on her lap. Her short grey hair was tidily combed and sprayed into the permed helmet-shape she favoured and she was wearing a neat pale blue dress with long sleeves, even though the evening was still warm. Mrs Larchet didn't hold with elderly women showing their arms, however hot the weather.

Plunkett was ambling around the garden, sniffing and poking his nose into clumps of tired-looking daisies and irises. As Jude watched, he lazily lifted a leg, directing a golden cascade over a particularly unhealthy-looking dahlia, drenching it from top to bottom. No wonder its leaves have gone all yellow, she thought. Its veins are probably full of pee not sap.

She'd forgotten to ask them who would be home for supper. Things had been too fraught that morning to think about domestic details. Jude looked at the kitchen clock. Half past six. Would she and Geoffrey be able to have a reasonable conversation without either of them losing patience with the other? It would help so much if only he would try and grasp how she was feeling. She knew he was occupied with the new television drama he was in the middle of filming but, busy or not, surely it wasn't unreasonable for her to expect him to switch his attention to her wholeheartedly every once in a while? Jude felt that she had managed not to show any resentment over the fact that even though she had been working non-stop since they married, all domestic dramas and crises had always been left for her to deal with. Sometimes it had been just a little difficult not to feel that she would have welcomed a bit more support from her husband – and her father.

Of course it was unreasonable to expect Flora and Oscar to understand. They were still too young – and blissfully unmarried – to know what she was feeling. Although they liked to pretend there was nothing left of any importance that they hadn't already seen or done – or tasted or drunk. Certainly neither of them had any memories of their maternal grandfather. He had never bothered to keep in touch with them, had never sent Christmas or birthday cards, let alone presents. As a grandparent, he was a total washout from their point of view. As far as they were concerned, he had been relegated to history and discarded. Each time she thought about it, a small wave of anger surged through Jude. It wasn't just that they had missed out. Her father had too. Even if he had somehow managed to convince himself otherwise.

She sometimes wondered, if he ever came into their minds, did they feel let down or angry or disappointed? Resentment had been the main emotion Jude had experienced whenever she'd thought about him. At school, she had watched her friends' fathers covetously. She noticed how quite a few of them seemed to have a special bond with their daughters. She could tell the unwilling ones who took part in the parent-teacher get-togethers and the obligatory sports days – the ones who she knew were resigned to being there and who were putting on a good front for the sake of their offspring. The handful of fathers who were a constant cringing embarrassment to their daughters, who insisted on holding their hands in public and who made unfunny jokes in too loud voices in their clumsy efforts to play the role of fond dad – even they were a source of envy.

Oscar and Flora would never know how wretched their grandfather had made Jude's mother. Jane Maybury had been courageous, somehow managing not to lose her sense of humour – although she found it nearly impossible to feel optimistic about the future in the early days after the separation. Jude realised many years later that her mother had taken quite a battering from her brief marriage to Jude's father. Not a physical one but the experience had left her with almost no self-esteem and very little confidence. For the first year or so after Liam Maybury had walked out on her, it was all she could do to keep the fragile household of two on the road. Jude would never forget how, as a small child, after her mother had kissed her and tucked her in for the night, she would wake later on to hear the sound of her weeping quietly in the bedroom beside her own. She would get out of bed and creep into the other room with its scent of sandalwood. She'd slip in beside the woman in the large double bed, with its Indian quilt and enormous soft pillows, and be instantly reassured that everything would be all right. Warm and comforted, she would eventually fall asleep with her mother's arms around her.

Slowly, Jane Maybury had gathered herself together. Step by painful step, she pieced together a life for herself and her small daughter. She got a part-time job in the local bookshop so that she was there for Jude when school finished. After the first year, she joined an evening class at the Italian Institute in Dublin. Two years later, she'd proudly graduated with her diploma. She had bought sparkling white wine and they lit candles and toasted her success until Jude became slightly tipsy with wine and pleasure at seeing her mother laughing wholeheartedly for the first time in a long while.

Jude's mother's French had always been good, having lived and taught in France for several years before her marriage. So that it wouldn't get rusty, she read constantly in both French and Italian. As Jude grew, her mother encouraged her to read poetry and plays. Jude's own love of language grew from those hours spent together but because she learned easily from her mother and didn't find her teachers nearly as interesting or encouraging, Jude was often in trouble at school. They complained that she was lazy and that she frequently distracted the other girls from their lessons by fooling around.

34

When her mother confronted her about this, she replied, "But, Mum, you do it so much better than they do. And you never tell me to do anything without there being a good reason. *You* never say, 'Do this because I tell you to'."

Jane Maybury admitted that was possibly true but did her best to plead the school's case. Jude wasn't interested.

"They might expel you if you don't keep your head down and at least pretend to fit in," said her mother one day after Jude had been sent home for sewing together a classmate's blazer sleeves during lunch break.

"She deserved it," was all that her daughter had to say on the subject.

As Jude shoved some potatoes in a baking-tin into the oven, she smiled to herself at the memory of her mother beating the school to it by removing her daughter before the headmistress had a chance to expel her. Although she hadn't been quite so quick off the mark at the next school that Jude briefly attended. They had branded her a troublemaker and asked her to leave after only a term and a half.

"What am I going to do with you?" Jane Maybury had asked in despair.

"Send me to a school that likes children," replied her twelve-year-old daughter promptly.

Which proved more difficult than either of them could have imagined. After a lot of questions and searching, her mother finally found a non-fee-paying school on the outskirts of South Dublin that was mixed, interdenominational and surprisingly liberal, with a headmaster who seemed to have a genuine interest in each individual child in his care. After the half-hour meeting, Dr Harrison appeared to thoroughly approve of both the child and her mother and she was accepted. When he said that she could start immediately, Jude was delighted.

Opening the freezer, Jude pulled out a plastic container of ready-made casserole. It was enough for four – if Oscar and Flora decided to eat at home that evening. That was unlikely, considering the dreadful atmosphere during breakfast that morning. The pair of them had probably decided to give family supper a miss.

She glanced out of the window again. Her mother-in-law had disappeared indoors and Plunkett was fast asleep in the middle of the rose-bed. I hope to God she won't make an appearance this evening, she thought. Could she not for once be a little tactful and keep out of the way?

Mrs Larchet had made sure to add her tuppence worth earlier in the day. Standing very straight and quivering with indignation, she held onto the back of a kitchen chair as though the sheer awfulness of what Jude was doing to the family might make her keel over.

"I don't want to interfere but I really can't just watch you upset everyone like this, Judith. I really don't know what's got into you these past few weeks."

Jude thought it best to appear not to have heard her mother-in-law. She reasoned that if she ignored her, perhaps the woman would take the hint and leave them to sort things out on their own. But Patricia Larchet was just getting up steam.

"Please don't pretend you didn't hear me." Her pale blue eyes were bloodshot and her voice had started to wobble with emotion. "Geoffrey is a marvellous father and husband and he really doesn't deserve this sort of behaviour from his wife. You are supposed to support him – not make life more difficult."

"That sounds a bit medieval, Gran," ventured Oscar.

His grandmother glared at him.

Jude, heartened by this show of support from her son, turned to Geoffrey.

"You know how much I've always supported you but it's got to be a two-way thing. Just now, I need *your* support and understanding." She gave him an anxious smile. "I'm sorry, Geoff. I don't want to feel the way I do at the moment. So confused . . . as though everything is getting on top of me. I've just got to sort myself out – and I feel that, if I can track him down, talking to my father might help."

Flora stared moodily at her mother from the far end of the table.

"I would have thought that at your age you would have got round to sorting yourself out by now. You've had long enough."

Jude took a deep breath.

"Just because a person has reached the ripe old age of forty-six, doesn't mean they have achieved Nirvana, Flo. You don't realise that it's just as difficult for us geriatrics to get it right as it is for you young ones." She softened her voice. "When Granny Maybury died, I can't explain how I felt – it wasn't just the shock of losing her – but I felt that I was suddenly in the front line myself and it made me start to look at things differently. All those years when my father wasn't around it seemed as though he was already dead. But he isn't. But he *is* seventy-four and I don't know how much longer he'll be alive. It seems to me that it would be dreadful for him to die with so many questions unanswered. And he is the only person who can answer them for me. Believe me, I feel as confused and troubled now as I sometimes did when I was a small child."

"Well, the way you carry on most of the time, you'd think you'd got it all brilliantly sussed out." Flora scowled at her mother. "Anyway, you don't have to go and *see* Grandpa Maybury. Why this sudden interest in bonding with him? You could phone him or send him a letter with all the questions you want answering. I bet he won't be too thrilled, you suddenly appearing on the scene after all this time. It's perfectly obvious he doesn't care a fuck about you or any of us."

"Flora!"

Mrs Larchet's wobble had developed even more of a vibrato to it.

"Flo's right, though. He's never shown the slightest bit of interest." Oscar looked over to where Jude was sitting, tense and white-knuckled, opposite him. "But I don't really understand either why you suddenly need to track him down now, Mum. Do you really think it will make any difference?"

"I don't know. All I *do* know is that I have to talk to him, to try and understand why he feels it's OK to treat his family the way he does. Perhaps there's some really valid reason for what he's done . . ."

"Yeah," sneered Flora. "Like he's been a little busy over the past twenty-odd years with wife number two and a bunch of mistresses. They must take up a lot of his time."

Geoffrey spoke sharply.

"That's quite enough, Flora."

Flora flushed angrily.

Jude wondered just how much other unhelpful information her daughter had gleaned from Patricia Larchet concerning the follies committed by Flora's maternal grandfather.

Suddenly Oscar pushed his chair back with a loud scraping noise and got up from the table. He went and stood behind his mother's chair.

"Well, I can't say I understand but I don't think it's fair to attack Mum for doing what she feels she has to." He shot a meaningful glance at his sister who immediately looked away. He bent over and kissed Jude on the cheek. "I'm going out. I think it would be better if Dad and you were left in peace to talk things over. I'll see you later, Mum, Dad." He paused at the door and stared at Flora again. "Come on, Flo!"

There was a silence and then, unwillingly, Flora got up. She looked as though she was going to say something but, seeing the grim expression on her father's face, decided against it. However, on reaching the doorway, she turned towards where Mrs Larchet stood, gripping the chair back for all she was worth.

"If they need to talk, I think Gran should go too."

Four pairs of eyes immediately fixed on Gran.

Patricia Larchet stiffened and then visibly gathered herself together.

"Well, if I'm not wanted, of course I wouldn't dream of staying."

She walked in the direction of the door into her flat with a martyred expression, her court shoes clicking like castanets on the hard floor.

When they had all gone, Jude felt some of the tension leave her. She moved her chair nearer to where Geoffrey sat, staring down at his half-drunk cup of coffee. He was a good-looking man, she thought, with his dark hair, now sprinkled with grey, and his intelligent, interesting face. But he did look tired and, just at this moment, he was frowning.

Putting her hand on his, she spoke quietly.

"Geoff, you know I love you. I think you love me too but perhaps we've both been so occupied with our jobs, the children, all the daily paraphernalia of just getting through life that we've both forgotten to show each other how we feel."

Impatiently, Geoffrey slid his hand away from under her own.

"Spare me the mumbo-jumbo, Jude. You sound like one of those ghastly agony aunts on the telly. If you can't cope with the idea that grown-up people who've lived together for over twenty years don't go around fawning over each other and behaving like honeymooners, then, there's something wrong with you. As for this sudden passion for soul-searching with your dad . . . do you know what I think?"

"Please tell me."

Jude sounded bleak.

"I know it's not the done thing to say to a woman of your age but I really do think you are having some sort of mid-life crisis . . ."

"Just *don't* say anything more." Jude got to her feet, fighting back tears. "If you can't understand and won't or can't listen, then that's your problem. I really wanted to

40

talk this over with you, to explain – but you're making it impossible. I think you're being incredibly arrogant . . . and unkind."

And that was how the morning's 'discussion' had ended. Her husband did not take kindly to being called arrogant. Geoffrey walked out of the house with a face like thunder, leaving Jude hurling cutlery into the dishwasher with tears rolling down her face.

Now, as she put the casserole in the microwave to defrost, she wondered if there was any point in indulging in a second round of the same. The idea of prolonging a conversation that would leave her feeling even more like a wet rag than she already did and still not managing to make herself understood, was not appealing. Perhaps it would be better to just weather the next couple of days and concentrate on booking her flight and organising herself for the trip. She hoped to God that he was still at the same address she'd found in her mother's address book after her death. She'd already decided that it would not be a good idea to warn her father of her impending visit. There was no way of knowing what he felt about her after all this time – if he felt anything. He might just disappear and she wasn't going to allow him the chance to run out on her a second time.

She dropped the oven gloves onto the worktop and went into the study to hunt through the desk drawers for her passport. It was eventually located among a pile of birth certificates and unused Eurocheques. Jude extracted it from the chaos in the drawer. It didn't expire for another six months. Thank God for that, she thought. She hoped it wouldn't take her that long to come to some sort of an understanding with her father. She was just about to shut the drawer when she became aware of her mother-in-law standing in the doorway.

Drat her anyway!

"Yes, Patricia?" she asked politely.

There was a pause before the other woman spoke.

"I don't want to complain but . . ."

Jude fought back a sudden compulsion to laugh.

"Yes?" she repeated carefully.

"But who is going to look after Geoffrey and the children while you are away? I can hardly be expected to prepare meals for them every day and make sure everything is running smoothly. Don't forget that I have to shop and cook for myself and I'm not as strong as I was. Have you given that a thought, Judith, or have you been too busy feeling sorry for yourself to worry about the rest of the family?"

It all sounded very carefully rehearsed. How dare she! Jude made herself count to five before answering.

"Catriona comes in three times a week and leaves both your flat and the house looking spotless. As for cooking, the freezer is full of goodies from Marks and Sparks and the shops are only round the corner. If three perfectly healthy adults can't organise the food side of things, then there's something very wrong with them." Seeing how indignant Patricia Larchet was looking, she attempted to defuse the situation. "I'm sorry if you're feeling upset, Patricia, but it's really not the end of the world. I'll probably only be away for a few days anyway."

"But what about Geoffrey?"

"What about Geoffrey?"

Jude could feel her self-control ebbing away fast.

"You're his wife. You should be here with him, not disappearing off to the far side of the world on a wild-goose chase."

"The Greek islands are hardly at the other side of the world, Patricia, and I wouldn't be going if I didn't feel it really necessary. I certainly would not go if I felt it was going to be a wild-goose chase." Her mother-in-law opened her mouth to speak again. "And if you don't mind, I have no intention of discussing it further with you."

Jude watched as Mrs Larchet snapped shut her mouth, paused and then turned and walked out of the room, chin in the air. As soon as she'd gone, her daughter-in-law felt remorseful. She should have dealt with her more kindly, she knew that, but it was so difficult not to get riled by the constant battery of spoken and unspoken criticism aimed at her. The woman *was* getting on for seventy. She *was* less robust than she used to be. It would just be a lot easier to be generous-spirited towards her if she could only let up on the sniping and attempt to be a little nicer.

Feeling shaken, Jude rested her elbows on the desk in front of her and put her hands up to her face. Oh, Lord! Was she behaving like a complete lunatic? she asked herself. Was it all worth the effort?

Chapter Four

The next day was an exhausting one. Jude booked her flight, changed money, contacted the studio and met Fidelma for a hurried lunch to enlist her help in covering her tracks for the next week or so.

Fidelma was shocked by her dishevelled appearance. She could see how exhausted and dispirited her friend was. She gave her a hug.

"Don't worry, chicken! I'll keep the buggers off your case. I won't exactly tell them that you've gone to Ios – they might get the wrong idea! But I'll just let them know there's some sort of family crisis and it's really important that you're not pestered. You could always leave the old mobile at home. Anyway, it's not as if the programme's pre-recorded and you won't be starting the next run until the beginning of October, will you?"

"No," said Jude in a tired voice, "but there was some talk of my hosting a new weekly discussion-group thing and Alan's keen that I do it. It's a pet project of his and, if they don't give it the chop and *if* he still has a job in another few weeks, I don't want to let him down. You know how nice he is."

"I've already had a word with him and he told me to give you his love. He said that you were to forget about everything at the studio and get in touch when you resurfaced again."

"You didn't mention the fact that I'm intending to hunt down my long-lost father, did you? It sounds so ridiculous. Sometimes I think bloody Gran has got it right and I'm just being absurd and should let the whole thing drop and try and forget about the wretched man."

"Listen to me, Jude! I've reached the ripe old age of forty-eight! You're talking to an expert here. I know how hard it is these days to get it right – to get the balance between feeling fulfilled in one's self and being generous to those around you. I reckon I know you pretty well by now and I've seen how good you are at making time for people. You're fantastic with Oscar and Flora, the way you've kept on top of things all these years, and what you've achieved in your work. It's only amazing and I'm full of admiration. Look at the mess I've made of my relationships with all the guys I've ever known because I so desperately wanted to have a career and needed to be financially independent. OK, so I don't have to rely on a man for my clothes and my entertainment and my holidays in the sun. But *look* at me! I'll probably get the sack in another few weeks. Who wants to employ an out-of-work TV researcher with a bad degree, who only wants to work in radio and television and who can't even get her life together long enough to hang on to a decent bloke for more than a couple of months at a time

– *and* who looks like the back of a bus? If I were being really honest, some days, I'd willingly chuck the independent bit and settle for some sex-starved guy who was crazy to look after me and smother me in orchids and *After Eight*. Pathetic, isn't it?"

Jude couldn't help smiling.

"You *don't* look like the back of a bus. You're lovely," she countered quickly.

And she meant it. All right, she couldn't put her hand on her heart and say that the other was in any way conventionally pretty – she was too bony, her face was rather gaunt and her fair hair was thin and tended to be greasy – but there was humour and sweetness in Fidelma that showed in her face and in her way of speaking which was gentle and extraordinarily attractive.

Fidelma laughed.

"Listen to the pair of us! What a disaster! Come on, eat something so that you'll have the strength to sort it all out."

They said goodbye after a herb omelette and a glass of good red wine in their favourite café. Jude felt a little better. She hoped desperately that Fidelma wouldn't be given the sack. There weren't enough of her kind around in the media world. As for nice blokes working in RTVI – they could be counted on the fingers of one hand. People like Alan Carruth, for example.

* * *

That night, after filling in time for what seemed like hours, hoping that Gran would keep her distance, Jude finally ate on her own with her plate on her lap in front of the television. *Inspector Morse* came and went, leaving her puzzling over why she'd been so sure one of the proven good guys hadn't committed the half-dozen gruesome murders that had taken place in half a dozen different Oxford colleges. Anyway, why did the killings always take place *inside* the university? she wondered. They must be running dreadfully short of dons.

When Geoffrey came back, it was nearly ten and she had only just finished her meal. He came into the room, dropping files and folders onto a chair, and sat down wearily beside her on the couch.

"I'm really sorry I'm so late. Everything that could possibly go wrong did, including the first AD having to be rushed into hospital halfway through the afternoon with a suspected appendicitis." He leaned over and gave her a light kiss on the cheek. "I'm sorry about this morning too. Perhaps you were right. Perhaps we've let things slip a bit. I don't mean to take you for granted, Jude. It's just that there's been so much going on and I never seem to be able to catch up with myself these days . . . I don't know. RTVI isn't the happiest of places in which to be working at the moment." He looked at her with a half-smile. "But you already know that."

Relieved, she smiled back. "You could say that! I won't ask what else went wrong at work. Have you eaten?"

"Yeah, snatched something off the trolley at eight. Anyway, I'm really not hungry."

"Shall we go to bed then?" she asked. "I think I'm badly in need of a hug." She looked at him more closely. "What's the matter?"

"Nothing! Nothing's the matter," said Geoffrey.

* * *

Later, although she was deadly tired, Jude lay wide-awake with one arm around her sleeping husband's back, her breasts and belly pressed against his warm skin. She didn't want to disturb him by moving but the pins and needles in her other arm that was folded under her were becoming more uncomfortable by the second. Gently she eased herself away from him and turned on to her back. He stirred in mid-sleep and changed position, kicking her in the right ankle in the process.

Their lovemaking had begun tenderly enough. But he had quickly become aroused and wanted to enter her before she was ready for him. Her pleasure evaporated, to be replaced by a mildly affectionate tolerance of his need but also an impatience to have the whole thing over as soon as possible. It all seemed so predictable – the same routine of kisses and minimal caresses followed by this disappointing lethargy of mind and body on her part. These days she was more aware of the odd stab of an improperly trimmed toenail or the fact that one or other of them was suffering from garlic-coated halitosis than of the surging, exhilarating desire she'd felt when they had come together in the early days of their marriage.

Tonight, although she'd thought she had managed to hide what she was feeling, Geoffrey sensed it. He suddenly became very still before abruptly withdrawing. He silently rolled back to his side of the bed.

Jude raised herself from the pillows, putting a hand on his shoulder.

"Don't stop now."

"It's no good. Nothing shrivels him up faster than you pretending, Jude."

48

"I'm sorry, Geoff. I really thought I did want to. I wanted to be close – especially after everything that's been going on these past weeks."

"Don't worry!" He almost sounded bored. "I'm too knackered anyway to make you feel good. I don't seem to have the energy these days. Forget it. Let's get some sleep."

As he made no move towards her, she leaned over and kissed him. Almost imperceptibly, he turned his face away so that her lips grazed his cheek rather than coming into contact with his mouth.

"Goodnight then," she said quietly.

"Goodnight."

How sad it was to sound so formal immediately after being intimate, she thought.

She was still wide-awake at two in the morning. The sounds from the street were fewer and less raucous. In the light that filtered through the curtains, Jude watched her sleeping husband. The night was warm and he lay on his back now, breathing softly and evenly, the crumpled sheet resting lightly across his knees. He did still have a beautiful body – smooth, physically very fit without being muscular. She'd always loved the way he stayed a warm brown all through the winter. He didn't have time for sunbeds, so it must be genetic. She wondered at how small and harmless his prick looked as it rested innocently on his left thigh, its head hidden in a silky cowl of foreskin like some dozing one-eyed monk. What was it he'd once said about the male sexual urge?

'Just think! All the wars, murder and mayhem caused by a miserable chipolata wanting a home!'

She had to admit that recently she hadn't felt like

offering a home to a chipolata – even if it were her husband's. She would have liked him to have held her more often, without the need to make love. Although, if she were honest, she knew that he hadn't been all that interested lately. Perhaps he's right, I'm thoroughly menopausal and I'm losing my sexual appetite. Perhaps I've lost it already and I'm well on the way to ending up a dried old prune, for whom physical passion is just a vague and faintly ridiculous memory, she thought dismally. The idea of that happening would have worried Jude quite considerably a couple of years ago. The way she felt just now, she could barely summon up the energy to mind.

Her mother would have understood. They would have laughed at it all together – nothing ever looked quite as bleak after a little while in her company. If only she were still around to talk things over with. 'Tumbling Jude'. It seemed that she was still in free fall. When would she hit the bottom? She gave a small sigh and then carefully rolled over onto her side. When I get back from Ios, I suppose I could investigate the HRT scene. I will . . . just in case, Jude promised herself unenthusiastically before finally drifting into a restless sleep.

* * *

Breakfast on the day of Jude's departure was eaten is a state of uneasy armed truce. Her mother-in-law and Flora both avoided catching her eye. While Oscar did his best to make small talk, Geoffrey seemed to have retreated into another world. This left Jude trying to respond to her son's pseudo good humour. She didn't fool herself for one moment that he wasn't almost as unhappy about her departure as everyone else sitting around the table, but more from concern for her wellbeing than from selfishness.

Flora didn't make any attempt to hide the fact that she was fed up. An observer might have commented that perhaps this was because, unconsciously, she had a monopoly on being selfish. Not that Flora looked at it like that. As far as she was concerned, her mother was out of her tree.

"She's *so* self-absorbed! I mean, *what* is her problem?" she moaned to Oscar shortly after Jude returned from Wexford and told them that she was going away again. "How can she do this to us? And Dad," she'd added as a hurried afterthought.

Oscar, who up until then had been feeling that his mother was rather letting the family down, was galvanised into disagreement by his sister's remarks.

"That's a bit rich coming from you!"

"And what do you mean by that?"

"Oh, Get real, Flo! You use Mum like a twenty-four-hour taxi service when she's not working. You've always taken it for granted that she'll ferry you around at the drop of a hat. You seem to have forgotten how she used to sit for ages in a cold car waiting for you and your pals to emerge from The Point after some diabolical pop concert or other. Then she had to put up with you as a raver with all your little dreadlocks shedding beads around the gaff – which blocked the Hoover every time you shook your head or lost your temper. As mothers go, I don't think she's all that bad."

For three long years the family had suffered Flora's addiction to The Cure. The affliction had only ended a couple of years earlier. She had been a dedicated Cure-head, spending her time dressed in black, strangely amorphous garments with her face half hidden by a swathe of lank hair. The half of her face that was visible was plastered in white make-up with black-rimmed eyes and purple lips that made her look as though she'd just been hastily dug up after a not-very-recent interment. Oscar considered that their mother had been especially good about it all. After one concert, when Jude had searched a sea of identically dressed females for some time before spotting her daughter, she had then driven Flora and a silent collection of her Cure-cloned friends home to various parts of Dublin. Oscar remembered how she had managed, with some difficulty, to hide her smiles after enquiring, when they eventually arrived home at nearly two in the morning, what it was Flora felt she gained by being a Cure devotée. Her daughter had muttered something about the importance and benefit of 'being different'.

If Flora was angry with her, Jude realised that Oscar was not sure how he felt. They had spent some time together the night before her departure. She'd got the impression that he wanted to be seen to be adult.

After talking about various things that had nothing to do with her going, she had been touched by him saying in a casual voice as he got up to leave, "Don't worry, Mum. The others will come round eventually. Don't let Gran upset you. She's completely batty and I know she doesn't show it but I think she'll miss not having you around."

Jude didn't argue but she very much doubted that Patricia Larchet would pine for her company. Although who would take the dog for walks? She might miss that contribution from her daughter-in-law. The woman had been very frosty since their encounter in the study two days earlier. Thankfully she hadn't gone on the attack again, just walked around with that look of martyrdom that Jude found so irritating. Even Geoffrey seemed to have found her a little hard to take these past few days. He had been unusually short with his mother when she dropped unsubtle hints about the possibility of her having to move into the main part of the house since his wife was obviously hell-bent on going ahead and leaving him.

"Mother, Jude is *not* leaving me and that sort of remark is extremely unhelpful."

"I only meant . . ." she began in pathetically weakened tones.

"I know perfectly well what you meant. Just leave it!"

For a brief moment, Jude almost felt sorry for her mother-in-law.

It was difficult for her to tell what Geoffrey was really feeling. For one thing, the problems at RTVI were real and time-demanding and resulted in him having to attend union meetings on top of his normal workload. There had been more talk of compulsory redundancies and lay-offs. She knew he was desperate to finish filming. There were only a couple more weeks to go – *if* there were no major disasters.

He had been pleasant enough in the short periods in which they came in contact but he seemed a little cool and detached. The way he behaved towards her made Jude feel guilty, which annoyed her, which in turn increased the guilt. Their abortive attempt at coming closer had apparently backfired. Obviously Geoffrey blamed her for that too. At the back of her mind, she couldn't help feeling that there was something else that was coming between them. Something he didn't talk about but it was there, hiding in the shadows. Perhaps, when filming was over and he was more himself, he would tell her what it was that bothered him so much.

Even though Jude felt anxious about what the outcome would be from confronting her father, she knew that, especially after all the scenes and arguments over the wisdom – or otherwise – of her decision, she couldn't change her mind now.

It was agreed that Oscar would accompany Jude to the airport and drive her car back afterwards.

"It might be a good idea to give Dad the keys. I don't want you to think that you can spend the next few days flying around the countryside visiting all your mates in Donegal and Galway," she warned.

"Ma! As if!"

"Instead, you might have another go at deciding on a future career?"

"I might!" he agreed, stretching his arms and yawning.

Geoffrey had already said goodbye before leaving for the studios.

He seemed to be torn between worrying that the venture would turn out to be a disaster and being thoroughly annoyed that Jude had not chosen to take his advice and, as he had put it, 'be sensible and let sleeping dogs lie'. Their parting had been public with him giving Jude a kiss over the breakfast toast and coffee, watched closely by his mother.

"Sorry I can't take you to the airport but you know how it is. Have a good trip. I hope it . . ." Jude was half expecting him to say, 'I hope it will prove that you should have taken my advice after all'. Instead he managed to finish with, "works out for the best".

"Thanks, Geoff," replied Jude, looking up at him and smiling with a confidence she was not feeling. "I'll ring you when I've found somewhere to stay."

She had a strong premonition that it would be very foolish to expect her long-lost parent to offer instant hospitality on her arrival.

Jude had asked Flora, if she didn't feel like going to the airport, to at least come out to the car and wave her off. Her unsmiling daughter did so after being given a look by her brother that hinted at trouble in Paradise if she didn't.

When it came to saying goodbye to Gran, Jude made an effort to smile and be pleasant.

"Goodbye, Patricia. Look after yourself. I'll be back very soon."

Mustering all her self-control, her mother-in-law didn't add anything more than a small but noticeable sniff to her chilly, "Goodbye, Judith."

Jude kissing Patricia Larchet's cool cheek and saying goodbye inside the house, pre-empted the necessity of the woman coming outside with Flora. She wanted to say goodbye to her daughter without a Greek chorus hissing menacingly in the background.

Standing by the car, she put her arms around Flora and gave her a long hug.

"Don't be too cross, darling. I love you lots and I'll be back sooner than you think."

Suddenly the rigidity left the other's body and Flora burst into tears. She seemed to crumple onto her mother's shoulder.

Jude pulled away slightly and put a hand under her chin, gently raising her moist face so that she could look at her properly.

"Hey! What's all this about?" she asked softly.

"You will be all right, won't you?"

"Of course I'll be all right, you lunatic! The worst thing that can happen is that your grandfather will take one look at me and say thank you but no thank you and then I will know that he's a hopeless case and I'll be on the next plane home – but at least I will have tried."

As she made this light-hearted statement, Jude felt her heart constrict at the thought that her father might say just that very thing.

Chapter Five

Jude said goodbye to Oscar outside the entrance to the airport.

"Don't come in. It's so expensive to park and anyway, with security the way it is, we probably wouldn't even have time for a cup of coffee together." He gave her one of his sudden embraces that made his mother feel as though she'd been mugged by a member of the New Zealand rugby squad. She smiled at him. "Wish me luck!"

He smiled back reassuringly.

"Good luck, Mum. I hope it all works out for you. In a way, it's rather exciting – having the chance, after all these years, to get to know the person who is your father. I expect there was a good reason for him not keeping in touch. Anyway, he's your dad, so he must be all right!"

She wondered if that remark was made to convince himself more than her that all would be well.

"I'm sure you're right!" She gave him a last hug before turning towards the entrance. "Be good while I'm away –

and for God's sake, keep an eye on that mad sister of yours," she added.

He grinned.

"Not so easy! Flo's a right little prima donna. Gran's definitely loopy and Dad's been so occupied with work he's been more absent than present for quite a while. In fact the whole family is suffering from some weird problem or other – with the exception of you and me of course!"

Amused, she watched as he directed a radiant smile at an advancing airport ban garda before climbing back into the car. Sticking a hand out of the window, he gave his mother a cheerful wave as he manoeuvred around the untidily parked cars and taxis. She saw him pick up speed and then come to a sudden halt as a group of trolley-pushing travellers, oblivious to the traffic, launched themselves onto the crossing in front of him without any warning. She turned away hastily. Better not to watch, she thought, hoping that he wouldn't mow anyone down on his way back to the house or come into contact with a signpost like he had the last time she'd let him use her car. He'd sworn blind that it hadn't been there the day before. Geoffrey's scathing comment that if he were blind as well as stupid it would perhaps be safer if he travelled everywhere on foot in the future had been the catalyst for a humdinger of a family row.

* * *

Jude paused in front of the long mirror in the lady's lavatory. How would a stranger see her? Because that's what her father was – a total stranger. If he held any sort of mental picture of her, it would be of a chubby four-year-old child with her face half-hidden by an unruly mop of red curls.

Staring at herself, she saw a tall woman with black-lashed blue eyes and long red hair gathered into a loose knot on top of her head. Her dark blue cotton skirt reached her ankles and the matching blouse billowed comfortably out over the waistband. A silver bracelet adorned her left wrist and she wore a large wristwatch with a blue strap on the right. The woman was slim with slender sandalled feet and long-fingered hands. An over-loaded brown leather bag hung from one shoulder. She wore a wide white-gold wedding band and, on the little finger of her left hand, a three-diamond ring in the shape of small leaves. Long, silver earrings swayed slightly as she moved her head.

Her father had lived abroad for the past ten years or so. Would he be put off by her sudden and unsolicited appearance? Would she prove to be a disappointment as well as being thoroughly unwelcome?

She would have been genuinely surprised to find out that several of the men with whom she came into contact through work considered her to be extremely attractive, even though she was rather understated in the chest region. That deficit was cancelled out by her long, slim legs and neat bum. The more intelligent male was also drawn to her interesting face and a way of carrying herself that was unconsciously elegant. The reason she appealed to them was difficult to pin down. Perhaps what attracted them most was the fact that she was different and unselfconscious.

She suddenly became aware that a woman standing at a nearby sink was staring at her with what Jude recognised as an increasingly familiar 'I know I've seen that face somewhere before. Is she someone important?' look. Quickly, she moved away from the mirror and walked towards the door, leaving the figure at the sink staring after her, frantically racking her brains for a name.

Several more people watched her as she queued at the departure gate. Opening her bag, she fished around until she found a large pair of sunglasses. Jude didn't realise it, but they only made her look even more like someone who *was* someone trying to hide their identity; which of course made her altogether more interesting to celebrity spotters. The fact that the flight was full of holidaymakers bound for a package holiday in Crete made them more relaxed and daring than they might otherwise have been. They made no attempt to lower their voices as they downed their in-flight lagers and gin and tonics and commented on her presence.

"You'd think *she'd* go Business Class, wouldn't you?" confided a fellow traveller to her husband.

"They don't have Business Class on this sort of flight," he replied, opening his second can of Bud while leaning out into the aisle to get a better look at the woman with her face hidden behind a copy of *The Irish Times*.

"I wonder if she'll be in our hotel."

"I doubt it," he said. "Her type don't stay in the sort of places we go to."

"There's nothing wrong with the place we're going to. It's dead posh!" His wife sounded mildly put-out. "Anyway, she *might* be. You never know!"

The woman would be disappointed to know that Jude had booked a 'flight only' ticket to Heraklion and was travelling on that same day by boat to Ios.

* * *

Leaning back on the freshly painted white bench seat on board the *Giorgios Express* to Santorini and Ios, Jude watched the crowds of fellow travellers with interest. Snatches of German, Swedish, Japanese and various versions of the English language – sometimes Scots or Liverpudlian or London, sometimes Australian or South African accents – filled the air. She loved the feeling of being surrounded by this polyglot mix of people. They didn't know or care who she was and she was free to watch them and make up improbable lives and backgrounds to fit the human beings moving around on the packed deck.

As well as people-watching, because she was by nature observant and curious, she also noted that the lifting gear for the lifeboats had received so many coats of glossy white paint that, if they did ever start to sink, she very much doubted the crew would be able to winch them down into the water. It was easy not to feel worried with the sun beaming down and landfall less than an hour away. It would be a different matter in a storm in the dark.

She glanced over the rail, squinting out at the wind-cobbled water that sparkled with thousands of dots of light like sequins. In the distance, she could just make out the rugged shape of Santorini, rising steeply from the sea. It looked misty-blue and mysterious. It was hard to believe that thousands of people lived out their lives on that chunk of volcanic rock. Ahead, a school of dolphin plunged in and out of the turquoise water. She found herself smiling as she watched them. They were so full of life and energy. Their appearance made you feel unexpectedly joyful. She thought it not at all surprising that they held such an important place in legend and myth as she watched them stitch the sea with their glistening curved bodies and secret smiles.

As the ship approached the island, passing shining black rock that looked as though someone had dumped giant shovelfuls of coal in a careless semicircle, she found herself wondering just how deep the volcano's crater was underneath the vessel as they approached the surprisingly small quay. Three other ships were already moored there while others appeared to be circling, waiting for the chance to roar in to dock. For roar they did. Taken aback, she watched as the *Giorgios* swung around and charged at horrifically high speed, backend first, towards its berth. The water bubbled and foamed as propellers spun and spat. Jude felt like closing her eyes as she waited for the inevitable crump against the concrete edge to the quay. Amazingly, it didn't happen. She wondered if all the equally loud roaring and shouting from the ship's officers as they directed proceedings through loudhailers was really necessary. They wore immaculate white shorts and shirts, decorated with various bits of gold braid. She got the distinct impression that they knew perfectly well they looked gorgeous.

Before the ship had stopped moving completely, there was a loud crash as the metal gangplank was dropped and dusty cars and lorries started to spew out from the bowels of the vessel and lurch onto *terra firma*, grinding their way towards the serpentine road leading to the town above.

Looking up, she marvelled at the thin sprawl of buildings perched along the tops of the cliffs like a line of unmelted snow. She could imagine how tiny the ships must look from up there. Perhaps one day she would come back with Geoff and visit the place properly. She'd read about its twisting streets full of fabulous shops packed with gold and precious stones and of the precarious restaurants that clung limpet-like to the sides of the cliffs where tourists ate while they watched the red sun sink into the distant sea while the sky turned from blue to rose to pale gold.

Within half-an-hour they had left the island and were on their way to Ios. As they got nearer, Jude began to feel queasy. It wasn't seasickness, she knew that. What if she couldn't even find her father? She was counting on him still being at the same address that she had found in her mother's address book after she died the previous year. What if . . . ? Trying hard to keep calm, she told herself to stop expecting the worst possible scenarios. Things had a habit of turning out for the best, even if it didn't always seem like that at the time.

Jude fished around inside her bag until she found the envelope. She slid a photo out and stared at it. Her father must have been in his mid-twenties when it was taken. It was ridiculous really that she didn't have anything more recent. Had her mother thrown out the others? She'd more or less refused to discuss him on the few occasions Jude had questioned her and Jude had soon given up. Perhaps they hadn't bothered to take any photographs? At seventy-four, it was hardly likely that he would still have black hair. The eyes were dark brown – deep set and compelling. His face was long rather than square, rather like her own. He was standing outside what looked like a typical English country pub and the picture had obviously been taken in the summer. He was wearing a white shirt, open at the neck, and slacks. Unsmiling, her father stared back at her. It would seem from his expression that the person taking the photograph had chosen a bad moment. There was a tension about him that made you think that perhaps he had just received unwelcome news.

* * *

It was nearly nine o'clock and dark before the *Giorgios* docked in Ios harbour. Far too late to do any parent-hunting. She would have to find somewhere nearby for the first night. Picking up her bag, Jude lugged it down three sets of metal stairs that shook from the impact of descending feet, before emerging into the car deck. Among the hordes of mostly young backpackers in their minimal shorts and wrap-around sunglasses, she felt almost elderly – and hot and tired. It had been a long day.

Once on the quay, her heart sank as she was met by an advancing wall of shouting locals waving signs bearing the scrawled names of various apartments and hotels: *The Hotel Homer, Golden Sun Apartments, Yani's Apartments, The Purple Palm*, amongst others. She didn't know where to start.

A small, skinny woman, dressed from head to toe in black, grabbed hold of her arm.

"You come," she said forcefully. "Very clean, very good. I have nice place."

"How much?" enquired Jude, doing her best to give the impression that she wasn't prepared to just throw in the towel without any discussion, however hot and tired she felt. A piece of crumpled paper was thrust under her nose for inspection: *Villa Rosa. Rooms 10,000 Drachmas*. Roughly £25 a night, she calculated. "Is it nearby?"

The woman pulled her arm, nodding.

"You come! You see. You like very much Villa Rosa."

Without waiting for a response, she let go of Jude and started to push her way through the crowd of shouting, gesticulating humanity. Jude did her best to keep up but it wasn't easy. Even though the woman looked well into her sixties, she fairly sped along. They crossed a well-lit open space that stretched from the quayside to a line of whitewashed buildings. They made their way around numerous groups of couples eating at tables arranged outside restaurants. Tray-bearing waiters nonchalantly ducked and dived in and out of the chaos. If Jude hadn't felt so tired, the smells and sounds and happy bustle would have pleased her. Hurrying along a narrow street, they emerged into a small square where she glimpsed a packed café bar and shops – all selling the ubiquitous postcards, chunks of polished onyx made into ashtrays and ugly vases, and rack upon rack of blue beaded necklaces and bracelets. Keeping as close as she could, she followed the woman as she bore left and started to scuttle along a gently climbing road lined with apartments. Beach towels were spread out to dry on the balconies in the hot night air. Jude could smell cooking meat and garlic but she wasn't hungry. She'd eaten a 'cheese roll' on board that had been revolting but it had successfully dulled her appetite.

Finally they came to a halt outside a bougainvillea-covered two-storey white house with wooden shutters. A scrawny cat darted across the path in front of them and melted into the shadow of nearby shrubs. The woman pushed open the gate and then turned to face Jude.

"This, Villa Rosa," she announced proudly, apparently blissfully unaware of either the lack of any roses around the place or the fact that the house walls were startlingly white, not rose-pink.

Her face looked very pale in the light from the street and Jude noticed that she had dark circles under her eyes. Was she a widow, running everything herself, getting up at dawn, busy all day and then having to brave her competitors each evening, fighting for customers when the ferries arrived?

Perhaps it was time for introductions. Jude thankfully dropped the case and held out a hand.

"My name is Jude."

She looked enquiringly at the other woman.

"I Rosa," she said with a quick gap-toothed smile that vanished almost immediately as if she hadn't got time to stand around smiling. "Come!"

She led Jude through the doorway, up a flight of stairs and along a short passage. Opening a door, she switched on a light and ushered the younger woman inside with small beckoning gestures.

The room was clean and simply furnished. It had white walls and a deep blue bedspread that matched the curtains over the shuttered windows. Jude glimpsed a spotless, if tiny, bathroom through an open door to the right of the bed. Almost before she'd had time to take in her surroundings, the woman called Rosa disappeared, leaving the bedroom door wide open. Jude dumped her bag and handbag on a chair and sat down thankfully on the bed. This would do her fine. She glanced at her watch. Even though it was only half-past nine, she decided that an early night was called for.

There was the sound of brisk footsteps and Rosa reappeared carrying a small tray. On it were two glasses containing what smelled like ouzo and a pretty china bowl filled with sugared almonds. She placed it on the bedside table and picked up the glasses, handing one to Jude.

"*Yamas!*" she said and proceeded to swallow almost half the contents in one hearty gulp. She smiled at Jude. "Drink, drink!"

"*Yamas!*" Jude said, obediently taking a sip from her own glass.

* * *

Next morning, Jude lay in bed and listened to the unfamiliar sounds percolating through the window she'd had to close during the night because of the mosquitoes. It was certainly a change from waking at home to the background noise of traffic and police sirens she was so used to. There was the slightly hysterical sound of a donkey braying, a cock crowed and goat-bells clonked unmusically somewhere nearby.

She rolled out of bed and went over to the window. Undoing the catch, she pushed back the shutters. Instantly, the room was invaded by a wave of warm air and light. There was no sign of the road she and Rosa had come along the previous night so the room must be at the back of the house. The view was of a gently sloping field with grazing goats and the now silent donkey. Further away and facing her were terraces of vines. Everything was bathed in bright sunlight. A sort of extra-luminous quality in the air over to the left of the terraces hinted at the presence of the sea close by. She leaned out and looked down to the garden below where plastic chairs and a couple of sun-loungers were scattered around on the coarse grass. A cat lay curled at the base of a small tree. Rosa, in a black skirt and blouse, her grey hair almost completely covered by a black scarf, was energetically sweeping the path with what looked like an old-fashioned broomstick.

After showering in a trickle of tepid water and banging her elbows on the shower doors in the minute bathroom, Jude went downstairs in search of some breakfast.

She chose a table set for two in one corner of the room. Several people were already eating. She nodded good morning to a couple of smiling girls at another table. Business must be good, she thought. There were at least a dozen people in the small dining-room. There was a general buzz of conversation and the coffee smelt good.

A young girl came over to her with a jug of coffee, hot rolls and orange juice on a tray. Jude accepted her offer of yoghurt and honey, having noticed the tall glass dishes filled with creamy-looking yoghurt and thick, dark-brown honey that some of the other guests were tucking into with obvious enjoyment.

As she ate, her mind was in turmoil. Had she been stupid to come this far without giving her father any prior warning? She was pretty sure that it was the best way but she wasn't entirely convinced. Ever since she'd made the decision to confront him, what bothered her most was the possibility of him refusing to talk to her after all these years. If he were ill and frail, her appearance might even result in him having a heart attack! Or, more realistically, he might be just furious. Perhaps he would lose his temper and tell her to go home and not bother him. Whatever he said or did, she knew perfectly well that it was not going to be easy – for either of them.

After breakfast, she went in search of Rosa, who was now busy watering the dozens of pots of geraniums that lined the steps up to the main doors of Villa Rosa. Jude blinked as she walked from the shade out into the heat of the morning. After greeting each other, Rosa glanced at the address on the piece of paper held out to her. Then she snatched it from Jude and read it again more carefully. When she'd finished, Jude wondered if she imagined the gleam of interest that suddenly flickered in the other's face before she handed it back to her. The woman's sharp eyes, that looked like small black raisins, observed her closely.

"You want House of Manolis?" Jude knew she was dying to ask why the Irishwoman needed to go there. "Is not apartment for holiday. You stay *here* in Villa Rosa." She stabbed a finger emphatically towards the house. "Here is good."

"Here is very good," said Jude carefully. "I am looking for a person who lives . . . might live . . . at that address." She got the feeling that Rosa was having some difficulty in stopping herself from asking questions. She looked as though she were boiling over with curiosity, her eyes fixed on Jude's face as she leaned expectantly towards her as if, by sheer willpower, she might be able to drag more information out of her.

Jude decided to put her out of her misery.

"I'm looking for my father, Liam Maybury. He used to live at that address."

Rosa frowned then gave a small nod. She pointed down the road in the direction of the port.

"You go to the sea. Then you go this way – to Yialos beach." She jerked her head to the right. "After beach you

69

go more down the road. You see house with big tree. Is House of Manolis."

Somehow Jude couldn't face asking her if the man called Liam Maybury still lived there. She'd find out soon enough.

Chapter Six

It took five minutes to walk the short distance down to the port. Jude tried to concentrate on her surroundings as much as possible, in an attempt to keep herself from performing a U-turn and retreating back to Villa Rosa. She passed a miniature church that looked almost as if it were made of white icing, complete with blue dome. A little further on there were some worn steps leading up to a well with a man and his spindly-legged donkey resting in the shade close by. The donkey, its head drooping, was almost invisible under a load of wood. The man looked out into the road but didn't seem to notice her walking by. The sense of being invisible increased after Jude passed half a dozen elderly men relaxing outside one of the houses bordering the dusty road. They too ignored her. Obviously tourists held no interest for them.

Once at the port, she turned right, glancing into the cordoned-off section of the quay that was Paradise Café. It was half full of people having breakfast, bathed in the gentle light that filtered through the green and white striped canopy above. The place looked cool and pleasant. A fat, bald man sat on a lopsided plastic chair beside the entrance into the kitchen. He was sipping a cup of coffee and every now and then craning his head, while he kept an eye on two waitresses, as if making sure that his customers were being well looked after.

To Jude's left, yachts of various degrees of size and luxury, were packed into their berths so tightly there was hardly any space between them. A grossly overweight man, sunburned to the colour of an old walnut, eyed her with interest from the deck of one of them. He made some remark in German to a younger blond man who was lazily coiling a rope. He looked up from what he was doing and he too watched as Jude continued on her way. When she was younger, she had got used to men staring at her, always assuming that it was because of her long red hair.

Slowly she crossed the plaza, aware of the heat radiating up at her from the ground. She'd forgotten what it was like to experience really hot weather – to feel as though she were being lightly chargrilled.

Once past a Flying Dolphin that was being loaded up with passengers for a trip to a nearby island, she could see Yialos beach ahead. A path led from the far end of the plaza and curved around the biscuit-coloured sand with its rickety shacks where bronzed young men hired out pedalos and wind-surfing boards to the adventurous and energetic – when they weren't chatting up topless, pretty tourists. Jude paused for a moment, gazing out between the far arms of the island where the sea lay in a flat metallic strip. The glare was so strong, that even with sunglasses she was slightly dazzled. What looked like a toy boat was balanced on the horizon, as though it might topple off the edge at any moment. The vivid colours of bikinis and towels and the bright blue and green of the umbrellas in the foreground gave the place an almost carnival atmosphere.

Unwillingly she forced herself on. At the far end of the beach, the road started to climb steeply. In some places, the sea became hidden by a tangle of trees and tall grasses on her left. The thick screen of foliage blocked any breeze and made the sound of crickets seem louder and the air more scorching. There was a scattering of houses on the other side of the road – perhaps four or five. As Jude rounded a corner, she immediately saw what Rosa had described as 'the House of Manolis'. It was perched high up, facing the bay below. In front of it, a tall pine reared above the surrounding vegetation. Whitewashed like most of the other buildings she'd seen, the house had sun-blistered shutters closed over all the windows. They looked as though they had once been painted green. The building appeared to consist of two storeys and was reached by an uneven track that was bordered by low trees and more dried-up clumps of grasses. Jude raised her glasses a little way off her nose and squinted up at the small building. There was a battered-looking car parked outside but no sign of anybody moving around.

By the time she reached the house above the road, she could feel a welcome breeze caressing her sweaty face and body again. That morning she'd put on a pale green cotton dress with no sleeves in an attempt to stay as cool as possible, but already she could feel the material sticking to her back and she was uncomfortably aware of the skirt clinging to her recently shaved legs. Pausing beside the dust-covered car, she wiped her forehead with the back of her hand. There wasn't a sound from inside the house – only the distant shouts of children on the beach and the sudden roar of a ferry's engines as it manoeuvred into its berth.

The wooden door was scarred and peeling like the shutters. It was more than half open. A slim triangle of sunlight shone down onto pale grey and white marble tiles and a further door. It looked invitingly dark and cool inside. Taking a deep breath, she leaned over the threshold and knocked and waited. Nothing! Jude hesitated. She didn't want to seem impatient if someone had heard her. After making herself count to twenty, she knocked again more loudly.

"Be patient! I'm coming!"

The voice was female – resonant, strong-sounding. It struck Jude as strange that whoever had spoken had done so in English.

She saw the door at the far end of the hallway open. As the figure approached, Jude could see that as well as broad, the woman was very tall. The most striking thing about her though was that she was black. As she stepped out into the sunlight, Jude saw that the other's skin was like polished ebony. She appeared to be dressed in some sort of a bright orange sarong and was wearing flip-flops. Her hair was close-cropped and touched with grey and she wore heavy gold earrings and a gold necklace. Several gold bracelets slithered down her arm as she put a hand up to unhurriedly swat away a large black bee that seemed intent on landing on the tangerine cloth stretched across her melon-like breasts.

Jude had tried to prepare herself for various possible kinds of encounters when she presented herself unexpectedly on the doorstep. She'd known that it was quite probable her father would be living with someone. From what little she'd gleaned, that was his style, but she hadn't been expecting this striking apparition. She hoped her father *was* still living here. Jude suddenly realised that she must look like a complete idiot with her mouth hanging open in surprise. The woman was watching her with a part-amused, part-interested expression.

"Can I help you?" she asked.

Her speech was lightly accented, her voice deep. It sounded as though her throat had been coated with honey. Hearing her immediately reminded Jude of her time in West Africa so many years earlier.

"Do you speak English or has the cat got your tongue?" The woman looked at the silent visitor expectantly, eyebrows raised.

Jude managed to pull herself together enough to answer the question.

"Yes! I'm sorry. I do . . . speak English." She swallowed dryly. "I am looking for my father, Liam Maybury. Is he here?" She hesitated before adding, "My name is . . ."

"Your name is Jude. I know," interjected the woman. "Yes, he is here. He is expecting you. I am Marguerite, by the way."

She held out her hand.

They shook hands and Jude stared at her in amazement. How could he have known? she wondered.

"He knew that I was coming?"

But the woman called Marguerite was already padding across the tiled floor towards the far doorway.

Jude stumbled after her, confused and troubled.

She barely registered any details of the inside of the house. They crossed a kitchen, darkened by the nearly closed shutters, and through another door out onto a stone-paved terrace that stretched along the back of the house. Marguerite led her around the end of the building and up a short flight of steps to a terrace that was raised above the surrounding hillside. Above her, green grapes hung down in heavy clusters through a trellis that ran the full length of the terrace. A man was sitting in a deckchair with his back to them. A table, loaded down with books and papers, stood to one side of him. An opened bottle of wine was placed on top of one of the piles of books and beside it, two half-full glasses.

Jude suddenly felt unable to walk any further. It was as if her feet were glued to the ground. The woman bent over the man's shoulder and said something in a low voice. Then she turned and smiled at Jude. She pointed to a chair facing the unmoving figure in the deckchair.

"Come, Jude! Come and sit down and I will go and get you a cold drink while you introduce yourself." As she passed her, she paused, placing a hand briefly on Jude's arm. "My dear, he won't bite, you know!"

Maybe, thought Jude. But neither is he showing any signs of delight at my arrival.

However, encouraged by Marguerite's friendliness, she walked stiffly over to the other chair and sat down, placing her shoulder-bag carefully at her feet. When she finally raised her eyes, she was struck by how unchanged the eyes watching her were from the ones in the photograph taken nearly half a century earlier. It was the only feature she recognised. Extraordinarily penetrating, they seemed to bore into her. They were the deepest brown, flecked with hazel. However, the black hair had been replaced by a mass of white. His skin was sunburnt and he wore faded blue shorts and a short-sleeved shirt that had seen better days. Like Marguerite, he too wore battered flip-flops. She noticed that there were knotted blue veins in his legs.

She had no idea for how long they stared at each other. Finally he spoke.

"Welcome to Ios."

Her mother had told her that he had a beautiful speaking voice. She'd been right. Jude had half-expected him to make a physical gesture towards her of some sort but then, what *was* the etiquette for a daughter meeting her father after so many years? Somehow a handshake didn't seem to fit the bill. She hadn't expected an embrace, however minimal, and she wouldn't have wanted one.

"I hope you don't mind me coming. I felt it was something I had to do."

"There's no need to sound so defensive. I suppose that it was inevitable that you would appear sooner or later."

He sounded neither angry nor upset. Come to that, he didn't appear particularly pleased either – just rather cool.

"How did you know I was coming to see you?

He looked at her appraisingly as he answered.

"Your mother-in-law took it upon herself to inform me."

"My . . . ?" Jude was stunned. "I don't understand."

"She's made it her business to keep herself informed of my whereabouts through the years. Perhaps she was concerned that your unannounced arrival on the scene would unsettle me." His tone was dry. "For whatever reason, she phoned me a couple of days ago."

Jude looked at him in amazement. What on earth was her mother-in-law up to? The devious old bat. "I didn't even know Patricia knew you! I knew she knew *of* you, of course."

"Yes, well, that's another story. Not a very felicitous one."

There was an awkward pause. It was obvious that he didn't want to discuss either Mrs Larchet or her reasons for feeling it was her duty to contact him about Jude's visit. Perhaps she would be able to broach the subject later when they had talked for a bit. Hopefully things would become more relaxed. She found his continuing gaze uncomfortable. She wasn't sure how to continue the conversation. With difficulty, she dragged her thoughts away from her mother-in-law. Perhaps, as he was a writer, it would be safe to ask about his writing. It was always flattering to be questioned about one's work.

"Are you still writing?"

"I am still writing and my literary agent and my publishers are still endeavouring to make sure I don't get my hands on too much of the small amount of money I make. They probably think that there is so little demand for my sort of writing, that I get what I deserve."

She had managed to get hold of one of his books earlier in the year. It hadn't exactly been what she would call a page-turning read – an intricate literary novel about people whose intellects were explored in fine detail but who never seemed to act spontaneously. To her, they were so busy thinking that they didn't seem to have the time to really feel or behave like real people. She'd found his characters disappointingly lacking in emotion or any real warmth.

And yet, she knew there existed a small band of devoted readers who remained loyal.

"I suppose it is out of the question to change your style?" she ventured and immediately wished that she hadn't.

"You would suppose correctly."

Was there just the smallest hint of amusement in his brown eyes? Jude wasn't sure. She turned away and let her eyes travel over the view, which was spectacular. In the distance she could just make out the vague shape of another island. Ios port and the beach were clearly visible and a little to the right and beneath them and the road, a smaller horseshoe-shaped beach nestled in between the rocks. In spite of it being August, it seemed completely empty. An invisible lark was singing somewhere in the blue sky over their heads.

"This is really lovely," she said, looking back at him.

"Yes, it's very pleasant." There was the sound of a door closing and the noise of approaching flip-flops. Her father looked relieved. "Ah, here's Marguerite."

Jude suspected that this meeting of father and daughter was every bit as awkward and uncomfortable for him as it was for her.

The woman handed her a tall glass filled with freshly squeezed orange juice. Ice tinkled as Jude took it from her, thankful to have an excuse not to talk for a moment. She had run out of things to say. The important questions couldn't be blurted out five minutes after seeing each other for the first time in forty-odd years.

"You haven't finished your wine," her father said to the tall woman standing near Jude's chair. "Sit down and relax for a few minutes. The painting won't disappear." It

79

sounded to Jude as though it had been a plea for her not to leave him alone with his daughter as much as a casual request for her to join them. He looked over at her. "Marguerite is an artist. A very fine one too. She's exhibited all over the place – Rome, London, Lisbon – even Los Angeles."

She saw a fleeting expression cross his face as his gaze returned to the other woman's face. Was it admiration? Affection? A combination of the two perhaps. Whatever it was, it had the effect of momentarily softening his expression.

"OK, I'll sit but only for a while," the woman replied, looking down at him and smiling slightly.

Jude couldn't help feeling that Marguerite wasn't an appropriate name for her. She was too large, too powerful-looking. Even her hands were enormous. The only flower Jude could think of that might suit her was the dark-faced sunflower, standing tall, fringed by golden petals, its face tilted confidently towards the sun.

Flora had been so named because, as a tiny baby, she had reminded them of a small flower – pale and delicate. Jude had a brief vision of her sullen-faced offspring shouting to the heavens how unfair they were, how unreasonable life was, how nobody understood. Delicate was not the right description for her these days, she thought with a sudden pang of affection.

Marguerite picked up her glass from the table and walked slowly over to the edge of the terrace. Lowering herself onto a sun-faded cushion on the surrounding low wall, she leaned against one of the wooden trellis supports and stretched her legs out in front of her. In spite of her size, there was something very fluid and relaxed about this woman, like a large jungle animal who feared no predator because none dared threaten her. Her gold jewellery flashed in the shifting splashes of sunlight that found their way through the jigsaw puzzle of vine-leaves above. The orange sarong seemed to glow against the background of grey-green olive trees. Jude thought how perfectly comfortable with herself and her surroundings she looked.

"Where are you staying?"

Her father's voice broke into Jude's thoughts.

"Villa Rosa."

"Ah, yes! With the industrious and immensely inquisitive Rosa."

She smiled slightly. "That sounds like her."

"I can't offer you accommodation here, I'm afraid."

"I wasn't expecting you to," she said quickly.

"Marguerite is using the second bedroom. The other one is very small and is used as my study."

So, he and the woman didn't share a bedroom. Perhaps they weren't lovers after all.

"I see."

In a way, she felt relieved. It was better like this – to visit him and to be able to escape when necessary. At least the first hurdle had been crossed. They'd met face to face and he hadn't told her to clear off. Would he *want* to see her again after this first meeting? Though they needed to talk without the woman being around – even though she seemed pleasant enough. Jude glanced over towards her. Marguerite's eyes were shut, her face smooth and relaxed – almost trance-like. The wineglass stood empty on the wall beside her. She gave the impression of being apart from them and their conversation.

Again she was aware of her father's eyes on her. What was he making of this daughter of his? Was he already bored and wishing she would leave?

Jude spoke softly, not wanting to disturb the other woman.

"I would like to talk to you – on our own."

"There's no need to whisper. Marguerite has an outstanding knack of wandering off into a sort of Yoruba version of Aboriginal dreamtime. Physically, she's present but her mind is elsewhere. She won't hear us unless we want her to."

"Marguerite comes from Nigeria?" Her father nodded. It didn't sound like a typical Nigerian name – but then she did remember once meeting a Nigerian taxi driver in Lagos called Hyacinth. Jude couldn't help feeling curious. How long had they been together? *Were* they together? Was their relationship an affectionate, platonic one? Dozens of questions crossed her mind. "How did you and she meet?"

"We met in London seven years ago in the restaurant in the Gallery of Modern Art."

"Are you interested in modern painting?"

"No, not really. I was in London for a book launch and a friend, who is besotted with anything painted, designed or sculpted after the middle of the last century, dragged me along to an exhibition. He informed me that I was out of touch, living on a Greek island on my own. Apparently he considered I had become far too self-absorbed for my own good."

"And had you?"

"You're not thinking of interviewing me for your programme, are you, by any chance?"

Jude coloured slightly. So, he knew about her work. Patricia again.

"No, of course not! It's just that I know next to nothing about you. I have to start somewhere. I don't mind if you ask me questions about my life."

"Patricia has kept me up-to-date on your activities. You sound as though you have a successful career, an equally successful husband, a pleasant home, two healthy children . . ."

"*Your* grandchildren, by the way," Jude could not stop herself from interjecting sharply.

Liam Maybury didn't reply. He stayed very still, staring out over the sea, his mouth slightly pursed. It was almost as if he were stopping himself from answering her.

Jude could feel herself becoming angry. The selfish bugger wasn't apparently the least bit interested in Oscar and Flora. She found his stillness an added irritant. What would it take to prod him into some sort of lively reaction? "Is there anything you'd like to ask about them?"

There was a long silence.

Then he sighed and said, "Is this wise?"

She looked at him in astonishment.

"What do you mean, is this wise? Aren't you interested in them, in me – in any of us? Do we really mean so little to you that you can't muster up enough enthusiasm to even pretend to care?"

Slowly, he leaned forward and picked up his wineglass before looking at her.

"I don't want to hurt you, Jude, but . . ."

"It's a little late to say that! You *have* already hurt me! Do you realise that I don't have one single memory of you? Nothing! I don't remember you picking me up when I was

83

a child – or you holding me. I don't even remember you being in the house. Then, when you left, I don't remember you leaving because you were never bloody well there. You were too busy enjoying yourself wining and dining other women."

Jude realised that she had raised her voice almost to a shout. She also became aware that Marguerite was standing in front of her, her face expressionless.

"It is better that you leave now, Jude."

So, the woman was going to take his part after all? Jude supposed that she shouldn't be surprised. If she were his mistress, it wouldn't do for her to be seen supporting the enemy. Furious, she fumbled for her bag and stood up.

"Of course, I'll leave. I wouldn't want to be any more of a nuisance than I am already." Choking back her tears, she faced the man in the chair. "But I'll come back. I'm not going away until I have some answers. We *have* to talk, even if you think it's not important. Even if I am only your daughter."

"No, I'm afraid that's where you are wrong." His voice was measured. "You are *not* my daughter."

Chapter Seven

Marguerite moved to Jude's side and gently led her away from the terrace. They walked through the house until they reached the glare of the open front door. For Jude, a feeling of unreality pervaded everything. The phrase, 'You are not my daughter', rang in her ears.

Afterwards she couldn't remember anything much that had been said, either by her or the man who claimed that he wasn't her father. She didn't know how she suddenly found herself standing with her back to the house with one of Marguerite's large hands resting around her waist, the other one under her elbow. There seemed to be a strange humming sound in her head and she found it difficult to focus after the darkness of the house. Her hands felt icy.

Marguerite was saying something to her but somehow her voice seemed strangely distant and the words jumbled. Jude shook her head, trying to force herself back into the real world. The other woman spoke again and this time the words made sense.

"You have had a shock. Will you not sit down in the shade for a while? There is no need for you to leave like this."

She pointed to an old seat under the tall pine tree.

Jude took a step towards it, then stopped and slowly turned and stared into the other's face.

"What does he mean, I'm not his daughter?"

"My dear, he would not say it if it were untrue. Of that you can be sure." The woman's voice was gentle. "I can see how upset you are. Go and rest for a while. Come back tomorrow."

"What would be the point in coming back? He doesn't want to talk to me." He must have been lying. His neglect over the past years must have filled him with guilt and he thought it would be easier to explain his lack of interest by making up this crazy fairytale and disowning her.

"On the contrary!" Marguerite's face was serious. "Liam didn't handle things too well just now. He gets tired very easily these days. But he has to talk to you. It is not easy for him but he must do it. For your sake as much as for his own."

She sounded quietly determined. Jude felt that perhaps he wouldn't have much choice in the matter. Perhaps, after all, it wasn't a question of Marguerite taking sides. It was a matter of doing what needed to be done. Somehow, the woman's pragmatism had a calming effect on her. She started to feel a little less shaken.

"You really think I should come back? *Will* he talk to me, explain it all?"

"Yes, of course you must come. You are owed an explanation."

"Will you be there?"

Marguerite smiled at her.

"I thought you preferred it if I weren't around."

So it was possible she hadn't been quite so 'absent' as she'd seemed when Jude and her father had been talking. Jude still couldn't stop herself from thinking of him as her father.

"I'm not sure what I want at the moment. I'm feeling incredibly confused."

"Let's wait until tomorrow then. But now, I suggest you go and relax, have a swim. It is the middle of the day. You will be alone on the beach below. Try and do something that will stop you worrying so much. Worry solves nothing. There is always a reason for things being the way they are."

"I'm not sure I believe that. People are largely responsible for the way their lives turn out," said Jude.

Marguerite didn't reply. After giving Jude an encouraging smile, she turned back to the house and went inside, softly closing the door behind her.

For a moment Jude stared at its flaking paintwork. The temptation to lean her forehead against its rough surface, close her eyes and weep with frustration was enormous. But that would leave her feeling even more drained and, anyway, she didn't think she could summon up the energy to cry.

She managed to make herself set off down the track towards the hidden road. It was unbearably hot now and she felt unsteady on her feet. Even the crickets seemed to have been silenced. As she walked, little eddies of dust rose around her feet, coating her sandals and skin with a fine white powder. Once on the road, she turned to the right and almost immediately saw a narrow entrance, half-hidden by small trees and bushes, to the small beach on the other side. Crossing the sticky tarmac, she made her way over the scorched grass until she reached the sand. Even though she was wearing sandals, she could feel the heat through their thin soles.

Marguerite was right. There was not a single person around. Tiny waves rippled at the water's edge, sparkling in the intense light. Usually so aware of her surroundings, Jude barely noticed the blending of turquoise and inky blue, marbled here and there with the deep purple of gently swaying seaweed. As she walked towards the sea, her mind ached with confusion. He said he wasn't her father. Marguerite told her that he had only spoken the truth. If so, who then was her real father? What was the connection with Patricia Larchet? Had she been in contact with him ever since he walked out when Jude was a small child? If so, why had she never mentioned the fact and why would she have bothered if he really wasn't her father?

The bay was surrounded on two sides by high rocks. At one end she noticed a large flat stone that seemed to jut out over the water. Part of it was in the shade. When she reached it, she sat down, feeling numb. Blankly, she gazed around her as she took off her sandals. Perching on the rock was a little like sitting on the hot plate of an Aga. Looking down into the transparent water, she realised how hot and sweaty she was. Suddenly, the only thing she wanted to do was to plunge into its welcoming coolness – not just because of the need to cool down but the necessity to try and minimise the feelings of misery and incomprehension she felt. No matter that she had no swimming-costume or towel. There was still nobody about and Jude couldn't remember the last time she'd gone skinny-dipping.

Quickly she stood up and stripped off her dress and pants, lowering herself into the welcoming water, feeling it close over her in a cool, refreshing caress. Swimming along the sandy bottom, Jude watched the small shoals of fish that changed direction at the same moment, becoming one flashing entity of movement, transforming from nearly transparent to silver as they shimmered in the fragmented sunlight. Somehow in this watery world it was easier not to think of the other place outside – or the people in it.

For a long time she stayed in the water, only emerging when she started to feel cold. Climbing back onto the platform of rock, Jude once again checked the beach for intruders but she was still alone. Carefully, she lay down on the hot rock and closed her eyes, head pillowed by her folded clothes, hair fanned out to dry. Whether it was due to the heat or just exhaustion after the events of that morning and too little sleep the night before, she fell asleep almost immediately.

It was the rattle of stones dislodged by passing feet that woke her with a start. Making a grab for her dress, she quickly turned onto her stomach, in time to see a tall man in rust-coloured shorts heading up the beach, his brown back towards her. Crouching now, Jude rammed the dress over her head. How close had he come? Had he stood looking at her while she was asleep? She felt sick at the thought of it. She struggled to get her head through an armhole. He must have seen someone was lying on the rock when he came down to the beach. There was no need for him to come anywhere near her unless he was snooping.

It was an invasion of her privacy and she hated the feeling of having been in such a vulnerable position. Was he a tourist or one of the locals? He had jet-black hair, cropped short and, from what she could see as he walked away from her, was possibly in his thirties. It was difficult to tell at that distance. The easy way in which he moved was athletic. Furtively, she eased her pants up her legs and over her hips. What an idiot she was to fall asleep like that. Already her skin felt a little sunburned. Well, she hoped he'd enjoyed gawping at her. She must have looked like a stranded starfish spread out on the rock like that.

* * *

Jude hadn't felt like eating anything after her swim and disrupted nap but the canopied shade of Paradise Café was too compelling to resist and anyway, she was dying of thirst. Not caring that she must look a mess with her sticky sea-tangled hair, which the small comb in her bag had been unable to tame, she sat down at a corner table, doing her best to push thoughts of her father – or the man she couldn't help thinking of as her father – out of her mind. It was well after three and the place was quiet. She supposed everyone sensible was enjoying an afternoon nap. In spite of trying not to, as she settled herself, she found her thoughts returned to puzzling over what possible connection Patricia Larchet could have with Liam Maybury. It was no good. She'd just have to prise more information out of him when she went back to see him on the following day. Giving herself a mental shake, she picked up the cardboard menu from the table.

The owner himself put down his cup of coffee and came

over and asked her in English what she wanted to order. It always surprised her that waiters and people serving in shops seemed to know, without her opening her mouth, that she spoke English. No doubt they would switch easily to Danish if she turned out to be a red-haired Dane. Jude forgot about trying out her few words of half-remembered Greek and ordered a glass of beer in English.

When she had finished the drink, he returned to the table and asked her if she would like another beer or perhaps something to eat.

Jude smiled at him, pushing her hair off her face.

"No, nothing more to drink, thank you. And I'm not hungry."

He paused, one hand on the back of the chair opposite her.

"Perhaps you come to eat here next time. The food very good," he said, pulling an expressive face, implying that the meals in Paradise Café were definitely something not to be missed.

She laughed.

"Perhaps I will. I love sea food."

"We make calamari that is best in Cyclades. When you taste cooking here you not go nowhere else, this I promise you." He looked at her carefully. "Excuse, but you not English, I think?"

"No, I come from Ireland."

The effect on him was immediate and dramatic. Beaming, he put down the tray and white napkin with a flourish. Moving around to her side of the table, he took hold of her hand and shook it fondly.

"Ah, Ireland! The beautiful island that is always green.

My son, Fotis, he go to Ireland as student. He say everybody very kind in Ireland. He had so good time there he never forget." Letting go of her hand he made a small inclination of the head. "My name is Adonis." With a plump hand he gestured at the surrounding plastic chairs and paper-draped tables with their small, ornate vases of plastic flowers on each one. "This, Paradise Café, my restaurant," he announced with pride.

Considering he wasn't a day under sixty, the belly sagging over the top of his trousers, his almost total lack of hair and the fact that he was barely five feet something tall, Jude couldn't help feeling that the name Adonis was just a little inappropriate. But there was something nice about him. There was kindness in the observant small eyes that were deep-set in his moon-shaped face. She felt too that there was something melancholy mixed in with the bustle and busyness of this man who stood, perspiring gently as he smiled at her.

When Jude had paid for her drink, she hooked her bag over her shoulder and stood up.

"It is a beautiful café and I will most certainly come back and eat here. Perhaps this evening."

Adonis looked pleased.

"You do this. You will not regret. I make you very good food at special price."

Once out in the glare of the sun, she glanced back. Adonis was gently admonishing a sleepy-looking girl for apparently not sweeping thoroughly enough under a recently vacated table. Taking the long-handled brush from her, he demonstrated how the job should be done.

* * *

That night, as she lay on the bed unable to sleep, Jude tried to sort out her thoughts. So much had happened since her arrival less than thirty-six hours ago.

She had phoned home on her return from the evening meal at the Paradise Café. Geoff had not been there. He was working late, Flora informed her before asking if her mother had seen her father yet. Before she had time to think properly, Jude had said, no, not yet but that she had an address. She didn't feel like saying anything about the matter until after the meeting on the following day. Flora had seemed cheerful enough in her usual rather off-hand way. Oscar was out at a film with 'his latest woman', she said.

"She's a bit of a slapper really. All tits and no brain," she announced.

"Have you met her?" asked Jude.

"Yeah, Mum, I have and believe me, you wouldn't want to know."

"She can't be *that* bad, surely?"

"Can we change the subject?" said Flora in the impatient tone she so often affected these days when dealing with either parent. It annoyed both of them but they'd agreed that it would probably soon pass – like bed-wetting, nail-chewing, conveniently lost homework and sibling rivalry – and all the various other delightful phases they had ploughed through over the years. Jude hoped it wouldn't take too long before Flora emerged from the present one. "Do you know when you'll be coming back?" her daughter asked.

"Not yet but it'll probably be sooner rather than later."

There was a pause before Flora said, "Good! Anyway,

I'd better go. Gran's on patrol. Jesus, Mum, it's like living with the secret police breathing down your neck. She's been monitoring all our phone calls. She says she hasn't but Oz caught her the other day lurking behind the door when I was on the phone to Carina. She's getting worse."

"Well, practise being nice to her."

"She probably heard *that* too. So it won't do me any good," replied Flora glumly.

As Jude hung up she thought again about the remark Liam had made about Patricia keeping in touch with him over the years. What exactly was it he'd said? "She's made it her business to keep me informed . . ." Something like that. What did the damn woman think she was up to? All the questions Jude had prepared were based on a meeting with her father but if he really wasn't her father, a mountain of other queries now filled her brain. She tried to push the next day's encounter out of her mind.

The meal at Paradise Café had been delicious. As Adonis had promised, the calamari was terrific, as was the creamy tzatziki, the spicy dolmades and the baklava. Retsina had flowed, followed by several thimblefuls of a particularly fiery liqueur. Adonis insisted that the drinks were on the house. She was feeling slightly tipsy by the time he asked permission to join her at the end of the meal. Their conversation had mostly centred on life in Ireland. He had asked about her family. Jude's work on radio and television had especially fascinated him.

"So – I have famous lady in my restaurant," he said, smiling broadly. When Jude denied that she was famous, Adonis waggled a finger at her and added, "Famous and most beautiful."

When she had asked him about his son, a look of regret crossed his face.

"When Fotis small, he want to help his papa all the time in the restaurant. He very clever boy, very quick. All tourists like him. I think when he grow big, he will work with me." He shrugged sadly. "But he want big house in Athens. Here is too small. He tell me his wife does not like to come to Ios."

"Can he not come to see you without her?" she asked.

"Last time was three years ago when my wife die." Adonis paused, tipping his head back and staring for a moment at the canvas ceiling. Then he looked at Jude and said in a resigned voice, "He is busy man now. Big job, many things to do. It is difficult for him. But I hope he come soon because now *he* has son too."

"I'm sure he will want to show him off to you," Jude said with an encouraging smile.

Adonis raised his glass.

"*Yamas!* We drink to all beautiful ladies and to our sons. May they never forget!"

As she downed her drink, Jude found herself fervently hoping that Fotis would soon see fit to visit his father, bringing his young child with him.

The bill had been ridiculously small, prompting her to leave a generous tip before setting off on the short walk back to Villa Rosa.

She had not seen Rosa that afternoon but the old lady ambushed her as Jude tried to slip upstairs on her return from the restaurant. The woman appeared in the hallway, duster in hand.

"You find your father?"

Even the whiskers on her chin seemed to quiver with curiosity.

Jude smiled down at her from halfway up the stairs.

"Thank you. I found the house and Mr Maybury," she replied ambiguously.

"House of Manolis very good house," said Rosa, looking at her expectantly.

But Jude was too exhausted to go into the merits of the House of Manolis just then. She smiled politely and continued on her way as fast as she could, leaving a disappointed Rosa standing, gazing after her.

Villa Rosa had been very quiet when Jude went to bed. It seemed that after darkness fell, most people liked to climb the hundreds of steps that led up to Chora – the town on top of the hill above Yialos port. It was apparently the place to go to if you were looking for a good time. She had noticed it on her way back to Villa Rosa that afternoon. It looked remarkably attractive with its white buildings, church domes and bell towers standing out against the so-blue sky. It hadn't looked real – like the sort of thing you would see on a postcard. She wondered if she would have the opportunity or the inclination to visit it while she was on the island.

Resolutely pushing all the unanswered questions from her thoughts, Jude lay back with her hands behind her head. I will just have to wait and see what tomorrow brings, she thought.

Chapter Eight

On her way to the House of Manolis next morning, Jude noticed that Adonis had propped a large board against the entrance to Paradise Café. Although feeling nervous as to what revelations awaited her when she reached her destination, she couldn't help chuckling. Among the neatly chalked list of 'Special Dishes', there was an item described as, 'Cock in wine sauce with garlig'. Adonis was not to be seen, but even if he were, how to explain that it would perhaps be more delicate to substitute chicken as the main ingredient?

As though in competition in the hilarity stakes, around the corner, one of the larger cafés was announcing a screening that evening of 'Babe 2 – Ping in the City'. She wondered what the uninitiated would make of that. Two Swedish girls, arms draped around each other's shoulders, long blonde hair glinting attractively in the sunlight, were considering the sign. They talked to each other in low voices, their expressions serious. Perhaps they thought it might be a sexy film. For a moment, Jude imagined Flora, who was famous for her sense of the ridiculous, saying in a bored voice something along the lines of: 'Yeah, Ma, and *ping is the sound made by the beautiful babe – Babe 1 having just passed away from a surfeit of sex – when she unhooks her bra!'*

Jude walked past the gaggle of yachts and on towards the beach. It was all very well to smile at the shaky English that was sometimes used on the island but how many of the thousands of invading visitors ever really tried to speak Greek, herself included? Very few, she guessed. And the Irish poke fun at the arrogance of the English!

She experienced a sudden pang. What was Flora doing at this precise moment? And Oscar too. Not driving their grandmother up the wall, she hoped. No doubt Jude would hear all about their dreadful goings-on the minute she got back. To mix well-known sayings, Patricia had never been one to bite her tongue and suffer in silence!

By the time she reached the track leading to the house, she was sweating, thirsty and tired, although it was barely eleven o'clock in the morning. She trudged up to the front door, which, as on the previous day, was half-open. And, as on the previous day, Jude knocked and waited, her heart thumping in her chest.

Almost immediately, Marguerite appeared through the door at the far end of the hallway and called out to her.

"Good morning, Jude! Come on through."

When Jude reached her, the other woman touched her lightly on the shoulder and indicated that she should go out onto the terrace.

"He is waiting for you," she told her with a smile.

Jude looked at her questioningly.

"You aren't coming out, then?"

"Not for the moment. As you can see, I am in the middle of a painting."

In the light from the open door, Jude saw that Marguerite was wearing some sort of voluminous white smock over long, baggy peacock-blue trousers. Both smock and trousers were covered in smudges and splashes of paint. She guessed that the woman worked with large brushes on enormous canvases and that her paintings were bold and colourful.

As if guessing Jude's thoughts, Marguerite added, "You can have a look later on if you are interested."

Jude stepped out into the heat and walked slowly towards the raised terrace at the end of the house.

This time, Liam Maybury's chair had been turned so that he was able to watch her as she approached. She felt suddenly desperately self-conscious. Like yesterday, she found his stillness unnerving. The brown eyes followed her as she walked to the chair opposite his own and sat down.

"Good morning! I trust you slept well?"

It sounded like a polite enquiry from a stranger.

"No, actually, I didn't."

"I'm sorry to hear that. Probably because you're not used to the heat –"

"I like the heat," she replied quickly. "Can we please cut out the pleasantries?"

Even as she said this, Jude was aware that she must have sounded like her daughter: impatient and rather rude.

"Of course! Where do you want to start?"

Oh, God! Where *to* start? she wondered.

"Well, how about beginning with your parting remark of yesterday – that I am not your daughter?"

"It's quite simple really. When I married your mother, she was already pregnant with you."

Jude stared at him. He must be lying! It wasn't one bit simple. Her mother wouldn't have gone to her grave allowing her to believe that this man was her father if it weren't true.

He spoke again. "I can see from your face that you think I am making this all up." He gave her an almost challenging look. "Why would I bother?"

Jude shrugged helplessly. "I can't begin to imagine. Perhaps because it doesn't matter to you if you cause other people hurt. Perhaps because you never cared for me. You left us when I was small – before I'd had time to develop into a person. To you, I was a boring child and then, the longer you stayed away, the easier it became for you not to think about us – and anyway," she said bitterly, "you had your hands full with family number two." Jude's eyes never left his face. "Oh, my mother told me how you had remarried almost immediately and then left *her* for someone else."

"Yes, you're right. I did remarry and that too was an awful mistake. I should have realised that marriage was not for me."

"But *why* say that I am not your daughter? Forgive me for asking but hadn't you and my mother slept together before you married her? It can't have been too unusual, even back then, for the woman to be pregnant when she walked down the aisle."

"Because, dear girl, I am *not* your father."

She stared at him for a moment.

"Then, would you mind telling me who the hell is?"

"I'm afraid I don't know who he was."

There was a long silence. When Jude next spoke, her voice was scornful.

"You mean to say, that you married my mother knowing she was expecting a child and you didn't think to ask who the father was? I'm sorry but I just don't believe you."

"Your mother had been . . . taken advantage of by someone she didn't know at some sort of a weekend house-party affair."

"What do you mean, 'taken advantage of'? That sounds as though she was some pathetically drunk teenager who didn't know what was doing. She was twenty-six when she married you, for God's sake!"

"Your mother was quite a wild young thing when I met her – a bit of a hippy, in fact. If I remember correctly, she was into free love, wearing flowers behind her ear, beads and quite a lot of pot-smoking – all that sort of carry-on." He looked at her sharply. "Don't tell me you ever thought she was conventional – even in her later years."

She remembered only too well her mother's individual behaviour and how Jude had sometimes, even as an adult, been torn between pride at her mother's eccentricity and wild embarrassment at some of the things she had done or said. It was only since Jane Maybury's death that Jude realised that she herself was capable of behaving in equally unconventional ways. She remembered her mother's hoots of laughter when, on a visit to London, thirty-odd years earlier, they'd been present at some function where 'God Save the Queen' was played, and Jude had refused to stand up because the woman wasn't an Irish queen. She had also demanded to know, in a loud voice, 'Who did she have to be saved from anyway?' The incident was still vivid. That and a hundred other occasions that she remembered with amused affection.

"Yes, I know that but Mum wasn't stupid."

"I'm not saying she was. She had a sort of innocence though. From what I gathered afterwards, on the last night of the house party, things apparently got a little out of hand. Someone slipped something in her drink. She'd smoked a lot of dope and the combination of the two made her an easy target for the miserable git who then took advantage of her. She said she never knew who'd done it and I believed her."

He couldn't be lying, she thought. The way in which he'd told her had the ring of truth about it – his voice, the constant, unflinching eye contact – everything about him while he spoke couldn't be an act. Could it? She reminded herself that he was a somewhat unsuccessful writer, not an accomplished actor. But if he were telling the truth, that left her facing up to the knowledge that for all her life, her mother had hidden what had happened and had encouraged her to believe that Liam Maybury *was* her real father. Why? It seemed so completely out of character. She'd always considered her to be a truthful and courageous woman.

Feeling suddenly defeated, Jude slumped back into her chair.

"Then I don't understand why she didn't tell me the truth."

"Maybe it was because she thought you would be

happier with the happy family story she'd concocted. Perhaps she felt guilty, ashamed about what happened." He gave an impatient sigh. "Or perhaps because, once a serious lie has been fabricated, it's easier to let things be, easier to go on deceiving than undergo the trauma of the unmaking and unmasking. I really don't know."

"There is one thing I'd like to ask and it's important." Jude pulled herself up in her chair, her hands gripping the ends of the wicker arms. "Why didn't you tell me when I was older? Why did you leave me to think that you were my father?" His eyes wandered over the twisted olive trees, crouching low in the unrelenting glare of sunlight. She could see that he'd heard her. There was a long pause – as if he felt he couldn't come up with a credible answer. She battled on, determined not to be ignored. "Because telling me would have been less cruel than what you have done. All these years, I thought you hadn't ever cared for me, or my mother or my children, whom I've always thought of as your grandchildren. They feel the same sense of betrayal and denial as I have. Don't you see how wrong that is?"

Unwanted tears sprang into her eyes. For the first time since they began to talk, the man turned away his head for a moment. But when he eventually looked at her again, his voice was as even as ever.

"I think your mother wanted to erase it from her mind. What had taken place was a negation of everything she believed that a woman should be – proud, individual, independent, complete and, above all, I believe that she was angry with herself for behaving so irresponsibly. She never for one moment thought of having a termination but she was terrified that, once you were born, she would find it impossible to really love the child resulting from such an unconsidered, careless act of foolishness. When you were born, she found she did love you with all her heart. I think she concentrated on nurturing that love and, for reasons only she understood, decided that you should never know. She begged me to go along with it and despite having doubts and because I loved her, I did just that. Later on, when you were older, I felt I had done quite enough damage without going against her wishes." He lifted both hands slightly, palms facing each other, in a hopeless gesture. "And now look where it has got us all!"

Like a dog worrying at a bone, Jude repeated her question.

"Perhaps that makes sense. I don't know. I'll have to have time to think about it. But why did you ignore us? Why did you pretend that we simply didn't exist?" A thought suddenly occurred to her. "Did you treat your other family in the same way?"

"There were no children from that marriage. A stillborn baby after several miscarriages – that's all."

The bleak way he said this made Jude realise that she'd better watch her step. Obviously he wasn't prepared to discuss this 'other family'. That fell outside the permitted boundaries of her questioning.

"So you have no children of your own?" A closed, private look appeared on his face but Jude couldn't stop herself from asking, "Didn't you want to have a child with my mother?"

He gave her an angry glance.

"It's a shame that she's not around to tell you how I was never there, how I was always having affairs, living it up.

104

But then I'm sure Patricia would be more than happy to fill you in on what a rotten husband I was. She knew your mother before I met her. They never liked each other. Perhaps that's one of the reasons she's always kept in contact with me. God knows, I never wanted her to. Perhaps it gave her pleasure, a sense of power, knowing how much your mother would have resented the fact that she and you were under her scrutiny and that she'd kept in touch with me all through the years. I really don't know." Gradually, his voice became more calm. "Your mother very soon realised she'd made a terrible mistake in marrying me. At the start, all her ideas and ideals seemed to fly out of the window. She suddenly wanted a husband to look after her, make her feel cherished and safe – I don't know. For an intelligent woman, she behaved very strangely. Motherhood must have temporarily warped her brain. Anyway, she picked the wrong man. All things considered, it's hardly surprising we didn't get round to producing a brother or sister for you to play with. There was a lot of bitterness between us. I felt used and she felt cheated. My marriage to your mother, Jude, was over almost before it began."

"Well, you didn't have to take it out on me because you made such a bloody awful mess of things," said Jude angrily. Again she could feel the damned tears prickling her eyes. Unplanned, she found herself blurting out, "I can't tell you how awful it was growing up without a father. I used to pretend that you were dead to try and make it easier – but it didn't. I used to watch my friends' fathers and play a game when I'd pick out the most handsome one and secretly adopt him for myself. Mum used to get so annoyed with me, the way I'd slither up to them on sports days and at concerts, trying to get the nice ones to notice me. I'm sure they thought I was pathetic – if they noticed me at all. And I kept on playing that game even when I'd started to go out with men. I invariably went for the older ones and it usually ended in disaster – until I met Geoff. And then, when the children were little, they seemed to accept that they hadn't got a proper grandfather once dear old Pop Larchet died and I found it easier to go along with that. But when Mum died last year, I *needed* my father." She looked at him, desperate for him to understand what she was trying to say. "Maybe it sounds ridiculous, but I wanted you to be there at Mum's funeral, saying goodbye with the rest of the family around you. I wanted to give you a hug and let go of all that had happened in the past. But you didn't come. You didn't even send flowers – and I knew that it must be because you just didn't care. And now you tell me all this and I . . ."

Jude was suddenly aware of an arm around her and Marguerite was leaning over her exuding a musky smell of sweat and turpentine and a jasmine-like perfume.

"That is enough for now. No more questions, no more angry words."

Jude fought valiantly to stop herself crying openly.

With her free hand, Marguerite lightly touched the side of the other's face. "Let the tears come, Jude. Let them come. You will feel better afterwards."

* * *

Jude turned down Marguerite's offer of lunch.

"That's kind of you but I'd rather be on my own for a while – to try and make sense out of it all." She smiled shakily at the other woman. "I've got rather a lot to think about."

They'd walked around to the front of the house and were standing in the stippled shade of the giant pine. Marguerite's white smock billowed around her in the sea breeze, making her look rather like a handsome ship in full sail.

She watched Jude's face carefully as she asked, "Does this *have* to make sense?"

"What do you mean?"

"My father was a diplomat – a very successful and wise man. He always said that people often came to grief because they wanted life to be logical, thought out, to have a meaning that they could understand. He maintained that the world is not a logical place. It is full of mystery and of the inexplicable." She laughed. "Look at religion! People are misguided, they react spontaneously, they make the wrong decisions – sometimes for the right reasons – and vice versa. It is not wise to always expect a logical reason for everything that happens in the world. My father thought that the secret of a successful life was the art of adapting to what life throws at you and only doing battle with what you find to be truly unacceptable. That way, you have enough energy left to live your life to the full."

"That sounds like a good philosophy but you can't blame me if I feel confused. I've just found out that I don't have a father and that my mother, whom I always trusted implicitly, lied to me." She didn't want to say out loud that she hated the thought of being the unwanted product of such a casual coupling between the mother she had loved so deeply and some unknown, unnamed, drunken lecher.

"Lied to you?" The woman shook her head. "No, I don't think so."

She gestured to Jude to sit with her on the lopsided seat under the tree. When they were both sitting, she said, "Did you consider your mother to be a kind, good woman?"

"Yes, I did," replied Jude emphatically.

"Then presumably, after that one moment of madness, the important decisions she made in her life would have been made in a considered and serious fashion – and with the best motives?"

"Yes."

"So, why does it matter so much to you what she did or didn't tell you . . . when she obviously loved you, looked after you well? The relationship you had with each other sounds marvellous to me when you look at what goes on in so many families. I think you have been very lucky, Jude."

Jude couldn't help being taken aback. *Was* she being unrealistic in expecting answers to it all? Perhaps this woman with the beauty of a slightly battered Benin bronze was talking a lot of sense.

"But what about his part in all of this?" she asked quietly, glancing in the direction of the hidden terrace.

Marguerite sat back, resting her large hands on her thighs. The golden bracelets tinkled. The wooden seat creaked under them as she moved.

"I think he is the one who has possibly suffered most in all of this."

Jude looked surprised.

"Why?"

The other woman looked at her intently.

"Can you not see from his face that he is unhappy?"

"I've seen him look very happy when he looks at you when you aren't aware of him watching."

"Oh, we are old friends. He is comforted by my being around but it is only a temporary remission. He soon sinks back into a state of depression." She leaned forward, speaking in a low voice as though she didn't wish to be overheard. "You know that there are two great passions in his life? The first is that he has always been desperate to write a novel that people will recognise as a significant work. The second is to have fathered a son. Neither has been realised and he cannot come to terms with that – and that, amongst other things, is his tragedy."

All Jude's own angst seemed to evaporate. She too leaned forward. Somehow, the task of sorting out her own feelings appeared suddenly unimportant.

"Are you saying that he has never been happy?"

The other woman nodded.

"Yes, I suppose I am."

"Do you mind me asking if you are married to him?"

Marguerite chuckled.

"Ask away! No, we are not married. He was right when he told you that marriage is not for him." She hesitated and then continued talking as though she had decided against saying too much and possibly being indiscreet. "I spend four or five months with him each year. I paint. I tell him what is happening in the world outside. We would drive each other mad if I stayed any longer. Most of the time, he prefers to be reclusive. But this way, between us, it works well."

"Would I be right in saying that he is not an easy man to live with?" Jude asked with a half-smile.

Marguerite threw back her head and laughed so that her whole body shook. Her breasts seemed to tremble like blancmanges and her gold earrings swung backwards and forwards.

"You could say that, I suppose!"

The contrast of the woman's sheer size and the rich-toned, cultured voice that emerged from deep inside her was striking.

"It must be wonderful to be so accepting. You seem to be, I don't know . . ." Jude searched for words to describe what she wanted to say. "You seem so complete – as if you had no worries, or at least, if you *have* worries, you don't waste time worrying."

"My dear, there are plenty of things I could worry about." Marguerite smiled at her. "For example, you feel as if you don't belong because you don't know your father. If I wanted to, I also could feel as if I don't belong. My mother was a Yoruba chief's daughter by a wife who fell from favour and was disowned. My father was half Yoruba, half Ibo – two tribes with a long history of mutual mistrust and who often indulged in open warfare. I lived in Lagos, Paris, London and Rome. I went to five different schools and made and lost track of more friends than I care to think about. The only thing that has remained constant in sixty years is the fact that I am in charge of making me the person I am. And *that* has been a full-time job – and an interesting one, I can tell you."

There was an amused gleam in her eyes as she said this. Jude reckoned that the woman beside her had been adept at following her father's recipe for living life to the full.

"So, if I were to say that the best thing for me to do now

110

is to turn round and go home to Ireland, you would probably agree?"

"I think it would be a pity for you to disappear before Liam has got to know you a little better. He has few friends. I too would like it if you stayed in Ios for a while longer."

Jude looked guilty.

"That's part of the problem. I would like to stay longer too."

"And that is a problem?"

"Well, I did rather walk out on my family. In fact, I've not been thinking straight at all lately. I left my job in the lurch. Although they'll probably put it down to some sort of a stupid female behavioural blip if I go back quickly enough. My husband thinks I am having a mid-life crisis."

"Does he?" Again, a light chuckle escaped Marguerite. "One moment! Let me get this straight. If Patricia has been accurate, you have one spouse, adult, male, with a good job. You have two children, one female of twenty-one, one male of nineteen, both of whom are capable of looking after themselves." She held up a hand as Jude started to say something. "I didn't mean that they *wanted* to look after themselves. A different matter entirely!"

"And there's Patricia – and her blasted dog," added Jude.

"That's called living with an extended family. You are lucky. In some parts of the world, one's whole village considers itself to be part of your family – especially if you attain any degree of fame and fortune! I speak from bitter experience!"

For the first time since her arrival on the island, Jude felt herself relax as she too laughed. She *would* stay for a few more days, not just to find out more about Liam Maybury. She also wanted to get to know this extraordinary woman who seemed to have the art of living well learned. A pleasant thought occurred to Jude, causing her to unconsciously smile: *Marguerite makes manageable molehills out of seemingly insurmountable mountains*. That would make quite a good tongue-twister.

"Yes, I think I might stay on for a couple of days," she said.

Chapter Nine

Geoffrey sounded fed up when Jude phoned him that evening.

"Well, have you found answers to all your questions? Has your father explained why he's behaved the way he has?"

"I'm afraid it's all a little more complicated than I thought. For a start, he isn't my father." There was silence at the other end of the phone. She could imagine the look of surprise on his face. "I'll tell you everything when I get back but I need to stay on for a few days and find out a bit more." Continued silence. "Are you there, Geoff?"

"Yes, I'm here. I might have guessed the old bugger would make life more difficult for you if he got the chance. Is he telling the truth?"

"Yes, I believe he is."

"Do you really think it's sensible to hang around? Wouldn't it be better to just come home? The kids are missing you."

"Are you missing me?"

"Yes, of course I am. That goes without saying."

He sounded impatient now, as well as fed up.

"Well, you know how we women like to be told these things," she said, trying to tease him out of his ill humour. Another silence. This conversation was turning out to be pretty pointless, she decided. "Listen, I'll ring and let you know my arrival time when I've booked my flight back. It has to tie in with ferry timetables this end. OK?"

"OK."

"How's work?"

"Bloody impossible, if you must know. I'm starting to wonder if this project will ever see the light of day the way things are here at the moment."

"Oh, I'm sorry! Look! Give Flo and Oz my love – and your mother too," she added diplomatically. "Bye!"

"Bye, Jude."

She hung up, wishing that their exchange had been more friendly. The phone had never been a means of satisfactorily communicating with another person as far as Jude was concerned. So much had to be left to guesswork when there was no eye contact, no visible physical reaction or body language. As soon as she put the phone down, she also found herself regretting that she hadn't been more sympathetic over Geoffrey's difficulties with his filming. But Ireland seemed an awfully long way off just at the moment and her head was buzzing with the morning's conversations with Liam Maybury and Marguerite.

Jude had used the phone in Paradise Café rather than the one in the entrance to Villa Rosa. The old lady had been perfectly amiable in her manner towards her but Rosa had a nasty habit of materialising silently in her felt slippers and making Jude jump. It seemed that whenever Jude wanted to sit quietly in the garden, the small black figure would be lurking somewhere nearby – sweeping, watering, weeding – ready to scurry over and engage in conversation at the slightest opportunity.

"You look sad, beautiful lady!" Adonis paused on his way back to the bar, carrying a tray loaded with empty glasses and coffee cups. "I make you cold drink. What you like?"

Jude pushed back the sweat-dampened hair from her face.

"I would love some local beer."

He beamed at her.

"*Endaxi!* You sit. I get very good Greek beer for you."

When he brought it over to her, he asked, "Why you not happy? You not have good holiday on my island?"

"I'm not really on holiday, Adonis. It's more business than holiday."

The moment she'd said it, Jude regretted being so honest. Adonis' eyebrows climbed wildly up his shiny forehead and his expression changed from one of concern for her welfare to one of intense interest and speculation. She could almost see steam coming out of his ears as he considered what possible sort of business could have brought this woman to Ios. However, when Jude changed the subject to the excellent quality of the beer, he refrained from asking any more questions concerning the purpose of her visit. As well as being kind, he was obviously a gentleman, she decided.

After finishing her drink and taking leave of the quietly

puzzled proprietor of Paradise Café, Jude turned up the road towards Villa Rosa.

Marguerite had invited her to dine out with them that evening. They would collect her before it got dark so that she would be able to enjoy some spectacular views on the way to the restaurant. All she wanted now was to have a much-needed siesta. Her thoughts were so muddled; she reckoned that no good would come of trying to sort them out while feeling the way she did. Perhaps, after a refreshing sleep, she'd be able to see things more clearly. As she walked, she could hear Marguerite's voice repeating her diplomat father's advice for a contented existence. The more she thought about it, the more it made sense. Why waste a short life in getting so uptight and demoralised by other people and difficult situations? Even though she felt tired after the morning's encounter with Liam Maybury, she seemed to have shed some of the awful feeling of gloom and doom that had dogged her during the past weeks. Jude concluded that had to be a good sign!

Just as she turned into the entrance of Villa Rosa, she experienced an uncomfortable sensation, a prickling of the hairs on the back of her neck. Looking around, she noticed a man standing on the other side of the road staring intently at her. A blue towel was slung over one shoulder. He looked Greek – dark-skinned, of average height with black hair cut short. She guessed that he was somewhere in his early thirties. A look of recognition flickered in his face before he walked slowly away from her. There was something familiar about him. It wasn't until she'd reached the steps up to the front door that she glanced after him again. Of course! He was wearing the same rust-coloured shorts, although this time, accompanied by a dark brown T-shirt. Although there was no one around to see her embarrassment, Jude found herself blushing. He was the man who'd seen her stark naked on the beach the day before. Damn! He was the last person she wanted to bump into again.

* * *

As she climbed into the back of the dusty car, Jude was aware of Marguerite's perfume. From what she could see of her, the woman looked magnificent in some sort of a jade-green caftan. Even though she wore hardly any make-up and her grey-tinged hair was close-cropped to her head, her appearance was unbelievably exotic. If she were really sixty, as she had told Jude earlier in the day, where were the lines and wrinkles that etched the faces of all the women Jude knew of that age? No wonder Liam Maybury liked having her around to feast his eyes on. He ought to consider putting her into one of his books. That might increase his sales – and cheer him up in the process.

As they drove, it suddenly occurred to her that there must be something special about him too. Why else would a woman like Marguerite put her time and effort into any sort of relationship with him? She'd said that he suffered badly from depression. It couldn't be pity that had her spending several months out of the year in his company. She was too intelligent and he too proud for that to be the case.

Apart from giving Jude a perfunctory greeting when she got into the car, Liam Maybury remained more or less silent on the journey to the restaurant. The occasional remark was made by him – but apparently intended for Marguerite's ears only. He made no effort to include Jude. Obviously, the evening's invitation to dine out had not been his idea. He probably wishes I would quietly vanish and leave them in peace, she thought. He drove erratically, but his driving seemed to her no worse than the other drivers who skimmed potholes at high speed and dodged the groups of sunburned tourists cluttering the roads as they stood outside the various cafés and restaurants, reading over the dishes on offer. Jude had noticed that most of the menus were identical with the same sun-faded, strangely blue-tinged photos of unidentifiable chunks of meat. She could imagine her mother-in-law's shudder of distaste. As was so often the case, she heard the Flora-like voice in her head. *"Like some barbequed horse then, Gran?"*

Marguerite looked over her shoulder, "We are going a short distance up into the mountains on the road to Kalamos. That is Mylopotas beach on your right."

It was beginning to get dark but not enough to stop Jude having a good view of a long, sandy beach sweeping towards the distant mountains. All the umbrellas were closed and the ski-jets and wind-surfers corralled for the night. The odd figure walked along the edge of the still sea. On their left stretched a line of cafés, bars, hotels and restaurants, each lit up for the evening's festivities. It was too early for much activity and waiters stood around, chatting and smoking, enjoying the lull before the storm. There were signs for Greek dancing, fire-eating, plate-smashing and table-dancing. She felt puzzled as to who would want to sit and watch plates being smashed. Did they hurl crockery at awkward diners? That could be quite therapeutic when you considered just how bloody-minded some people's behaviour was in restaurants.

When they reached the far end of the beach, the car slowed and Jude saw that the tarmac came to an abrupt end. What looked like a track climbed steeply in front of them. It proved to be just that – a track – and a fairly dusty, uneven one at that. A signpost she could not decipher but that looked as though it might indicate the road to Kalamos, seemed to consist of letters she recognised mixed with something resembling a tent and a squiggle like an electrocuted earthworm. She knew that one! Jude had seen IOS on the map of Ios. The Flora-like voice chimed in her head. *"Oh, brilliant, Mum! With those powers of deduction, you'll qualify for the next expedition up the Amazon!"*

The ascent was hair-raising. The road was made for one vehicle at a time and there were infrequent indentations hacked out of the side of the mountain to enable vehicles to pass each other. Parts of the road had crumbled away leaving horribly narrow sections to be negotiated in low gear. Some of these were criss-crossed with substantial cracks. Jude had the distinct impression that this mountain route had been built by guys with donkeys *for* guys on donkeys – certainly not for tourists in cars. When she caught a glimpse of the sheer drop below them, her queasiness increased. Thank God, it was almost dark. At least some of the more precipitous detail was being erased. Glancing round and seeing her expression, Marguerite laughed.

"Better not to look! You are lucky we aren't going on up to the monastery. It gets even narrower there and the coaches find it difficult. Concentrate on the stars and the lights in the distance instead!"

To Jude, the idea of rounding a corner, with the rear end of your car sticking well out over a vertiginous drop, only to be confronted by a full-size coach complete with a cargo of merry pilgrims on board, was too mind-blowing to contemplate.

Behind them, distant lights twinkled magically. Until a fold of mountain blocked the view, she could see Chora glowing like a fairytale town on top of its rock. Each dome and bell-tower shone like ivory, clearly etched against a velvet blue-black sky.

* * *

The restaurant proved to be well worth the journey. Whitewashed walls enclosed a large courtyard with a low building at one end. Geraniums of every conceivable colour trailed from stone containers and the apricot petals of an enormous bougainvillea lay on the ground like origami flowers made of tissue paper. Large amphora stood, sentinel-like, in each corner of the courtyard. There were small lamps on every table, the light reflecting off the white walls and tablecloths so that the restaurant seemed to glow welcomingly. In the distance Jude could see the sea, a distant expanse of watered silk, silvered by bright moonlight. She could make out the shape of a ferry silently ploughing through the shimmering water on its way to other hidden islands. The restaurant was already half full and the smell of roasting meat and herbs made her realise that she was hungry.

Jude could hardly believe her eyes when, halfway through the meal, their table was approached by the man she'd seen earlier that day staring at her outside Villa Rosa. Not looking in her direction, he greeted Liam and

Marguerite. Marguerite seemed uncharacteristically cool in her manner towards him. Liam, on the other hand, appeared delighted. For the first time that evening, his face lit up and he became almost animated.

"Manolis! Come and join us! Pull up a chair. I didn't know you were eating here this evening." He introduced the newcomer to Jude. "This is Manolis, Jude. He owns the house I rent at Tzamaria beach."

So this was the Manolis of the House of Manolis, she thought as they shook hands over the table. No wonder he had been down there yesterday morning. He probably owned the damned beach as well! Doing her best to appear suitably polite, she glanced briefly at his face. Was there a hint of a smirk lurking there?

After he'd seated himself, he turned, leaning attentively towards her and enquired, "You are on holidays here?"

She was aware of Liam's eyes fixed on her. She was pretty sure that he wouldn't want the real reason for her visit exposed.

"Yes. Just for a few days."

The man turned towards Liam.

"How did you meet?" Manolis paused and then added, "Perhaps on the beach?"

Almost imperceptibly, his eyes slid over to Jude and then quickly back to Liam. Quite separate from the memory of her feelings of discomfort at her state of undress when he'd first seen her, there was something about him that made her want to squirm – a sort of seedy, provocative quality. She felt he was the sort of man who liked to embarrass. There was also an oily familiarity in the way he spoke that she instinctively disliked.

"We met many years ago," said Jude crisply before Liam could answer. Turning to Marguerite she asked, "Would it be possible to order some more water?"

"Of course, Jude."

There was something about the smile Marguerite gave the younger woman that hinted of approval – as if Manolis' manner grated on her every bit as much as on Jude.

By the time they had finished drinking their coffee, a trio of musicians had begun to play and couples started to drift onto the small square of open space between the tables to dance.

"You would like to dance?" Manolis asked Jude. He looked as though he was about to get to his feet, sure that she would accept his invitation. In fact, she thought it sounded more like a statement than a question.

"No, thank you," she replied brightly.

"But you cannot say no," the man replied, eyebrows raised in what he obviously felt to be an irresistibly appealing manner.

"I'm afraid that I can," Jude said with a saccharine smile. "You see, it's against my religion."

She was immediately aware of a slight commotion beside her. Marguerite's bosom heaved and she seemed to be choking. After some coughing and throat-clearing, she dabbed at her eyes with a handkerchief.

"I'm sorry! An almond must have gone down the wrong way."

Manolis gave both women a contemptuous glance.

"What religion is it that does not allow you to dance?"

"The Church of the Western Celts," said Jude without

hesitation, her face expressionless. "We are *very* fundamentalist in our approach to life."

More half-suppressed coughing erupted from the woman beside her. Jude was careful not to catch her eye.

To her left, Liam appeared preoccupied with his thoughts and seemed not to have noticed the exchange. Manolis was looking unamused.

"Are there many other things you are not allowed?"

Jude was tempted to say, 'Oh, yes. Sex, laughing and blood transfusions, amongst others'. But she was dreading the journey back down the mountain and felt it might be tempting fate as, in the event of falling off the edge, she might very well need a blood transfusion – that was if she survived.

All of a sudden, Marguerite rose to her feet.

"I need to powder my nose. Are you coming, Jude?"

Jude got to her feet gratefully.

* * *

It was nearly midnight by the time they eventually arrived back at Villa Rosa. Jude had achieved relative peace of mind during the journey down from the mountain by leaning back against the upholstery, closing her eyes and pretending that they were crossing a bumpy field at sea level and not dicing with death at an angle of forty-five degrees, hundreds of feet up in the air. It had almost worked.

She'd also found herself going over the evening and the unwelcome arrival on the scene of Manolis. She couldn't work out his relationship with Liam, who seemed not to be irritated by the other man's trivial conversation or his over-familiarity. Instead, he seemed to be almost fond of him. To Jude, watching with an outsider's eye, it struck her as extraordinary that someone as apparently reticent as Liam Maybury should not object to Manolis throwing an arm around his neck as he laughed loudly at his own unfunny jokes. Nor did he appear to mind when the other man took it on himself to order another round of liqueurs that none of them wanted and for which, Jude noted, Liam paid. Manolis only returned to his two male companions when Liam had settled the bill and was preparing to leave.

She'd asked about his unwelcome appearance at their evening meal as she stood beside Marguerite, washing her hands in what was delicately described on the door as, the ladies' 'Rest Room'.

"Why does Liam like him?"

There had been a hesitation before Marguerite replied, "Even intelligent people have their blind spots."

"You mean that Manolis is Liam's blind spot?"

Their eyes met in the mirror.

"You remember I told you that Liam has always wanted a son?"

Jude nodded.

"Well, for some reason, I think that Manolis seems to be the nearest he has got to having one. I know that young man appears incredibly stupid but, in fact, he's quite cunning. He knows how to flatter and to even be reasonably entertaining on occasion. I'm not really sure why he cultivates Liam. Perhaps he thinks it improves his image locally to be seen consorting with a published writer from Ireland who looks so distinguished. Perhaps he thinks Liam will leave him everything in his Will. I don't know.

But Liam seems to like Manolis and so I put up with him when I have to if it makes Liam happy."

"I can't stand the man," Jude said vehemently.

"I rather gathered that was the case." Marguerite laughed. "May I compliment you on your good taste? And I would also like to congratulate you on your quick thinking – although I had trouble not swallowing my tongue trying not to laugh!"

Jude then told her about the episode on the beach. When she finished, Marguerite threw her eyes to the ceiling. "Oh, my dear! What a tale of disaster! No wonder you felt at a disadvantage when he materialised at the table. What bad luck! But, you know, I don't think you are in any danger from that Greek demigod!" Her full lips pursed together in a wry smile. "Well, let's just keep our fingers crossed that he's got the message and stays out of your way from now on."

Jude fervently hoped so. Otherwise she felt she might just be tempted to cause him grievous bodily harm.

Now, as she got out of the car, she leaned into Marguerite's open window, taking hold of the woman's proffered hand. Jude smiled across at Liam Maybury. She thought how tired he looked. Tired and unwell. The lines either side of his mouth appeared more deeply etched than ever and the brown eyes seemed to have sunk into their sockets.

"Thank you for a lovely evening and a delicious meal."

The meal had been good at least – and she'd enjoyed Marguerite's company.

"I didn't talk to you as much as I should," he said unexpectedly. "I hope you didn't mind Manolis joining us."

"Of course not," she lied.

"Will we see you tomorrow?" he asked.

"Would that be all right with you?"

"Yes, yes. Come if you wish."

His impatience to end the conversation and leave was palpable.

"We would love to see you, Jude. I will show you my paintings when you get tired of talking to him."

Marguerite gave her hand a slight squeeze before letting go.

The car immediately turned and rattled off down the road towards the port. She noticed that one of the rear lights wasn't working.

As Jude climbed the steps up to the Villa, waving away a persistent mosquito that whined around her eyes, there was a rattle of a window catch. Unexpectedly slicing through the hot night air, a sudden chink of light escaped from a slightly opened shutter. Apparently the ever-watchful Rosa was still awake.

Chapter Ten

She'd go for a swim before calling in on Liam and Marguerite, Jude decided next morning. But this time, she promised herself, she would wear a bathing suit.

Once she had negotiated the already bustling port and passed Yialos beach, the road was empty. It was still early when she arrived at the small beach below the House of Manolis. The morning light was golden, making the spiders' webs look like translucent loops of beaded necklaces stretching from one clump of dry grass to another. The real heat of the day had not started yet and the air was still comfortably warm. Around her, house martins made graceful, swooping runs, skimming low, almost touching the sea, before disappearing over the tall grasses behind her.

Looking out across the water, sitting on the same rock she had chosen on her first visit there, she wondered how much more she would be able to prise out of Liam Maybury. Did he have to tell her anything if he didn't want to? After all, he wasn't her father. On the other hand, he *had* married

127

Jude's mother. They shared her in common, even if the marriage had only lasted a couple of years.

Jude hugged her knees, staring unseeingly ahead, hardly noticing the wash that suddenly surged around the rock from a distant ferry. The truth was, that after having reluctantly taken on board the fact that he wasn't her father, she felt no bond of any kind with him. And that saddened her. But the furious resentment that had burned inside her after her mother's death appeared now to have dwindled into a kind of melancholic acceptance. The reality was that she had lost both her parents and she'd better come to terms with it.

Jude couldn't help feeling disappointed that Liam seemed so taken with 'the idiot Manolis', as she thought of their dinner guest of the previous evening. Did he so desperately want a son? Could he not have settled for the next best thing? she thought, with a sudden stab of jealousy. After all, he had a ready-made, adopted daughter who had spent her entire childhood pining for him. He also had two step-grandchildren – who apparently counted for nothing.

She was still curious to know quite how Patricia Larchet fitted into the picture. Why had the woman made a point of keeping in touch with him for all these years? And why hadn't Jude's mother told her that they'd known – and disliked – each other before her marriage to Liam?

Suddenly she stood up and dived into the water, scattering the small shoals of fish. It was refreshingly cool in the glass-like water. Tiny particles of sand rose, catching the light as they turned, churned up from the seabed as she swam away from the beach.

* * *

When Jude appeared up at the house two hours later, Marguerite kissed her lightly on each cheek before accompanying her out to the terrace. This morning the woman was wearing a loose turquoise shift that matched exactly the colour of the sea.

"That looks marvellous on you," Jude said admiringly.

Marguerite smiled.

"Thank you! It's one of the benefits of having a dark skin. No colour is too bright to wear. You can get away with murder – rather like my paintings! But you need heat and bright light to do both of them justice."

How true! Jude glanced at her own arms. "I feel rather like an anaemic stick insect beside you."

Marguerite halted a moment, looking at her. "You are beautiful in your own way, Jude. You wear your beauty lightly and that's a very attractive quality – to be unaware of how one looks. With that perfect skin and red hair of yours, you could only be Irish! But I have to admit that if you lived in some parts of Nigeria, any prospective husband would pack you off to a fattening farm as soon as he set eyes on you. When you'd put on a few stone and he felt you'd do him justice, then he would have you back. A thin wife looks as though her husband can't afford to feed her properly and that is very bad for his image!"

"It's a good thing I live in Ireland then."

"Yes. Especially as I believe that is the only place where the 'Church of the Western Celts' is to be found!"

They were both laughing as they drew close to where Liam Maybury sat, his face and body strangely camouflaged by the dappled light escaping through the vine leaves above his head. Jude was aware of crickets chirruping

129

loudly in the surrounding bushes as she walked towards him.

Before Jude had time to greet him, the man looked up at Marguerite.

"Can you leave us for a little while?"

She smiled slightly.

"Of course, dear Liam." She turned to Jude. "When you have finished with him, come and see my paintings before you go."

Without a sound, she padded away on bare feet, her shift billowing around her as she walked.

Jude took her place opposite the man as she'd done on the two previous occasions. He still looked tired, she thought.

"I suppose you feel that there is very little left to say," she said tentatively.

"Yes, I suppose I do. I was hoping that you would feel the same."

"Well, I can't pretend that it wasn't a shock to find out that you weren't my father. I also can't pretend that I don't still feel disappointed that it never occurred to you that, even though I was only your adopted daughter, I deserved a little attention and effort on your part." She suddenly wanted to challenge him in some way, to make him snap out of his lethargic state of non-involvement. "I'm not *that* uninteresting or unlikeable, am I?"

A look of irritation crossed his face.

"Why do women have to be reassured all the time? Why in God's name do they have to be told that they are intelligent, amusing, attractive – all the rest of it? Have you got so little self-confidence that you can't stand on your own two feet, a complete person in your own right without having to be propped up by constant male approbation?"

Jude was stung into stunned silence. That was hardly fair, she thought. She hadn't expected him to go on the attack like this.

He suddenly leaned forward in his chair, making the cane seat creak. "Do you know why I enjoy Marguerite's company so much?"

"Because she knows who she is and is content?" Jude ventured.

"Exactly! That woman doesn't need me or anyone else to tell her what sort of person she is. She certainly doesn't need outside approval to make her existence justified or valid in her own eyes." He leaned back into the cushion behind him. "You can't imagine how refreshing that is." Then he suddenly seemed to relent. "My dear girl, I am a gay man who would have loved to have had a son of his own." Ignoring the look of astonishment on Jude's face, he continued, "For years I did my best to hide the fact that I was gay – and it blighted my life. It spoiled my relationship with your mother and my second wife and when I eventually admitted it to myself and was prepared to admit it to others, it was too late." He gave a sardonic smile. "I fear I've shocked you."

"No, of course not," Jude said, hastily. "It's just that I hadn't considered that as a possibility – a reason for you leaving my mother. I thought you weren't around because you couldn't be bothered, because you'd found someone new." It was true. She wasn't shocked – just taken aback by the unexpectedness of it. She paused before asking, "What do you mean, too late?"

131

"Even then, when I had 'come out' as they call it, I hadn't learned how to go about having a loving, fulfilling relationship with anyone, male or female, and now it is certainly too late in the day."

"Why? You're not too old surely? The Greeks thought platonic love was a good thing." She added shyly, "And you seem to have a very good relationship with Marguerite."

He didn't answer but just shook his head slightly, a withdrawn look on his face. She got the impression that he regretted having spoken so openly.

Then, with a laconic smile, he added, "What is it they say in the press? We are just good friends. She is one of the kindest, most genuine people I've ever had the good fortune to meet."

Jude remembered a recent conversation with Marguerite. Had she hinted that he was gay during their brief exchange the evening before? Or had it been Manolis she'd been referring to? She couldn't remember. Perhaps she felt it was up to Liam to decide whether he wanted Jude to know or not.

He spoke again.

"And now, Jude, I would like to ask a favour of you."

"Of course," she replied quietly.

"I am glad I have had this opportunity to meet you. I hope that the reason for things being the way they have been is a little clearer to you now but I really don't think that either of us would benefit from your staying any longer. I would like you to know that I am sorry if I've caused you hurt." He smiled in a self-deprecating way. "As you have no doubt concluded, I am and always have been a very selfish man and it is too late for me to change now."

"That sounds very arrogant – as if you're not even prepared to try. Surely it's never too late to attempt to become a better sort of person?" Jude demanded angrily.

"Maybe I don't have the energy to make the effort. Anyway, for both our sakes, will you please leave now?" He was watching her intently, as though he were willing her to get up and go. "Don't forget to call into Marguerite before you do. Her studio is at the far end of the house." He hesitated before adding, "She seems to like you very much."

"That's ironic! When it was you who I wanted to like me," said Jude in a low voice.

She waited, hoping that he might add something, anything, to soften the moment of parting. But he had closed his eyes. His wrists rested against his chest, his fingers clasped in front of his lowered face. She had been dismissed. There appeared to be nothing more to be said. Slowly, Jude got to her feet. She leaned over and picked up her bag and swimming things, then turned away from the statue-like man in the white cane chair.

"Goodbye, then," she said.

There was no reply.

* * *

The paintings were every bit as large, bold and colourful as she'd expected them to be. Jude had stumbled through the door, her mind in turmoil. Marguerite, seeing her distress, immediately put down the canvas she was holding and moved swiftly to her side.

"Are you all right, Jude? He can be brutally honest when the mood takes him."

She led the younger woman over to a stool that stood in

front of an easel. Picking up a bottle of water, she poured out a glass for Jude and handed it to her. All around the walls, paintings were stacked. A table under a large, open window was littered with bottles, tubes of paint and brushes. A battered cream-coloured fan whirred in a corner.

Jude pulled a face.

"I feel a little as though I've just been trampled by a rhino but I'll survive!"

She swallowed some of the water, holding the glass with both hands to keep it steady.

"What did he say? What is it that has upset you so much?"

"He told me he was gay."

"And? You find that disturbing?"

"No, I don't. But he also said he thought it would be a good thing if I didn't hang around here any more; that it would be better for both of us if I left."

Marguerite shook her head.

"Oh, my God! He never learns! I'm afraid that Liam was never one to search for soft words. He tells it as he sees it." She moved away to the table and picked up a cloth and a paintbrush, which she started to clean, her face thoughtful. "But he is right, you know. If he has decided that he doesn't want to explain any more about himself or his actions, you would only be wasting your time if you hoped that you could persuade him otherwise." She looked over to where Jude sat. "Would you like to see something of what I do?"

Together they worked their way through the stacks of paintings. Jude was enchanted by the other's work. The canvases were inhabited by people, animals, birds and strange figures that appeared to be half-human, half-animal or half-bird. Everywhere lush vegetation curled and twined around them.

"A lot of these characters come from the Yoruba legends my mother told me when I was small," Marguerite explained.

"Is she still alive, your mother?"

"No, she died when I was twelve. She was a great storyteller. She knew all the legends and she told them over and over again and made me repeat them after her until I became word-perfect. She said that a people, a tribe, a nation will never cease to exist as long as its history and its fairytales and its stories continue to be told. For me, my mother lives on in my paintings, as fresh and as vivid as though she were here in this room with us."

Jude caught sight of a large canvas standing on its own in a corner of the room. It was the portrait of a woman in a purple headcloth, wrapper and wide-sleeved blouse. She was sitting in a high-backed, ornamented chair, her hands resting on its carved arms. Her dark skin, like Marguerite's own, was smooth and unwrinkled. And like Marguerite's, it seemed to catch the light, unexpectedly reflecting different colours. With her chin raised and her mouth unsmiling, she looked proud. Her dark eyes seemed to stare back at Jude. She moved closer and saw that the painting was textured with what appeared to be seeds of different sizes and colour glued on to the canvas. All around the seated woman, among the curving stems of flowers and trees, Jude could make out the shapes of the figures she'd seen in some of the other paintings.

"Is that your . . .?"

Marguerite gave a deep-throated chuckle.

"It is one version of her. People are multi-faceted. They often allow you only a brief glimpse of a small part of what they really are. My mother was a very complex woman. I thought she was kind; others saw her as cruel. My father once said that she was the most extraordinarily compassionate person he had ever met. That is why I will never get tired of attempting to capture her true essence. I fear I will never succeed but I enjoy trying!"

By the time all the paintings had been examined by Jude, the studio had become stiflingly hot and she realised that it must be nearly midday.

"I must go, Marguerite. I have to organise my flight back from Heraklion to Dublin. Thank you so much for showing your paintings to me. They are so powerful. But having met you before I saw them, I'm not surprised that they are the way they are. They're magnificent."

They said goodbye at the top of the track that led down to the road. Marguerite rested her hands on Jude's shoulders.

"Go back to your family, Jude, and enjoy them. Leave me to do what I can for that stubborn old man back there – not that there's very much I *can* do. I think you know that I have his best interests at heart."

"Yes, of course, I do. I think he is very lucky. I'm not entirely convinced that he deserves you though." She paused for a moment before asking, "Tell me, is Manolis gay?"

Marguerite gave another of her throaty chuckles.

"I'm not really sure. And I don't think Manolis knows either. That not-so-young man seems to drift in any direction the wind takes him."

"When you've gone, will he spend more of his time up at the house?"

Jude didn't want to ask if the younger man's visits to Liam were as surrogate son or as lover – the latter possibility, she found particularly difficult to come to terms with.

"Don't worry! If Liam doesn't want him there, he will tell him."

"I know it sounds rather stupid but I feel happier when I know you are here to keep an eye on things."

Marguerite gave her a quizzical glance.

"You sound as though you care about Liam, even though he's been hard on you."

"I suppose I do," said Jude, surprised. "I can't think why!"

"Well, he will only have my company for another six weeks and then I have to go back to London to get ready for an exhibition at the start of October. I shouldn't worry about him. He's become quite a recluse during the past few years. He seems to enjoy his own company – even if it's not all that jovial! Things will work out for the best. You concentrate on your own life and don't fret over him. He wouldn't thank you for it – or appreciate it!"

They embraced and then Jude turned and began the dusty descent to the road below. As she walked, she realised, that in spite of everything he'd said, she *was* glad that Marguerite would be there for him for a while longer. She glanced back over her shoulder but there was no sign of the tall woman in the turquoise dress that was the same colour as the sea.

* * *

A large part of the afternoon was spent with Jude booking her return flight and attempting to organise a seat on a ferry that would get her to Crete in plenty of time to catch the plane back to Dublin. She'd decided that she wanted to spend one last evening on Ios before she left. She would treat herself to a meal at Paradise Café. Eventually everything was sorted out and she was booked on the early morning boat, leaving at six the following day. If all went well, she would only have to spend a couple of hours queuing in the inelegant concrete innards of Heraklion airport before she caught the eight o'clock evening plane home.

Not feeling hungry, Jude bought an ice cream which she absent-mindedly licked as she wandered slowly along a back road to Villa Rosa.

When she got there, she tried to phone Geoffrey at work but the woman on the switchboard said he was out on location. His mobile appeared to be turned off. Then, hoping that Patricia Larchet would not answer, Jude phoned the house. The answering machine clicked on and her own voice instructed her to, '*Please leave a message after the bleep*'. She did so, giving the two a.m. time of her arrival in Dublin. "But don't worry about meeting me. I'll get a taxi," she added cheerfully, silently hoping that one of them might want to collect her – even at that ungodly hour.

Unusually, Rosa was not to be seen. Jude slipped up the stairs as quietly as possible and let herself into the relative cool of her room. The windows and shutters were closed and it felt stuffy. After opening the windows and replacing the shutters again, she shook off her sandals and collapsed onto the bed. What a strange couple of days she'd just lived through! She fell asleep in the middle of trying to make sense of it all.

* * *

Adonis welcomed Jude with a beaming smile and a flourish of his white handkerchief.

"You come to eat at Paradise Café? Excellent!"

He led her over to a table that overlooked the yachts nestling in to the side of the quay. Then he hurried off to fetch a menu. She noticed how quickly he moved through the busy café, bustling along with the small steps of a short man carrying more weight than he should.

She chose her favourite Greek dish to start with – a bowl of creamy tzatziki accompanied by hot, freshly baked pitta bread. Then dolmades with a plate of the ubiquitous Greek salad. She finished her meal with a slice of halva dripping with dark brown honey. Throughout dinner Adonis kept a close eye on things, serving her himself and making sure she didn't have to wait a moment longer than was necessary between courses. When he brought her a cup of coffee, she invited him to join her. He fetched his own ever-present cup from the table by the kitchen door, pausing to give rapid instructions to one of the waiters. Then he sat down at her table with a sigh.

"My wife, she always said I must not drink too many coffees because it is not good for me but I like so much to drink it. And now my wife is dead and I am still here!" He raised both hands in the air with the universal gesture of helplessness in the face of uncaring gods.

Jude smiled sympathetically.

"I know what you mean, Adonis. Sometimes I think it

is just better to enjoy the things you like and hope for the best. A short life perhaps – but a happy one!"

A waiter appeared and put down two glasses and a bottle of Baileys in front of Adonis who looked at her expectantly.

"Especially for you, this very good drink from Ireland. I hope you like?"

"I like it very much, thank you!"

When the not-so-small glasses were filled to the brim, Adonis raised his high above the table.

"I drink to the most beautiful lady on my island! *Yamas!*" His glass was drained before Jude had the time to take more than a first mouthful. He waited patiently until she had finished her own and, in spite of her protests, immediately refilled them. "Drink!" he commanded. "We must enjoy the good things in life, no?" His pleasant moon-shaped face and bald head were shiny with sweat as he raised his glass again, nodding over to her own encouragingly.

Jude, who had eaten well, wasn't over-keen on downing much more of the rich liqueur. She wondered how she could extract herself before he tried to persuade her to help him polish off the entire bottle. Just as she was taking a small sip from her glass, she noticed a couple of men at a table in the far corner of the café. Their body language spoke of a sexually charged intimacy. Their faces were close together, eyes fixed on each other and one of them was stroking the arm of the other with sensual caresses. She recognized the recipient of all the attention as none other than Manolis. So, he *was* gay, like Liam. She stared at him for a moment. So, at the restaurant near Kalamos, he'd decided to play the part of attentive son to the man who longed for a son – not Liam's young gay partner. Marguerite had said he was clever. Perhaps he was hoping to inherit from the older man. Jude felt a sudden stab of sadness. It was obvious that Liam was not well. It seemed quite possible that Manolis might not have to wait too long before getting his hands on the old man's possessions.

She suddenly became aware that Adonis had spoken to her.

"I'm sorry, what did you say?" she asked.

He had a disapproving look on his face. His eyes slid from the lovers in the corner back to her face.

"Do you know those people?"

"I was introduced to Manolis the other evening when I was dining with friends but I do not know him."

Was it her imagination or did Adonis look relieved at this piece of information? She was about to ask him if he knew the couple when Adonis abruptly turned his head away from the two men, shifting his chair as he did so, as if to block them from her sight.

"They do not come to my café very much. For that I am thankful. That Manolis, he make trouble."

As he obviously didn't want to pursue the topic any further, Jude asked him to tell her about the legend that Homer was buried on the island. Adonis beamed and began to tell the tale.

Some time later, she glanced at her watch. It was getting late. She smiled at Adonis as she leaned down to pick up her bag from the floor. "Thank you so much. I really enjoyed hearing you talk about Ios. You seem to know so much about its history."

He put down his glass and got up and went around to pull her chair back from the table.

"History is important. We should not forget from where we come. It helps to understand sometimes why life is the way it is."

For a moment, his usually jolly face looked wistful.

Jude got up, holding out a hand. "I must go but I enjoyed the meal very much. It was delicious. Thank you!"

Adonis took one of her hands in between his plump ones.

"You send a postcard from Ireland so when Fotis visit I show him? He will be very happy his papa entertain so special Irish lady in Paradise Café."

Jude promised that she would, at the same time hoping that Adonis' wretched son would make the effort to visit his father. She said goodbye and made her way out of the restaurant on the opposite side to where Manolis and his companion sat. If he had noticed her, he made no sign of having done so. He's probably decided that I'm of no use to him so it's not worth his time, Jude thought wryly – and thankfully – as she set off up the dusty road. She stepped hastily to one side as a rowdy bunch of young Greek boys on bikes passed her at high speed, shouting and laughing as they wove in and out of the parked cars. It made her think of her own son and she was suddenly filled with a longing to go home and pick up her life again.

As she turned into the gate, Rosa appeared, cleaning cloth in hand, at the entrance to the villa.

"You have good time?" she enquired brightly.

Jude smiled at her.

"Yes, thank you, Rosa. I had a good time."

Chapter Eleven

"Hi, Mum!"

Oscar suddenly materialised in front of her. His clothes were crumpled as though he'd gone to bed in them for a while before setting out for the airport. He gave Jude a hug and then made a dive for her luggage.

"You're a star, Oz! I really didn't expect you to come all this way in the middle of the night though," she said, relieved that he had.

As they walked to the car, Jude was aware that her son kept giving her sidelong glances as though he were trying to work out how things had gone and what sort of a state she was in. *He's wondering if he's got his old mother back or am I still a gibbering mess and likely to disappear into the blue when the going gets tough,* she thought as she intercepted one of the questioning looks.

"It's all right! I haven't got everything straight in my mind yet but I've found out quite a lot of stuff that explains a bit about what's happened."

"That's good."

But somehow Jude still got the feeling that her son wasn't his usual laid-back self.

"Can I drive?" he asked as soon as her bag had been stowed in the boot.

"Yes, of course, if you're not too tired."

"Mum, you should know by now that I'm just getting into my stride at this hour of the morning."

She laughed.

"I don't know where you got the gene from that means you can party all night without a bother. It certainly wasn't from my side of the family."

She stopped short. What was she talking about? she asked herself. She knew nothing of her real father's characteristics or of his parents – and she never would.

"You OK? You look done in."

Caught in mid-yawn, Jude laughed. "I'm fine but it's been a rather exhausting few days."

"What's he like . . . your dad?" he asked, backing the car out from the parking space at a speed that made her wince. No wonder car insurance for lads was as high as it was. Why was moderation such an unacceptable word in their vocabulary?

"Sorry?" she said, distracted.

"I asked what your dad was like," her son repeated patiently.

"Well, he's not exactly the friendliest man I've ever met and . . . I've discovered that he's not my dad after all," said Jude.

The car slowed slightly. Oscar looked over at her in surprise.

"You're joking! What do you mean, not your father?"

It took all the way from the airport back to the house before she'd finished telling him about what had happened on her trip to Ios. She wasn't quite sure why but she felt reluctant to tell her son that Liam was gay. What would be the point? It was irrelevant really, she thought, tiredly. After they had pulled up in the drive, Oscar switched off the engine and sat for a moment, deep in thought.

Then he said, "So, what it comes down to is that you haven't found your father and Flo and I don't have a grandfather, not even a useless one."

"That's about it," said Jude. She peered at him in the glow from the streetlight outside the gate. "Do you mind very much?"

For a moment he gazed out through the windscreen, frowning slightly.

"Not really, I suppose. I can live without the granddad bit. Although it might have been nice if you'd come back saying that there'd been some gigantic mistake and your dad was great and longing to meet us . . . I don't know. Some of my friends seem to have a good relationship with their grandparents and, what with you and Dad being only children, it's not as though we have cousins or aunts and uncles like most people." He pulled a face as he gave a small shrug. "I'm not sure what I was expecting. Flora will be disappointed though."

"I thought she reckoned her mother was one sandwich short of a picnic and had gone off on a wild-goose chase."

"Oh, you know Flo! She's never been able to say out loud what she's really thinking – until it's too late."

Jude was amused. She hadn't thought of her daughter

like that but what he'd said was true. Flora did seem to spend a lot of her time posturing so that what mattered and what she really felt got submerged. 'One bloody great production after another', as Geoffrey once remarked after they had been subjected to another of their daughter's tantrums.

Before she opened the car door, Jude asked casually, "How's your dad then?"

Was she imagining it or did he stiffen slightly and hesitate before answering her?

"Tucked up in bed, fast asleep, I should imagine."

It seemed to Jude that he was in a sudden hurry to get out of the car.

Oh, Lord! she thought to herself. The filming is going really badly and Geoff's been taking it out on them. She decided not to pursue the subject any further. Jude climbed out of the car and shut the door as quietly as she could.

"But Flora's OK?"

He nodded.

"Flora's busy being Flora, if you know what I mean."

His mother smiled. "She mentioned something on the phone about you having a new girlfriend."

"Did she? I bet it wasn't complimentary."

Jude didn't say anything.

"That's another thing about my sister. She hates not being the centre of attention."

He was sounding annoyed so she let the subject drop.

"And Gran?"

Oscar looked across the top of the car at her and rolled his eyes expressively.

"The same!"

146

"Lovely!" commented Jude as they walked towards the house together.

* * *

It was Geoffrey's mother, more than Geoffrey, who occupied Jude's mind on and off during the following days. He was irritable and rather withdrawn and had not wanted to discuss her trip after the initial conversation the morning after she got back. Jude put it down to pressure of work. He'd told her that the filming would be over by the end of the week. The wrap party was on Saturday. Then it was only the post-production period to weather. Thank God for that, she thought and turned her attention to his mother.

On the surface, the woman seemed more or less the same as when Jude had last seen her. Jude reminded herself that she'd only been away for a little under six days and things couldn't have changed that much. But she was convinced that Patricia Larchet had lost weight. Not very much admittedly but there was a slightly bony look about her face that she hadn't noticed before and the woman was rather more quiet than usual. She still liked to cause trouble. That hadn't changed, Jude noticed.

"I suppose he's living with some floozy or other," Mrs Larchet remarked to her daughter-in-law on Jude's first morning back.

"No, Liam lives on his own for most of the time."

Patricia Larchet snorted.

"Well, if you believe that, you'll believe anything. He probably had her hidden away while you were around."

"He has an extremely nice artist staying for the summer, that's all," Jude replied mildly, at the same time thinking

147

that he'd be hard put to it to hide someone of Marguerite's size and character.

"One of *them*! And a woman artist, I'll bet."

"She happens to be a woman, yes."

"There you are, then!" said the other, in triumphant tones.

Jude looked at her in despair. She was not going to run the risk of telling her that Marguerite was tall and black and amazing. That would only lead to problems. Instead, she continued, "And he didn't hide her away. In fact, we all went out to dinner together one evening."

"That must have been nice."

"It was, actually. She's very good company." Jude shut the washing-machine door and turned the appropriate dial with a sharp click. She glanced out of the window, just in time to see Plunkett trotting purposefully down the garden. He appeared to have a small shrub in his mouth. "What has Plunkett got hold of now?" she asked.

Patricia Larchet went over to the sink and looked out.

"Only a few twigs and leaves, Judith." She looked at her daughter-in-law critically. "You always do that."

"Do what?"

"Change the subject. You know! When you don't want to talk about something you either change the subject or . . . you pick on Plunkett."

Jude stared at her for a moment. The woman was unbelievable! But at least she hadn't accused her of changing the subject and then picking on Geoffrey.

"If you'll excuse me, I'm going upstairs to finish unpacking. Perhaps you could investigate what your dog has got in his mouth."

And then whack him with it, she thought savagely.

Up in the bedroom, she absent-mindedly flapped the duvet back into position and punched the pillows. Jude wondered how she was going to ask Mrs Larchet about her relationship with Jude's mother and why she had decided to warn Liam of her daughter-in-law's visit to Ios. She was also extremely curious to know why the woman had kept in touch with him for all these years and yet said nothing to the rest of them.

Accused of changing the subject herself, Jude knew perfectly well that her mother-in-law was an expert when it came to dodging awkward questions – from scrambling to her feet in response to imaginary telephone calls to having what Oscar referred to as an attack of the vapours. This invariably involved him pretending to search for imaginary smelling-salts while various member of the family dashed around opening windows, bringing glasses of water and fetching cushions to keep the sufferer more or less vertical in her chair. By the time Gran was sorted, everyone had forgotten what it was that had caused the upset in the first place.

Jude would just have to pick the right moment to ask her. In the meantime, she thought she'd better make contact with her producer at RTV Ireland and see if they still wanted her back. Perhaps they had found a replacement. She felt tempted to suggest they give Fidelma a chance at the job. She deserved it. Thinking of her friend made Jude want to phone her. She looked at her watch. Not a good time to ring. She'd have to wait to do it nearer lunch. Fidelma had always been more sensible than Jude and more able to look at a situation objectively. It would be good to talk things over with her.

* * *

Although it was September, Jude was surprised at how warm the weather still was. She'd expected to feel chilly after the baking heat of Ios. Must be a record for Ireland, she thought as she wandered along the beach behind an ecstatic Plunkett. She hadn't asked, but Jude was sure that the last walk the animal had been on was when she'd taken him out on the day before leaving. When he wasn't racing in circles over the sand, chewing on a chunk of seaweed, he danced in and out of the water's edge, barking at nothing.

"Shut up, you fool!" she shouted.

He turned his head to look at her, tail wagging furiously and then continued his hysterical, high-pitched barking at the horizon. An inquisitive black Labrador trotted up to him. They circled each other, sniffing at each other's rear ends, with the concentration of wine buffs sampling superior vintages, until, apparently satisfied, the other dog trotted away again to join his owner.

Jude glanced at her watch. It was nearly six o'clock. She whistled and Plunkett galloped over to her and then shook himself so that she had to retreat a few steps until he'd finished. Slipping the lead back onto his collar, she started to make her way back up the beach.

It hadn't been a particularly good day so far. Flora and Oscar out and Geoffrey preoccupied at breakfast before he'd dashed off, muttering something about not being back for supper.

His mother had joined them for the first meal of the day. Patricia Larchet noticed Jude's look of surprise.

"I know that, apart from Sunday lunch, you like me to eat most of my meals in my end of the house, Judith, but with you away, I got into the habit of having breakfast here so that I could make sure things were all right," she said in the self-righteous voice that always made her daughter-in-law want to kick the furniture.

Jude knew that the other woman knew perfectly well that right from the start, Patricia Larchet had always insisted that she preferred to eat in peace and quiet in 'her end of the house'. Be *nice* to the woman, Jude reminded herself.

"I'm sure that wasn't necessary, Patricia, but it was very kind of you."

"It wasn't a case of being kind, my dear. My conscience wouldn't have allowed me to do anything else."

Bloody martyr! Jude couldn't help thinking.

"Well, there's no need for you to fuss after them any more," she found herself snapping. "I'm back now."

"And none the better for your holiday, it would seem," replied her mother-in-law. "And I do *not* fuss."

Jude stared at her. Was it any wonder she'd decided against telling her that Liam Maybury was not her father? Why should she? Or did the bloody woman know about that too and had been enjoying her ignorance of the real situation?

"You know perfectly well that I didn't go on holiday."

At that point, Geoffrey exploded from his end of the table.

"Can't you both put a sock in it? You sound like a couple of argumentative kids in the school playground."

"Geoffrey! Really!" Wounded, Mrs Larchet stared at her son.

"Actually, you *do* sound rather pathetic," Flora chimed in.

151

"Shut up, Flora!" said Jude.

"Oh, happy families! Can't *wait* for Christmas," replied her daughter, raising her eyes to heaven.

Both Jude and Patricia Larchet glared at her.

"If you can't be pleasant, then I suggest you stack your things in the dishwasher and go."

"Don't worry! I'm not hanging around to be attacked just because the 'grown-ups' have decided to begin World War Three!" retorted Flora, pushing back her chair.

She always has to have the last bloody word, thought Jude, irritated with herself that she hadn't dealt with the situation better.

It was then that Oscar decided to offer his contribution to the proceedings.

"I think you're all being pretty horrible to Mum. I mean, she's only just got back and you're . . ."

He tailed off, aware that three of the other four family members around the table were now glaring at him. "I was only saying . . ."

"Jesus! Put a sock in it, Oz," interrupted Flora. She turned to her mother. "I thought once you'd sorted things out over there, everything would be back to normal again but you're still chewing everybody's heads off. Why can't you just relax, Mum?"

"That's rich coming from the resident drama queen," replied Oscar under his breath, leaning back in his chair so that only the two front legs remained in contact with the floor.

"I heard that!"

Flora, her face stormy, was now standing, cereal dish in one hand, spoon in the other.

"Oscar, don't do that! You'll break the chair," Geoffrey growled from the end of the table.

"I really can't take any more of this tension," said Mrs Larchet, making for the back-door. "I will see you later when you've all come to your senses – and remembered your manners."

She walked to the door, with a pained expression and one hand raised to her head as though registering the onset of yet another migraine. The door closed with a click behind her.

"Watch and learn, Flo! Can't beat Gran for the grand exit," remarked Oscar, looking at his sister with a grin. "She should be giving tutorials in that college of yours."

He started to lean back in his chair again, caught sight of his father's face and slowly returned to a vertical position.

"Sod off!" said Flora, making her own more noisy departure from the kitchen.

"Living with a difficult diva is not easy for the rest of us, you know!" Oscar called out as she left the room.

From the hall, Flora bellowed, "Divas *sing*, you fool!"

Grimacing, Jude looked across the table at her husband. But there was no shared glance of mutual frustration at their offsprings' behaviour. Geoffrey was already on his feet.

"I'll have to go or I'll be late. Don't forget I won't be back for supper tonight." She was about to say goodbye when, halfway out of the door, he added, "You'd better check on Mum and make sure she's not too upset." Then he was gone. Jude heard the front door slam behind him.

They'd stopped giving each other an affectionate kiss of greeting or farewell years ago but she thought he might at least have said goodbye. And why couldn't *he* have checked on Patricia? She was his mother, after all. Unconsciously, Jude sighed. Before leaving Ios, she'd allowed herself to imagine that, when she got back to Ireland, everything would be all right, that they'd make a new start. But it seemed as though nothing had changed. If anything, the tension between herself and Geoffrey was more palpable.

* * *

"Jude? It's Fidelma." Her voice sounded unusually cheerful down the phone. "Welcome back. They told me you'd rung the office earlier but that you wouldn't be in until Monday."

"Hello! You beat me to it. I have two more days of freedom before I'm back to the grindstone. I was just about to try and get hold of you. How are things?"

"Work wise, pretty gruesome really."

There was something about the way Fidelma spoke that hinted that work might be gruesome but other aspects to her life were not.

Jude was intrigued.

"I get the strong impression that you are dying to tell me something but are taking your time about it."

"I never could hide anything from you, could I?"

"Extremely foolish to even try. Well, go on! Spill the beans!"

"I think that, for the first time in my life, I am really and truly in love with a man who deserves to be really and truly loved."

"And that man is?"

"Can't you guess? You said yourself only a little while ago how nice he was."

"My mind's blank. I'm afraid I can't think of *any* nice men at this precise moment," said Jude, suddenly anxious. The last couple of men Fidelma had gone out with had been less than ideal.

"It's Alan!"

"Alan Carruth?"

"Yes!"

For a few seconds, Jude experienced several emotions. Surprise, pleasure and, to her shame, a brief pang of jealousy.

"Fidelma, that's marvellous! He's certainly a nice man. This is all very sudden. I only introduced you to him ten days ago."

"I know, I know! He rang me up the next day and asked me out. You were so busy getting ready to go away, I didn't mention it at the time and, anyway, I didn't think it would be anything more than two people sharing a pleasant meal together. But how wrong I was! Oh, Jude! I feel like a bottle of champagne that's been shaken – all fizz and bubbles!"

She sounded so happy it was contagious. Jude couldn't help smiling.

"You sound as though you've died and gone to heaven."

"I think it's possibly even better than that! Jude, he's lovely! I've waited forty-eight years for someone like this. He's patient, funny, clever, interesting . . ."

"And no doubt fabulous in bed."

There was a giggle from the other end of the line.

"Unbelievable!"

"That's marvellous. I'm really happy for you. I hope it works out – you deserve a decent bloke in your life."

Jude could hear Fidelma's name being called.

"I'm sorry, Jude, but I'll have to go. Things are really hectic here. We've just heard that we're to lose two researchers – and they'll still expect us to deliver. You know how it is! I'll call you. I'm dying to know how it went with your father."

Jude could hear a phone ringing in the background and Fidelma's name again being called.

"Of course. I'll speak to you soon," she said, thinking as she did that it was unlike Fidelma not to ask about Jude's trip earlier on in their conversation. She must be very much in love.

After she'd hung up, Jude remained sitting on the bed. So Fidelma and Alan were an item! She had never heard her friend sounding so animated. She felt genuinely pleased for her. Fidelma *did* deserve to be happy. Would it last though? Look at how excited and blissful she'd been at the start of her own relationship with Geoffrey. Just like Fidelma, she'd only seen his good qualities. That state of selective blindness had worn off after marriage but slowly and reasonably painlessly. Unconsciously, she threaded her slim fingers in and out of each other. Now things between Geoffrey and her had never been so bad. Was it all her fault? Should she have left all the questions unanswered and not insisted on tracking down her father? Jude stared down at her hands. No, surely it was much better to have found out the truth. Wasn't it?

Chapter Twelve

"Don't you want to go, then?" asked Geoffrey.

"Would you mind if I didn't? It's just that there'll be all the same old faces and . . . well, I don't feel like it."

"There's no point in going if you wouldn't enjoy it."

So Geoffrey had gone to the wrap party without her. At first Jude was taken aback that he had accepted the fact of her not going without more of a fuss. Thinking about it a little later, she reckoned it wasn't all that surprising when she considered how distant they'd been towards each other over the last few months. He was probably glad he could go and let his hair down without her hanging around like a spectre at the feast.

Jude had no illusions about him remaining partnerless for much of the evening. She'd been to too many similar get-togethers herself and knew all about the bonding that took place amongst the crew after a few weeks of meeting impossible deadlines, dealing with desperately wannabe-noticed extras and furious motorists who suddenly needed to be at their destinations yesterday and who weren't prepared to wait for a moment until the camera stopped rolling and the road was unblocked. All those, plus unexpected burglar alarms going off in the middle of love scenes, misplaced lenses, non-stop drizzle when sun was wanted and cloudless skies when a deluge was required – not to mention that most exhausting phenomenon of all – actors with easily bruised egos having to play opposite other actors with a breathtaking belief in their own genius and skins as thick as rhinoceros hides. It had always struck her as extraordinary that the odd assortment of characters who spent nearly the entire life of a film completely knackered, frazzled and irritated had the energy to do anything else. But working sometimes eighteen hours a day, six days a week with the same bunch of people seemed to have a strangely aphrodisiacal effect and flirtations were abundant. Apparently working and eating together all the time wasn't enough. They had to fit in the sleeping bit as well. From what she'd observed, these affairs usually ground to a halt when filming ended.

She and Geoffrey agreed that on-set flirtations were part of the game. Jude had never developed a taste for them and she was pretty sure that he had never taken it further than just the odd hug and kiss. Up until now that was. She guessed that some very tempting offers had been made over the years. Could his aloofness be due not to her being 'difficult', as he'd recently suggested, but to the fact that he was having an affair? The thought made her stomach churn.

She reminded herself that her husband, even though he was a man who – like most men – was not blind to the charms of a beautiful woman, was no lecher. He'd told Jude about some of the women he'd been involved with during his two years at the BBC before they had married. He explained that he'd been very honest with them. He'd informed them that he had no intention of proposing to any of them but if they wanted some reasonably intelligent conversation, good food and wine and better than average sex, he was prepared to do his bit. It was obvious that he felt he'd been more than fair. Reading between the lines, Jude deduced that he had inadvertently treated them rather badly – at the same time acknowledging that she was probably biased towards the woman's perspective.

Not having seen him since their Trinity days, when she'd come across him at a party on his return to Dublin, it was apparent that he wasn't pining for any of his lady friends. She had surprised herself by ending up in bed with him at the end of the first evening.

Their lovemaking had not just been passionate. There had been a mixture of urgency and tenderness in the way he'd made love to her that evening that was out of the ordinary. It was quite different from the often clumsy, sometimes lustful couplings she'd occasionally experienced up until then. She'd sensed that he felt he'd not only come back to Ireland because he'd been offered a better job but also because of her. He'd proposed to her after they'd made love again the next morning.

Lying on his side facing her, his hand stroking her long thighs, he said," I suppose you realise that I'm mad about you."

"Of course," she'd replied.

"And how do you feel about me?"

"I'm not sure. Reawakened affection, attraction, interest . . ."

"Well, that's not bad for starters. What would you say if I asked you to marry me?"

"I would say that it was perhaps a little early for you to ask me that," she'd replied gravely.

"I am in love with you and that's not something I've ever said to any woman. I didn't realise that I loved you when we were at Trinity together but seeing you again has brought it all back. I loved you then and I'm falling for you all over again after only a few hours. Could you, by the remotest chance, feel the same?"

Unsure, Jude had replied, "I love my mother deeply but I don't know what real love between a man and a woman is like. It's unknown territory, I'm afraid."

He'd kept on proposing and after a few weeks, she'd given in. Jude had never felt the same way about any other man. Geoffrey could take her breath away when she saw him unexpectedly in the street. When he touched her it was almost like experiencing a sudden surge of electricity – shocking – but deliciously so. He seemed genuinely interested in what she did and said and thought. That moved her even more than the sexual attraction they felt towards each other. Especially after the superficially romantic encounters she'd shared with other men. All of a sudden she realised that, up until then, she would gladly have given up any of her lovers in exchange for being loved and valued by her father. Now, that feeling receded. It occurred to her that perhaps loving and being loved by this man would be enough.

They married three months later. Seven months after the marriage, Flora was born. Geoffrey's mother nearly had a nervous breakdown trying to work out a way to stop her friends and acquaintances from finding out about this unacceptably short gestation period.

"Flora's a marvellously healthy child when you think how premature she was," she was heard telling the rector's wife.

"Another bloody miracle!" her son had commented with a laugh. "It could only happen in holy Catholic Ireland!"

Geoffrey's parents had been unenthusiastic members of the Church of England before moving to Ireland where, like Jude, he had gone to an interdenominational school. At university Geoffrey had been critical of the Catholic Church, especially the role played by the Church in Ireland but after his time at the BBC he seemed even more prepared than before to poke fun at the very human flaws of the people in charge. It also struck him as extraordinary that intelligent human beings could find solace in what he thought of as ritual mumbo-jumbo. "And they think that the savages got it wrong," he once remarked.

As far as Jude was concerned, the Church, any church, was irrelevant to her life and needs. What mattered was living that life to the best of your ability. Belonging to a Church wasn't a prerequisite – even to the Church of the Western Celts!

Jude smiled to herself, remembering the effect her membership of that imaginary sect had had on Marguerite. She wondered what the other woman was doing at that moment; painting, talking to Liam, standing, gazing out over the sea looking like a handsome ship's figurehead or did she have her work cut out, protecting him from the persistent Manolis?

Just then the doorbell rang. It was a short, almost

tentative peal as though the visitor wasn't sure if they should ring or not. When she opened it, she found a girl standing on the doorstep looking anxious.

"Hello," said Jude, smiling.

The girl smiled back nervously.

"Is Oscar in?" she asked hesitantly.

She really was incredibly lovely, thought Jude. Her skin was lightly tanned. A mass of fair hair fanned out from her head in waves, framing a heart-shaped face from which enormous blue eyes regarded Jude questioningly. In her jeans and short white T-shirt that displayed several inches of bare skin and slim waist, it was obvious that she had an exceptionally curvaceous figure. All of a sudden, Jude remembered Flora's dismissive comment on the phone about her brother's new girlfriend being 'all tits and no brain'. Well, she didn't know about the intellectual capacity of the visitor but she certainly had an amazing shape – the sort of shape, she guessed, that the minimally endowed Flora might secretly yearn for.

"No, he's out but he said that he would be back at six and it's nearly half-past now. Come in! I expect he'll appear any minute. My name's Jude, by the way."

"I'm Ellen."

Jude shook the warm, slightly moist hand the other offered.

"Well, come in and wait for him in the garden. It's nice and cool there."

The girl hesitated slightly before asking, "Is Flora here?"

"No. I don't expect her back for a while."

Ellen gave her a sudden smile that lit her face, making her look even more stunning.

162

"It's just that he said I should come over at six. I'd like to wait for him for a little bit – if I'm not in your way."

"Of course you wouldn't be." As Jude led her through the house and out into the back garden she considered the possibility that Ellen's reluctance to cross the threshold might just be as a result of having been subjected to Flora's less than friendly scrutiny and the girl realising that she hadn't scored many Brownie points. "Would you like something to drink? There's some orange juice in the fridge," she said as they emerged into the garden where large trees on one side cast long fingers of shadow across the less than even lawn.

"No, I'm fine. Really. I'll sit out here and wait for him. Please don't let me keep you. I'm sure you're busy." Then she added shyly, "Oscar told me you had been away."

"Oh, I wasn't doing anything special just now. Daydreaming, really." Jude could hardly stop herself from staring at the creature sitting beside her on the Plunkett-chewed garden seat. Why wasn't Oz home if he knew the girl was going to call? She hoped he wasn't going to be off-hand in the way he treated her.

"It's a nice garden," Ellen remarked, looking around at the neglected flower-beds and spindly rosebushes.

"Well, it's fairly green and reasonably quiet. I wouldn't say more than that," said Jude, smiling. "I wonder where Oscar is . . ."

"He's so nice, Mrs – ah – Jude," said Ellen. "I know I've only known him for a couple of weeks but he's different from the other lads. Sort of special, like." She blushed suddenly as if embarrassed by her sudden outburst.

Poor thing! She's got it bad, Jude said to herself,

163

remembering how smitten she'd been over her own first boyfriend all those years ago.

"Yes, he is nice – most of the time," she agreed with a laugh.

There was a sudden burst of furious barking as Plunkett tore out of the house towards them. She watched as he charged up to Ellen who calmly fondled his ears and told him he was 'only gorgeous'. To her astonishment, the usually frenetic dog settled at the girl's feet, having first licked her hand.

Jude could see her mother-in-law lurking in one of the windows of her flat, pretending not to be taking a good look at the stranger. She knew that it would be a battle between keeping up the appearance that she was far too busy to be the slightest bit interested in other people's visitors and succumbing to an overwhelming desire to know what was going on. Curiosity won.

Just as Patricia Larchet emerged, there was a bang of a door and Oscar loped into view. Seeing Ellen, he lifted a hand in casual greeting and started to saunter towards them. Ellen's reaction was more dramatic. The blush returned, then she got to her feet hastily, beaming with delight at the approaching Oscar. Oscar, however, appeared to be playing it cool.

"Hi!" he said in the girl's general direction. "Hi, Mum! Hello, Gran."

Mrs Larchet drew level with Jude just as he joined them. She gave Ellen a gracious smile before turning towards her grandson.

"Good evening, Oscar. Aren't you going to introduce me to your guest?"

It always amused Jude when her mother-in-law played the part of gracious lady. Eyebrows raised, she looked expectantly at her son.

"Sorry! Gran, this is Ellen. Ellen, this is my grandmother," he rattled off. Duty done, and before his grandmother could say anything else, he turned to the pink-cheeked girl. "Come on then or we'll be late."

"Are you going anywhere nice?" enquired Mrs Larchet.

Oscar gave her a look that implied that cross-examination would go down badly.

"Just out," he said vaguely. "'Bye, Mum. See you later."

"'Bye, Oz," replied his mother. "Goodbye, Ellen. Nice to meet you."

Apparently the girl was finding it difficult to tear her eyes away from Oscar.

"Oh, you too, Jude, Mrs Larchet. Goodbye and thank you!"

As Mrs Larchet joined her daughter-in-law on the seat, Jude watched them go back to the house, shadowed by Plunkett. She noticed the way Ellen seemed to lean slightly towards Oscar as she walked, intent on what he was saying.

No sooner had they disappeared from view than Flora appeared around the corner of the building. She was wearing a shapeless, layered garment in a colour that reminded Jude of over-cooked sprouts. Her eyes were hidden behind the latest wrap-around sunglasses and her long hair was tied up on top of her head. She sat down on the arm of the garden seat with an exaggerated sigh.

"Phew! I missed a riveting chat with Sue Ellen! Just managed to duck round the side of the house before she saw me," she exclaimed. "So, you've met Wonder-girl! Oz never learns, does he?"

"She seemed very nice," said Jude. "And she doesn't live at South Fork with JR and her name is not Sue Ellen. It's Ellen."

Jude found herself wondering what malign fairy had been present at Flora's birth. She felt suddenly protective towards her son's new girlfriend. Perhaps she wasn't the brightest creature on the planet but she seemed harmless enough and she was obviously mad about Oscar.

"Did you actually manage to have a conversation with her, Mum?"

"No. We didn't really have time for one. Oz appeared just after she arrived."

"Well, if you had, you'd have realised what a complete airhead she is."

"So, in your book, being nice doesn't matter – only being clever," interjected Patricia Larchet unexpectedly.

Nice one, Gran! thought Jude. The two women looked at Flora, waiting for a response. It was difficult to tell what she was thinking because of the sunglasses.

"No, I didn't say that." Flora sounded annoyed, aware of the rare sense of accord between her mother and grandmother. "There's not much point in being nice if there's absolutely nothing else to you. Nice won't get you far on its own. That's why she'll never do more than waitressing and bar-work until she marries some dumb man who only wants a dumb blonde for a wife. I mean, it's not like I'm saying you have to have a degree or anything to get places. After all, Gran didn't and I expect she thinks she did all right for herself."

"Young women didn't go to college in my day - not the attractive ones, anyway," Gran retorted.

"They just hung around until they could persuade some poor unfortunate to marry them," said Flora.

Aware of the affronted expression Gran was now wearing, Jude frowned at her daughter. She really was pretty unlikeable some of the time – and this was definitely one of those times. Sometimes she found herself wondering which of them was the more awkward.

"She seems very keen on Oz," she remarked dryly. "And that shows good taste at least!"

"Wait and see! He'll go out with her for a bit before he dumps her. It's good for his flagging ego."

Jude's irritation rose another notch. "For goodness' sake, Flora! Do you have to be so nasty?"

"Jesus!" exploded her daughter. "I'm not even allowed to have a point of view on anything these days – not unless it's the same as yours!"

"That's not true and you know it. Dad and I have always encouraged you to work things out for yourself, have your own opinions. I just thought you were hot on the idea of 'live and let live'. Also it wouldn't hurt to be a little more charitable sometimes."

"You always have to twist everything. No wonder Dad is fed up," retorted Flora.

She got up angrily and turned away from them.

As her daughter marched back to the house, shoulders hunched, Jude asked, "Just what do you mean by *that*?"

The back door slammed shut behind Flora.

"Unwise, Judith," commented Patricia Larchet.

Jude stared at her. Flora had been utterly unpleasant and now Jude was being accused of being unwise.

"*What* was?"

The affronted look was gone. Mrs Larchet's voice was all sweet reasonableness.

"You know how much young things that age hate being criticised. Now you've upset her and she will start banging doors and playing music too loudly."

And that is just what happened.

Damn both of them, thought Jude a little later on as she turned up the volume on the kitchen radio in an attempt to lessen the impact of Flora's CD player overhead. Were her friends as rude to their parents as Flora was? If not, why not? Where had she gone wrong? she wondered. Socrates had moaned about the youth of his day so perhaps it was all just part of a pre-ordained pattern and it was a foolish waste of time to wonder why. She looked at the clock on the mantelpiece. What time would Geoffrey be back? If he'd had a good evening, perhaps he would be feeling mellow and they might be able to manage a hug without antagonising each other when he came to bed.

During the evening, Jude found she couldn't concentrate on anything. She felt unsettled by Flora's throwaway remark about Geoffrey being fed up, the implication being that she was the one at fault. Another thing that disturbed her was her ongoing inability to get on with Patricia. This particularly worried her when she remembered how drawn her mother-in-law had looked that evening in the garden. Jude had let the opportunity slip by when she should have asked her if she was feeling unwell but the woman's criticism of her handling of Flora had rankled.

These anxieties came on top of the realisation that she was not really resigned to the idea of having no relevance in the life of her stepfather and also the fact that she felt let down by the mother she'd so trusted.

Just as she had decided that a good night's sleep would be preferable to staying up and feeling depressed, the telephone rang. When she answered it, Jude hardly recognised the voice at the other end as belonging to her mother-in-law, it sounded so weak and breathless.

"Judith, can you come through? I'm not feeling very well."

"Don't worry. I'm coming straight away," she said as calmly as she could.

As she hurriedly put the receiver back, Jude knew that Patricia Larchet was not pretending this time. There was something wrong. She had sounded as though she was in great pain. She had also sounded frightened. Slipping her feet into her sandals, Jude quickly made her way through the house with a feeling of foreboding.

Chapter Thirteen

It was nearly three in the morning by the time Jude got back from the hospital. She was greeted by an anxious Flora, who had stayed behind while her mother followed the ambulance in to Casualty. All attempts to reach Geoffrey by phone had failed. His mobile was switched off and the only information Jude had managed to winkle out of the restaurant where the wrap party had been held was that a group of them had gone on to a nightclub. The tired-sounding girl at the other end didn't know which one.

Oscar had got in shortly after Jude. She noticed in passing that there was a smudge of make-up on his shirt and his lips looked a little swollen.

Now the three of them sat round the kitchen table pretending to drink their mugs of coffee and waiting for Geoffrey to come home. Jude didn't know which of them looked most worried.

In typical Flora style, the earlier confrontation between them had been forgotten. Jude didn't doubt it would be resurrected in the future if it suited her to use as evidence against her mother. But for now, she was doing her best to be helpful by rinsing mugs, grinding coffee beans and providing them with more caffeine than they wanted.

The worst part had been waiting for the ambulance to arrive. Jude had found Mrs Larchet lying on her side on the couch in her flowery sitting-room with both legs drawn up towards her chest. She was breathing in quick, short gasps. When she became aware that Jude had come into the room, the woman tried to get up but immediately fell back onto the cushion with a muffled moan. One glance was enough to tell her daughter-in-law that she should act quickly. Once she had made the call, Jude knelt at the side of the couch. She wanted to comfort her mother-in-law but she knew instinctively that any touching or holding would be construed as taking advantage of the situation. So, fighting back the impulse to lay a comforting hand on the other's arm, she spoke in a low voice.

"Hang on there, Patricia. The ambulance will be here in a few minutes. Can I get you anything? A sip of water?"

The woman shook her head slightly and then closed her eyes, overcome by pain. Jude didn't like the way her forehead and upper lip were covered in small beads of sweat or the ivory-like pallor of her skin.

She'd felt impotent, waiting there beside this woman who she knew resented her distress being witnessed and yet who needed her help.

"Mum?" Oscar's voice broke into her thoughts. "Why don't you and Flo go to bed and I'll stay up and wait for Dad? There's no point in all of us being knackered, especially if you've got to go back to the hospital in a few hours' time."

What he said made sense. She smiled at him wearily.

"Are you sure?"

"Sure I'm sure." He looked at his sister. "Go on, Flo! Take Mum up to bed."

"I don't mind keeping you company," said Flora, attempting to sound enthusiastic at the idea of sitting up until dawn if required. She felt that, as his older sister, really she should be the one holding the fort.

"Go on, Flo! You know you're impossible if you don't get your beauty sleep."

Jude got to her feet slowly.

"Well, all right, Oz, but promise you'll wake me as soon as Dad gets back."

"I promise," he said with a reassuring smile.

Jude didn't bother to take off her clothes. She lay on the bed, trying to relax, to will herself to drift into sleep. It was difficult. What she hadn't told Flora and Oscar was that their grandmother was indeed very ill. The exhausted doctor who had examined Mrs Larchet said that, judging from the X-rays they had taken and the intensity of pain the woman was suffering, it looked as though there was a severe blockage in the intestine and they would have to operate. To do that they needed Geoffrey's permission.

Where is he? she wondered tiredly. Surely he hadn't chosen this night of all nights to do a disappearing act?

She must have eventually fallen asleep because the next thing she knew was that Oscar was shaking her shoulder and daylight was seeping through the closed curtains.

"Is Dad back?" she asked, pulling herself up into a sitting position and leaning back against the headboard.

"Yes, but he's gone to the hospital. He said I wasn't to

wake you until you'd had a couple of hours' sleep. He'll ring you when he has any news." He pointed to a cup of tea on the bedside table. "I thought you might like some tea. Flo's dead to the world so I just left her to sleep. You know what she's like when she hasn't had enough to recharge her battery."

Jude nodded and patted the bed.

"Keep me company while I drink it." As he sat down, she noticed that dark stubble peppered Oscar's chin and cheeks and his hair stood up in untidy spikes. Rather like an overgrown hedgehog, she thought fondly. She saw that he had remembered to exchange his make-up-smudged shirt for a clean one but he hadn't been able to do anything about camouflaging the love-bite on his neck. As she sipped her tea, Jude wondered why Geoffrey had gone off without saying anything to her when Oscar must have told him that she wanted to be woken when he got back. Neither, it seemed, had he wanted her to go to the hospital with him. "What's the time?" she asked blearily.

"Just after nine."

"And it's Saturday, right?"

Oscar laughed.

"Yeah, Mum! It's Saturday. I thought it was only Gran who muddled up the days of the week." He suddenly looked serious. "Will she be all right?"

"I don't know. It didn't sound too good when I spoke to the doctor." Jude ran her fingers through her tangled hair in frustration. "I wish I knew what was happening. I *wish* he would ring."

At that very moment the telephone rang, making them both jump. She picked it up quickly.

"Geoff?"

"Yes, it's me."

He sounded tired.

"What's the news?"

"I didn't phone earlier because they took her down to the theatre a couple of hours ago and there wasn't any point in waking you up until they found what the problem was." His voice was flat. Jude waited for the inevitable bad news. "It's not good, I'm afraid. She's got cancer – and it's spread. There wasn't very much they could do for her – apparently there are secondaries all over the place. They've given her a colostomy."

Oh, God! thought Jude. She will hate that.

Out loud she said, "Oh, Geoff, I am sorry. How is she now?"

"Very sleepy and full of morphia. She's not really with it at all. The Sister said I might as well leave her to sleep off the effects of the anaesthetic for a few hours. I'm going to leave now. I'll see you in about half an hour."

"OK. See you soon."

As she put down the phone, Jude hoped she'd sounded more cheerful than she felt. Suddenly, the realisation that life in the Larchet family had changed hit her. Nothing would ever be quite the same from now on. Her mind raced. Would her mother-in-law be well enough to come home in the next week or so? And if she did, who was going to look after her? Would Jude and Geoffrey be able to provide a united front to cope with it all? Panic welled up inside her. She remembered the feeling she'd had in the past when things got out of control – a sensation almost of falling. What her mother always called the 'Tumbling Jude

Syndrome' – which was nothing to get worried about, she'd insisted. "You spent most of your childhood falling over and that doesn't happen any more – or not too often! We're all allowed the occasional wobble," she had joked after Jude had had an attack of panic over some exam results. It would pass, she'd reassured her daughter cheerfully.

"What's the matter, Mum? Is it bad news?"

Jude looked at her son and felt a sudden surge of affection.

"Not good. Gran's got cancer and it appears that the doctors can't do anything much for her." She held out her arms. "Oh, Oz, give us a hug!"

Just as he leaned forward, a loud barking, followed by a mournful howl, reminded them that Plunkett had not been fed and was obviously feeling neglected. They both laughed. Oscar stood up and then bent over Jude and put an arm around her shoulders, giving her a squeeze.

"I'd better go and see to him before he demolishes the joint – or wakes up the Sleeping Beauty!" He looked down at her as he took her empty cup. "Don't worry, Mum. Everything will be all right. We'll manage fine, whatever happens."

At that precise moment, Jude wasn't feeling quite so confident.

* * *

It took two weeks before Patricia Larchet was strong enough to be discharged from hospital. Up until then, Jude had gone back to work, sharing the evening visiting times with Geoffrey while Oscar and Flora sometimes called in to their grandmother in the afternoons. This regime meant that Jude saw very little of her husband. It was usually late in the evening before they met, which meant they were both too tired to tackle the problem of their deteriorating relationship. She had assumed that Oscar and Flora were so busy with their own lives they hadn't realised how bad things had become between their parents. She had noticed that they both seemed to spend more and more of their time out during the evenings. But on the day before Mrs Larchet returned, Jude was unexpectedly confronted by her daughter after the evening meal.

Flora had been unusually quiet while they ate their supper, half watching a soap on the television. When the programme finished and the set had been switched off, she remained silent for a few minutes, staring down at her empty plate with a slight scowl. Usually this meant an outburst of some sort was immanent.

"Are you feeling all right, Flo?" Jude enquired.

"Mum, I need to talk to you while there's no one else around."

"That sounds serious!"

But Flora was looking pensive. She didn't respond immediately. Jude got the impression that her daughter was searching carefully for the right words. Dear God! she thought. I hope she's not about to tell me that she's pregnant. That would be too much to cope with on top of everything else that's going on.

"I've talked this over with Oz and he said I shouldn't say anything that would upset you, especially at the moment, what with Gran and everything."

Again Jude experienced the internal vertiginous nudge of worry she found so disturbing. She made an effort to smile.

"Well, now you've started, you'd better go on and tell me what this is all about."

"You won't be mad at me afterwards, will you? Only you should know what's going on."

"Flo, am I so unreasonable?" Jude put a hand on her daughter's arm. "I promise not to shoot the messenger. Now, what's wrong?"

Taking her by surprise, she noticed for the first time that there were tears forming at the corners of her daughter's grey-green eyes. Flora abruptly turned her head away for a moment as though angry at this sign of emotion. She swallowed noisily before shifting round again to face her mother.

I'm right! She must be pregnant. Jude tried to keep herself from shouting at Flora to get a move on and to get the whole thing over with once and for all.

"Oh, Mum! Dad's having an affair."

The sentence seemed to hang in the air above them. For a moment, Jude considered responding with a remark that would show how ridiculous she knew that statement was. She wanted to pour scorn on the very idea of Geoffrey being unfaithful. But she found herself unable to utter words of denial. Deep down inside, she had already known. She had been trying to smother the knowledge of it ever since the night of the wrap party – perhaps even a little before that awful night when Geoffrey's mother had become so ill. A strange sort of calm spread through Jude. She heard herself speak as though it were someone else.

"How can you be so sure?"

"Dad left his mobile behind by mistake one day when you were away . . . and I'd run out of credit on mine and so . . . I used his to send Oz a text."

177

"And you read his text messages?"

A stubborn look crossed Flora's face. "It's a good thing I did."

"And what did this text message say that convinced you that your father was having an affair?"

"I can't remember the exact words," her daughter mumbled.

"The gist of them, then."

Flora looked uncomfortable. "Mum, I can't! Don't make me, please. It was all sleazy and how she couldn't wait for him to . . ." She broke off, looking distressed.

"It's all right, Flo," Jude said quickly. "I understand. You don't have to say any more."

She put an arm around her daughter's shoulders and rested her cheek for a moment against the long dark hair that smelled faintly of honey and stale cigarette smoke.

"Mum, what are we going to do?"

She sounded like a miserable child. Jude didn't know how best to console her. It wasn't as if there were anything much to be cheerful about just now.

"Nothing for the moment, Flo," said Jude, trying hard to keep her voice steady. "Gran is coming home tomorrow and she's going to need a lot of looking after. We mustn't upset her." She smoothed back the hair from Flora's face. "Promise me that neither of you two will let her know that something is wrong?"

Flora gave a small nod and then said bitterly, "Gran thinks Dad is marvellous. She wouldn't believe it if anyone *did* tell her the truth."

"So if she found out, it would be even more of a shock to her."

"I suppose so." Flora looked at her mother. "Are you going to say anything to Dad?"

"Flo, leave me to sort out things with Dad. You just concentrate on college." Jude gingerly got up from the couch. She'd been sitting with her legs folded under her and she now had pins and needles in both feet. She picked up the tray from the coffee table. "You've only got a few weeks before your play starts, haven't you? I'm looking forward to seeing you in it. I think you'll make a good Margaret Roper."

A Man for all Seasons was the first chance Flora had been given for a named part in a college production and Jude knew that it was desperately important to her that it went well.

"*You* may be there to see me but will Dad still be around in four weeks' time or will he have gone off to live with bloody Sonia . . ." Flora stopped and went red. "Oh, Mum, I'm sorry. I hadn't meant to . . ."

"It's all right, Flo."

Jude was pretty sure she could guess that the Sonia alluded to was the pretty trainee assistant director she'd seen Geoffrey talking to on a couple of occasions at the studios. She'd observed both times that he'd not bothered to introduce Jude to her, which was unusual. She remembered how the girl had made some excuse or other and scuttled off as soon as she'd been able to get away.

"But it's not all right, Mum! How can you say that? *Everything's* going wrong," Flora wailed.

"Flora! Stop! Don't make a difficult situation more ghastly by imagining the worst. I need you to be strong and not go to pieces over this. It will be all right."

Her daughter looked as doubtful as Jude herself had when Oscar tried to cheer her up on the morning of her mother-in-law's operation.

Jude leaned over and placed a kiss on her forehead. "Come on! Mop up those tears."

As she walked down the passage to the kitchen, she felt her anger rise. It wasn't just what this meant in terms of her relationship with her husband. Flora and Oscar were going to suffer because of what he'd done. Was it a just a brief fling? Or was this the start of a full-blown affair? Damn him! she muttered, putting the tray down on the draining-board with a thump. How *could* he?

* * *

Summer appeared to be finally over. A cool wind was blowing grey clouds across the sky when, the following day, Jude watched while Geoffrey held his mother's arm, supporting her, as she slowly walked the short distance from the car to the front door. Even though Catriona had been happy to come in every morning and Geoffrey had taken the day off work, Jude felt it was important to be there for this uncertain homecoming.

Although Jude had seen her looking frail in hospital, Mrs Larchet seemed to have shrunk more than she had realised. It was obvious that she was doing her best to walk as erect as she could but to Jude, her mother-in-law, from being a smart, elderly woman, had suddenly been diminished into a replica of the dozens of other old women one saw shuffling along with no expectation of joy in what remained of their lives. This metamorphosis made her sad.

She stepped out to greet the woman, avoiding looking at Geoffrey as she approached them.

"Welcome home, Patricia."

Patricia Larchet looked up with a startled expression as if she hadn't expected to see her.

"Judith! I thought you would be at work."

Her voice sounded weak.

So, Geoffrey hadn't even bothered to tell his mother that Jude would be there when she came home.

"What? And not be part of the reception committee!" She gave her a bright smile. "The kids and Catriona are inside. They're all looking forward to seeing you." Mrs Larchet gave her a small smile. She looks completely done in, thought Jude. "Would you rather go straight through and see them later when you've rested?"

The woman looked at her gratefully. "If you don't mind, I think I'd like to do that."

It was painful to watch her climb the two steps up to the front door, leaning on her son's arm. In the hall, Geoffrey glanced over his shoulder. "I'll take Mum through, then."

Jude nodded mutely and looked quickly away. This was not going to be easy, even with Catriona's cheerful and willing help. They all knew that Gran must come first now – and that meant putting other problems on hold for the time being. Would it be possible to hide the tension that existed between herself and Geoffrey?

At least he hadn't lied when she'd tackled him on the previous night about his affair with Sonia. He seemed almost relieved that she'd brought it out into the open.

"I suppose you want me to move into the spare bedroom? Or would you like me to leave altogether?"

But Jude had done a lot of thinking in the hours between her conversation with Flora and Geoffrey's arrival home later that night.

"No, I do not want you to move out of our bedroom. It is *our* bedroom. I most certainly don't want you to move out of the house." Seeing his surprise, she added, "I am not going to let her come between you and me after two children and more than twenty years of marriage." When he still hadn't said anything, she said, "Geoffrey, I intend to try and save what we have. I consider it worth saving. Perhaps you don't and perhaps I'll fail – but I'm not giving you up without a fight. The world's too full of broken marriages."

She knew that he was waiting for her to ask the sort of questions she supposed wives in this situation were expected to ask. Why? When had it started? Why with a girl who was only a little older than his daughter? Was it Jude's fault that he had wandered? Did he still love her? Did he care about her at all?

She wanted to ask them – all of them. But she needed to come out of this intact. If she went on the attack, it would only make things worse. The most important thing, apart from protecting his mother from the truth, was to ensure that Flora and Oscar weren't hurt any more than they had been already. Jude hated to see them torn between very real anger and shock and their feelings of love for him because he was their father. Even if they were no longer small children, she, who had lost her own father, didn't want them to lose Geoffrey. Jude realised how difficult it would be for him to regain their trust, even if he did end his involvement with Sonia.

She had watched them that morning at breakfast. Geoffrey hadn't joined them at the table but stood, silently drinking his coffee beside the sink. Neither Oscar nor Flora had spoken to him. His daughter sat at the table scowling while Oscar kept giving Jude anxious glances. It was all she could do to swallow a few mouthfuls of coffee herself before escaping from the room that seemed to resonate with unspoken anger and apprehension – and the unasked questions.

As she shut the front door behind her, Jude tried to hold on to the idea that the whole thing could be resolved and they would be the stronger for it. One aspect that worried her was the thought that perhaps her own recent preoccupation about finding her father had made it seem to her husband that he didn't count – that the only person who mattered appeared to be this father of hers – a man who, consequently, turned out to be no father at all. She knew that for some time she'd been confused and miserable. Had her longing to find out the truth jeopardised her relationship with her husband? *Was* it her fault that this had happened?

Chapter Fourteen

"Oh, my God!" said Fidelma. "I'd no idea things were so bad."

Jude and she were having a snatched lunch together in the canteen. Not having had the chance to talk to each other for some time, Fidelma hadn't known about Mrs Larchet's illness. When she'd gone back to work, Jude caught sight of her friend once or twice during her lunch break but Alan was with her and she didn't want to intrude. They looked so happy together; absorbed in each other and completely oblivious of the people around them. Three would definitely have been a crowd.

"Well, there wasn't any reason why you should." Jude smiled at her. "Anyway, you've been too occupied with the new man in your life to think about much else." There was no doubt that things must be going well for her friend. Jude had never seen her look so well. She'd had her hair cut shorter so that it framed her face rather than hanging down in a lank curtain onto her shoulders. And her face had a fuller, softer look that made it seem less angular and bony. Even the way Fidelma walked had subtly altered. She looked more assured, more alert. In fact, she was positively glowing. "Would I be right in thinking that you and Alan are getting on well?"

Fidelma made an unsuccessful effort not to look smug. "You would!"

"And would I be right in thinking that you and he have just come back from a wicked weekend somewhere nice?"

Fidelma laughed. "You most *certainly* would!"

For a second Jude caught a glimpse of remembered pleasure in the other's eyes.

"Well, I'm really happy for you, Fee. I was going to say that you were looking really well but I think the word smouldering comes to mind as more apt!"

"Easy on now! I never thought of myself like that. Although, I feel more alive than I've ever done. It's not just the way he seems to understand me so well and why I say the things I say, why I do what I do. I've never met anyone so intuitive before. It's as though . . ."

The happy expression on Fidelma's face faded as she watched Jude absent-mindedly push a piece of tomato around her plate with her fork. She looked as though she were miles away and had suddenly tuned out of the conversation. She was also beginning to look horribly thin and the over-sized sweater she was wearing did nothing to hide the fact that she had lost a lot of weight over the past weeks.

"Listen to me, rabbiting on! I really am sorry about Geoffrey."

Jude looked up. With an effort, she focussed on her

friend's face. There was no point in pretending to be hungry. She put her fork down beside the uneaten slice of quiche.

"I suppose it's common knowledge – this *thing* he's having with Sonia O'Dowd?"

"Yes, I'm afraid it is. You can't help everyone knowing in a place like this. You know what it's like." Fidelma gave her a searching look. "Are you going to be all right with all of this – your mother-in-law, the father business and now Geoffrey?"

Jude's gaze travelled unseeingly around the busy canteen before she answered.

"I have to be. There's too much at stake for me to throw tantrums or go all weak-kneed." She looked over at Fidelma. "I *must* be all right. There's no other way to do it. Flora pretends she's fine but she's not. I'm really worried about her, Fee. She seems to seesaw from being unexpectedly supportive to behaving like a raving lunatic from someone's worst nightmare. Oscar's angry with his father too but he seems more able to detach himself from all the drama going on at home. He's being incredibly sweet to me but he disappears as much as he can. I don't think it's affecting him quite as much as his sister. Perhaps it's a man thing – this ability to be more pragmatic than dramatic. I think it's his way of dealing with an uncomfortable situation. It seems to be working for him anyway."

"Do you have a plan of action?"

"You mean, apart from slitting bloody Sonia O'Whatsit's throat?" Jude gave a mirthless laugh. "Nothing definite yet. Most of my spare time at the moment is taken up with doing what I can for Patricia. I can't imagine she's going to last very long. She's got one of those self-administering things on her wrist that helps the pain. But I don't think it's as effective as it was a week ago. The doctor's been great about visiting and Catriona's marvellous." She smiled at Fidelma. "So things could be worse, I suppose."

Not a lot, you poor love, thought Fidelma, smiling back.

"You will tell me if there's anything I can do to help, won't you?" she asked.

"Yes, of course," said Jude, knowing that there was nothing her friend could do or say to ease the situation.

They parted at the door to the canteen. Fidelma gave her a kiss.

"Please ring me if you need anything, Jude."

"Of course. But you know me. Invincible! In case you hadn't cottoned on, I'm really Superwoman in disguise!" replied Jude. "Or Bionic Woman – or Batwoman. I forget which of them is supposed to be the most amazing!" She gave her friend's arm a hasty squeeze before quickly walking away.

* * *

There was no doubt that the atmosphere between herself and her mother-in-law had improved. Although Mrs Larchet refused to let Jude anywhere near her when it was time for her to have her shower. Catriona and only Catriona was allowed to help her change the colostomy bags.

"How is she managing with the colostomy?" she asked the girl one day after Catriona had been closeted with Mrs Larchet for the best part of an hour.

Catriona pulled a face. "Well, she don't like it one bit poor old thing but I told her that I've seen more ladies with

187

no clothes on than she could imagine – and some of them in a much worse way than she is – with no legs, one hand, no boobs, stitched all over like one of them patchwork quilts, like some maniac's got at them with a darning needle. I told her she didn't have nothing to get her knickers in a twist about. Mind you, I didn't tell her everything about what I'd seen when I was working in that kip of a nursing home last year. Anyways, that kinda made her look at things a bit different, like." She shook her head. "No, she don't like it but she lets me do the necessary now without any fuss." Catriona gave Jude a grin. "She even thanked me the other day, so I must be doing something right!"

In the past, Patricia Larchet had hardly bothered to acknowledge her presence around the place. 'Domestic help should be seen only occasionally and definitely not heard,' she'd remarked once to her friend Joan Ryan. Catriona had overheard her and instead of being insulted, to Jude's relief, had giggled over the woman's silliness. "Ah, I wouldn't mind her!" she commented afterwards. "Well, I mean, she's English, isn't she?"

In spite of her attempts to pretend that everything was normal with Geoffrey, Jude found herself wondering if her mother-in-law hadn't grasped the fact that all was not well between them. She'd caught her looking at her in a strange way a few days earlier as if she'd been on the point of saying something but couldn't bring herself to actually come out with what was on her mind.

"Is there anything I can get you?" Jude had prompted.

Patricia Larchet smiled slightly and shook her head. "No thank you, Judith. You've done quite enough as it is."

It was late in the evening and the light from the bedside

lamp showed up the hollows around her eyes. There were dark brown shadows under them and the woman's skin had taken on a dry, parchment-like quality. The grey hair that had always been so neat now looked sparse and, in spite of Catriona's best efforts, stood out from her skull in wisps. Another thing that had changed was the woman's nose. It seemed to have grown while the rest of her face had collapsed inwards. She now looked rather like a pathetic small bird with a large beak, Jude thought – at the same time sympathetic and depressed at being a witness to her disintegration.

She wasn't quite sure what her husband felt about his dying mother. He spent time with her each evening but didn't seem to want to talk about her condition with Jude. When she'd asked him how he was coping with the situation, he brushed her question aside.

"I'm fine, Jude. I really am. It's you who's looking worn out," he added and she knew he felt guilty.

Damn it! she thought. I mustn't go around looking like a wreck. That will be no competition for the elfin Sonia.

She smiled and said in a matter-of-fact voice, "Well, it's hard on all of us at the moment."

He'd left the room, mumbling something about having paperwork to sort out.

And that was the extent of their conversation these days: both of them polite but with Geoffrey usually finding an excuse to escape as soon as he could when he found himself alone with her. It seemed to her that his ostrich-like behaviour was an attempt to deny the fact that his mother was terminally ill. If he didn't talk about it, perhaps it wouldn't happen.

At Jude's insistence, they still slept in the same bed, but never close enough to come into contact with each other. It's as if he's afraid to touch me, she thought. Then she would tell herself she was a fool. What man, leaping regularly into bed with a new woman twenty years his junior, would want to embrace his wife? I have to be patient, she kept reminding herself when, sometimes, all she wanted was to scream at him, to remind him that what he was doing was unacceptable and unfair.

* * *

During the week, Jude had been touched by the appearance of Ellen, bearing a large, multi-coloured bunch of mixed flowers that Jude knew instinctively would be the sort of bouquet Patricia Larchet would have sniffed disdainfully at in the past. Instead, her mother-in-law looked unexpectedly delighted, holding the scentless flowers to her nose with pleasure. Jude was immediately dispatched to find a suitable vase.

"Come and sit down beside me and tell me what that grandson of mine is getting up to these days. I think you see more of him than the rest of us do," Mrs Larchet said to Ellen with a slight smile.

When Jude returned, she paused, unnoticed in the doorway. Ellen was in the middle of describing a recent evening she'd spent with Oscar in a club that specialised in laser shows. Mrs Larchet's eyes were fixed on the girl's animated face as she tried to describe the sequence of coloured beams of light, synchronised to the music so that they seemed to pulse and dance quite independently of any human assistance.

Jude walked over to the other side of the room and placed the vase on the dressing-table. Ellen was now telling the fascinated woman about the difficulty of getting past bouncers outside the various nightclubs.

"You mean if they don't like the look of you," her mother-in-law asked, "they can refuse to let you in – even if there's room?"

Ellen laughed. "Oh, Mrs Larchet, you've no idea! Talk about the Mafia! Those lads would turn you away if you looked at them sideways. I've seen them letting in girls they fancied and stopping their boyfriends. They can push you around and be really rude too!"

"They sound like a bunch of thugs to me," said Patricia Larchet with some of her old spirit. "We never came across that sort of thing when I was growing up in London. If a place had a man on the door, he was always very polite – and if he had to turn someone away, he did it courteously. They *certainly* never wore walkie-talkies and *sunglasses*. I never heard of anything so ridiculous!"

"They stopped Oscar from going in one night last week because they thought he wasn't dressed smartly enough."

"Well, really!"

Mrs Larchet sounded so outraged, Jude found herself smiling.

"Patricia! You are always telling Oz that he's too sloppy about the way he dresses and that he doesn't comb his hair properly. You should be pleased that there are others out there trying to reform him as well!"

Patricia Larchet gave one of her sniffs. The sort of sniff that implied Jude was being extremely silly.

"One's family criticising you is one thing. A bunch of

191

layabouts having a go at you is quite another. They probably took against him because he speaks nicely."

Jude shook her head despairingly. Well, perhaps it was foolish to want too much. She couldn't expect her mother-in-law to change completely and drop the bad habits of a lifetime of indulging in petty snobbery. On the whole, being so ill had made her into a much easier person to get on with. It was nice to be able to have a conversation without ending up feeling thoroughly at odds with each other. And what was more, there was Ellen, perched on a chair beside the bed, looking a little like an over-ripe peach, with her bosom positively falling out of her skin-tight top and Gran didn't seem to have noticed. If she had, she hadn't said anything. So that was an improvement! A few months ago, the sniffs would have been deafening!

Mrs Larchet seemed to suddenly fade. She lay back on her pillows, looking exhausted. Jude saw her lips compress as she experienced a wave of pain.

Putting a hand on Ellen's shoulder she said gently, "I think it's time Oscar's gran had a rest."

Ellen hastily got to her feet, looking down at the woman with a worried expression.

"I'm so sorry! I hope I haven't made you tired."

Patricia Larchet gathered herself together and gave her a smile. "Not at all, dear. I really enjoyed our little chat. I'd love it if you came back to see me again – if you have the time."

Jude could see the effort she was making to sound cheerful. By the time Ellen had left the room, promising to visit her again and telling Jude not to worry, she would see herself out, the woman appeared to be nearly speechless with pain. She was fumbling with the morphine-dispenser on her wrist.

"Is the morphine not working, Patricia?"

There was a silence. Although her eyes were tightly closed, it looked as though Mrs Larchet was fighting back tears. Jude was appalled. In all the years she had known her, she had never seen Geoffrey's mother cry. A sudden movement on the sheet made her lean forward impulsively and take hold of the small, claw-like hand. There was no resistance to her touch. Suddenly, the woman's eyes opened wide. She stared up into her daughter-in-law's face, her other hand hesitantly moving out from under the bedclothes, hovering uncertainly for a second before descending to cover Jude's own hand.

Mrs Larchet laughed weakly.

"It's like that old game we played as children. You know, pat-a-cake." The smile vanished. "I'm ashamed to say that I feel frightened, Judith. I didn't think I would be but I am."

Jude knelt down at the bedside. What could she say? She felt so unprepared for all of this. Why wasn't Geoffrey here to comfort his mother? As soon as she'd asked herself the question, she instinctively knew that Geoffrey was even less well equipped to deal with his mother's suffering than she was. In fact, the whole thing terrified him. She looked down into Patricia's troubled eyes.

"I don't know what to say to you – except that I will do everything I can to make you comfortable. I'll ring Dr Kelly and tell him you need something more for the pain." She squeezed the other's hand gently. "You know that I'm not the least bit religious but in the last few years you've been going to church some of the time. Isn't that something you can draw strength from?" A thought occurred to her. "Would you like me to ring the rector? I know you like her."

The eyelids flickered shut and then opened again.

"Goodness no! I know she's very nice but I really can't be doing with all that gathering around the invalid stuff. I know I look an absolute fright. I don't want an audience. She might want to pray over me." Mrs Larchet looked appalled at the idea. "And anyway, now it comes to the crunch, Judith, I'm not at all sure about religion – or anything any more." The medication must have been helping because her voice sounded slightly stronger now. "In some ways, I rather hope they're wrong and God doesn't exist."

"Why?" asked Jude, surprised.

A wry smile appeared at the corners of Patricia Larchet's mouth.

"It's not as though I've been a very nice person, is it?" Jude was about to deny it when her mother-in-law looked straight into her eyes. "It's no good you pretending I have. I've always been difficult. The trouble is, I never had anyone to tell me to stop. My parents were too soft because I was an only child and they couldn't have any more and Robert was too mild-mannered for his own good." Jude remembered how her gentle father-in-law had just smiled and walked away at the first sign of any difficult situation that might lead to an argument with his wife. He'd obviously decided early on in his marriage to Patricia that it was the only way he would survive. "I knew the reason that he spent so much of his time on the golf course at weekends was because I made him feel in the way."

Jude could see that the effort of talking so much was exhausting her further.

"Patricia, don't upset yourself, please. I'm sure he loved you very much. Nobody's marriage is perfect."

"No, dear, I know that." Jude was aware that Mrs Larchet was looking at her closely. "I *am* sorry about Geoffrey."

Jude looked at her, startled.

"You know?"

"Yes, I know," the woman said wearily. "And thank you for trying to hide it from me, for trying to spare me. I appreciate that." Her eyes wandered to the garden beyond the window where a grey curtain of autumn rain was falling soundlessly. "I heard them on the telephone one day when you were away in Ios." She turned her head to look at Jude again. When she next spoke, it was almost as if she were pleading to be understood. "I feel I owe you an apology. I didn't say anything to him and I should have. I thought that it was some casual affair that would be over quickly – and I hoped that you would never find out about it."

"Well, I can only say how sorry I am that you should have found out," said Jude grimly. "I'm sorry that you and Flora and Oscar know – and everyone at work it seems as well." For a moment there was a silence in the room, broken only by the busy ticking of the alarm-clock on the bedside table. Jude realised that she was beginning to feel cold. She started to withdraw her hand, preparing to get to her feet.

"Don't go yet!"

There was a note of urgency in the other woman's voice.

Jude left her hand where it was and shifted her weight back onto her knees.

"I was only going to turn up the heating," she reassured her quietly. "It's starting to feel a little chilly in here."

"No, wait! There's something I want to tell you."

Jude was concerned by the agitated look in the woman's face. She could sense a strange feeling in the room – of heightened awareness and a sensation of prickling between her shoulder blades. She wasn't even aware now of the clock's ticking – it was almost as if time were standing still. She guessed that what was said now was of great importance and that it was difficult for Patricia Larchet to say it.

"What is it, Patricia?"

The woman ran a discoloured tongue over her dry lips.

"I know you wondered why I kept in touch with Liam and why I warned him you were going to visit him. I understand too that it must seem very strange that I never mentioned the fact that I knew him before – even before your mother did." Her eyes glanced away from Jude, who realised that she was uncomfortable at being the focus of her daughter-in-law's gaze. There was a pause and then she looked back at her. "In fact, I only knew your mother by name when he . . . when he married her."

"You knew my fa – Liam – before he and my mother got married?"

"I was his mistress," Patricia said in a bleak voice. "Perhaps that's another reason why I didn't say anything to Geoffrey about his carrying-on. I was too embarrassed. You see, I was married to Robert at the time. Like mother, like son, or so it would seem."

Jude stared at her. She hadn't known what the connection between her mother-in-law and Liam had been but this revelation took her completely by surprise. She knew from what her mother had told her that there had never been any love lost between the two women but she'd always put that down to their being incompatible in the first place and having a basic, animal-like dislike of each other. All of a sudden a thought occurred to her.

"Was my mother responsible for him . . . leaving you?"

Mrs Larchet gave an almost imperceptible nod.

Jude felt bewildered. "She never said anything. She certainly never told me that you and he had been together before . . ."

The sentence trailed away into the still room. It must be later than she'd thought. It was getting dark. Objects that were sharply defined in daylight had now started to blur at the edges.

"I know it's difficult to imagine now but I really was quite pretty when I was younger. Not clever or ever very interesting. He told me that he had never known anyone as fascinating as your mother. He made it very clear that I had begun to bore him. Liam was not the sort of man to hide his feelings."

"So I noticed," said Jude. It occurred to her that, perhaps, he had always been a self-indulgent sod, believing that he had the right to say exactly what he thought and to hell with other people's feelings.

"I hated your mother so much, Judith." Mrs Larchet's voice sank to a whisper. "When he left her, I was glad, God help me. I was glad that she had been made to feel like I felt." A small frown appeared on her parchment-like forehead. "But she won in the end. She had you to love and she made herself stop loving him. She was always a much stronger person that I was. I was never able to do that. That's why I was such a miserable wife to poor Robert –

because I could never stop loving Liam." She gave Jude a challenging look. "That's why I've kept in touch all these years and that's why I told him you were coming to find him – because I still love him." She gave a small laugh. "The truth is my whole life has been a waste of time. Pathetic, isn't it?"

"No, don't say that," said Jude quickly. She felt overwhelming compassion for the small figure in the bed. She searched for comforting words. "No, it's just terribly sad. But you had Geoffrey and all your friends." At that moment, she could only think of the names of a couple of women friends. There must have been others. "I just wish I'd known more. It might have helped us . . ."

"It might have helped us get on better? I don't think so, Judith. I'm the sort of person who has to have something really important happen in their life before there's any change." She gave Jude a sudden, quizzical glance. "And it can't get much more important than what's happening right now, can it? It's a shame I can't do anything about it. Bad timing. Isn't that what you people in television call it?"

All of a sudden, the pent-up pain and emotion that had been bottled up inside them both over the preceding weeks bubbled over and Jude found herself with her head resting on the woman's hands while they both laughed weakly.

Chapter Fifteen

The front door slammed shut. A snowy flurry of old paintwork from the banisters fell to the hall floor. In the study, Jude peered over the top of her glasses and through the gap in the door to see if the culprit was, as she suspected, Flora. Just inside the front door, her daughter was fighting to open it again so that she could retrieve the end of her long black cardigan that was wedged between the frame and the now well-closed door. She was looking furious.

"Fucking thing!"

"Hi, Flo!" Jude called out, hoping to defuse the situation.

"Ma! Come and give us a hand."

"What's the matter? Are you stuck?" said Jude, coming out into the hall.

"Of course I'm bloody stuck. My cardie's jammed in the – door," Flora snapped.

Between the two of them, they managed to wrench the door open. Flora looked down in despair, holding the bottom of the cardigan out in front of her like a bird with a damaged wing.

"I knew it! There's a hole in it now. *Look!*"

Her tone seemed to indicate that she blamed her mother for what had happened.

But Jude didn't notice. She was staring at her daughter's hair, which seemed to have undergone a radical change in both cut and colour. What had been long and dark with a natural auburn shade was now short, spiky and mauve.

Flora caught her mother's glance. Her expression changed from furious to wary.

"Now I suppose you're going to tell me you don't like it."

"I think it's different," said Jude as diplomatically as possible while she walked slowly around Flora, inspecting the cut more closely.

"You *don't* like it, do you? I knew you wouldn't."

It crossed Jude's mind that Flora was only asking for trouble if she had already known no one in the family would go for it. Gran would most certainly hate it. Oscar wouldn't be too pushed one way or the other. Although he was surprisingly old-fashioned sometimes and liked girls to look feminine. Geoffrey, if he noticed in his present state, would think it was just Flora being ridiculous and looking for attention again.

"I'm sure I'll learn to live with it," said Jude. "But have you thought about playing Margaret Roper with spiky purple hair? You might have a bit of a century clash in your long robes with that hairdo. She was an intelligent, outspoken girl for her time I know, but she was also an obedient daughter. And, I seem to remember, isn't there a scene where she has to kneel in front of the king, looking demure and giving a speech in Latin?"

From the look on her daughter's face, it was easy to see that Flora hadn't thought of that when she'd done the deed. Jude could guess what had happened. Geoffrey and Flora had had a row earlier on in the day and she had stormed out of the house – and while she was still angry, she'd decided on the spur of the moment to do something drastic, with never a thought to any possible consequences.

* * *

Jude had seen the beginnings of trouble brewing before breakfast when Flora decided to cross-examine Geoffrey about where he would be the following day.

"What do you mean, 'you want to know'?" he'd asked her, irritation written clearly on his face.

"Tomorrow's Saturday. Saturday is supposed to be part of the weekend. And at weekends, families are supposed to spend time together but *you* don't seem to want to be around nowadays at weekends, or any other time for that matter," she added unwisely.

"And what is it that you want us to do together on this particular Saturday, Flora?"

"I don't know, stuff! Family stuff!" She thought hard. "Why can't we go to the cinema? Something like that. Why can't we be a proper family?"

"Do you seriously think that if we trotted off to see *Harry Potter*, we would all start behaving like one big, happy family?"

"There's no need to be so bloody sarcastic – and anyway, *he* had nice parents – even if they were dead."

"I'm sorry we don't seem to be able to fit in with your idea of the perfect parents." Geoffrey's voice was ominously soft. "And there's no need for you to be so bloody rude. Shut up and let me have my coffee in peace."

When Flora had turned round and glared at her mother, Jude said, "And you can stop looking at me like that too. If you can't be pleasant to your dad, then it might be a good idea to shut up like he says."

Flora snorted. "I don't know why you're tiptoeing around him all of a sudden, Mum. It's not as though he deserves to be treated politely after what he's been doing."

"Jude, I'm taking my coffee into the front room," said Geoffrey in a cold voice, "and I don't want to be disturbed."

He ignored Flora as he picked up his cup and left the room.

Jude turned to her after she heard the further door close.

"Flo, why do you stir things up like that? It doesn't help. In fact, it only makes things ten times worse."

Her daughter threw her an exasperated look before cramming her mug, spoon and cereal bowl noisily into the dishwasher.

"I don't know how you can be civil to him. I hate him!"

Jude walked over and put a hand on her daughter's shoulder.

"No, you *don't*. You don't hate your dad, Flo. He's your dad – the only one you've got. And that's the important thing to remember – whatever he's done."

"Yes, I do!" shouted Flora, violently shrugging off her hand. "I thought he was nicer than most of my mates' dads but he's not, he's far worse than they are. When I think of all those lectures I got about not behaving like a tramp when I started going out with boys! I hate him . . . and I think what he's done to you is vile."

Angrily wiping away the tears that had begun to trickle down her face with the back of her hand, she walked quickly out of the kitchen. The house shook slightly as a door banged behind her.

* * *

So, thought Jude with exasperation several hours later, the day continues as it began.

She seemed to feel slightly sick all the time these days. The nausea had been lurking in the pit of her stomach ever since her daughter told her about the message on Geoffrey's mobile. She didn't appear to be able to shake it off. It made her feel not just miserable but annoyed. The way she felt at the moment was making it difficult for her to eat very much and Jude knew that she needed all her strength to deal with what was happening around her. Standing in the empty kitchen, she again experienced the sensation of being in free fall. But this time, with no sign of a bloody parachute, she thought to herself wryly.

Jude decided to make herself a cup of tea. Flora had stomped up the stairs, having first announced, "What's the problem if my hair is purple – or emerald green for that matter? Margaret Roper wore a sort of bonnet affair, so most of it would be hidden anyway."

So that's all right then, thought Jude. She hoped the college would agree.

As she waited for the kettle to boil, she wondered how Flora could be so pleasant one minute and so hellish the next. But she knew the answer. She'd always been moody and now the girl had been badly hurt by Geoffrey's affair. She felt let down and disillusioned and these feelings were manifesting themselves in a way that made everyone else upset. The sad thing is, Jude thought, it might be a sort of safety-valve for Flora but, in the end, it didn't seem to stop her from feeling just as miserable and bloody-minded as ever. Oh, Lord! When would things get better? *Would* things get any better? she asked herself as she sat down despondently at the table.

Fidelma had asked her if she had a plan for dealing with Sonia. Such as? she wondered angrily. Jude had told Geoffrey that she would fight to save their marriage but so far, she had barely succeeded in keeping her head above water – and not much else. Realistically, she hadn't exactly managed to *do* anything at all about it.

Just then, Oscar came into the room to find her sitting quietly alone. She was stirring her tea, a pensive look on her face. He thought how handsome she looked and how terribly sad. For the first time, he saw his mother as others might see her – not in the taken-for-granted way in which a nineteen-year-old son usually views his mother – as part of the fixtures and fittings – but as an individual, interesting person with her own personality and her own very real hurts and disappointments. He experienced a sinking feeling in his gut. What could he do to make things easier for her?

As soon as she saw him, Jude made an effort to look cheerful.

"Want a mug of tea?" she asked. "The kettle's just boiled."

Oscar slid into the chair beside her.

"No, I'm fine, thanks, Mum." He peered into her half-drunk mug. "Would you like a top-up?"

She shook her head.

"Is there . . ."

"Would you . . ."

They had both started to speak at the same moment. They stopped and laughed.

"What are you doing for the rest of the day, Oz?" she asked.

"Ellen's coming around in a moment and she wants to pop in to Gran for a little while – if Gran's feeling up to it."

"Gran seems to like Ellen."

"I know," said Oscar, beaming suddenly. "I thought she wouldn't approve. You know what an old . . . well, you know how critical she can be."

"Yes, I do know. But your gran has been surprising me lately."

"What did Dr Kelly say when he came this morning?"

"He's increased the dosage for the pain but he said she'd spend more time asleep because of it – that she wouldn't be really with it." She smiled at him. "Still, if that means she's not in pain, that's a good thing."

The doorbell rang.

Oscar got to his feet.

"That'll be Ellen. I better rescue her before Flora gets to her first."

He'd just reached the kitchen door when they heard Flora's voice in the hall.

"Oz! Ellen."

He hurried out of the room, passing his sister on her way into the kitchen. She'd apparently left the other girl standing at the front door.

Flora raised her eyes to heaven when she saw her mother.

"Guess who? Dolly Parton in person," she whispered.

Jude was in mid-glare when Oscar and Ellen appeared in the doorway.

"Hello, Ellen," said Jude, hastily adjusting her expression. She gave her a friendly smile. "Would you like a mug of tea before you go through to Gran?"

Ellen glanced across the room to where Flora stood impassively beside the sink.

"No, thank you, Mrs Larchet – Jude. If it's all right, I'll go in now."

Oscar followed her out of the room. As they reached the far door, he turned and looked at Flora. Raising his hand, he pointed an accusing finger at her and mouthed, 'Be nice!'

'Right!' Flora mouthed back, in the general direction of his departing back. Then she looked over at her mother. "Is it all right if I make myself a mug of tea, Mrs Larchet – Jude?" she mimicked the other girl's voice, giving a small, uncertain gesture with her hand as she did so. Jude had to admit that it was a very good imitation.

"Put a sock in it, Flo. She means well – and Gran likes her."

"Must be all the medication she's on then," replied Flora. Seeing the expression on her mother's face, she suddenly relented. "Oh, I suppose Ellen's not *that* awful. It's just that she does my head in with all that indecisive standing around stuff she goes in for. She looks like Barbie trying to decide if she should wear the frilly pink frock or the one with the little blue spots on. I can't help it and I can't understand what Oz sees in her. I thought he was supposed to be the brainy one out of us two."

"Well, you're not the one going out with her," replied Jude in a calm voice.

For the first time in a long while, Flora gave a small giggle. "Thank God for that!" All of a sudden, she went over to where her mother was sitting. She leaned over the back of her chair and put her arms around Jude's neck. "I'm sorry I'm such a bitch, Mum. I don't mean to be. It just sort of comes out."

"You're not a bitch, Flo. You're rather unkind and unthinking sometimes, that's all." She held her daughter's two clasped hands in her own. "You know, with a little practice, you could be quite nice."

"Thanks!"

Flora released her and collapsed into the nearest chair.

For the first time in what seemed like ages to Jude, mother and daughter sat beside each other in companionable silence.

After a little while, Jude became aware that Flora was watching her. She was fidgeting with her hands and looked as though she wanted to say something.

"Yes?" Jude prompted.

"Mum, how is Gran?"

"Not good but at least she seems more comfortable now that the painkiller's been increased."

"Will she . . . is she going to die soon?"

"I don't think it will be long now, Flo," said Jude gently.

"It's just that I find it really difficult to see her, Mum. There's that funny smell in her room now . . . and I don't know what to say to her. She never was the easiest person to have a conversation with, even before all this. I can't *do* anything. I feel sort of hopeless. When I'm in there with her, I can't wait to get outside into the fresh air. I know that sounds terrible."

Jude took hold of one of her daughter's hands.

"We all feel a bit like that, if we're honest. *Especially* Dad. It must be awful for him to see his own mother dying and to feel so powerless. Catriona's probably the best person to be with her."

"Why? She's not even family."

"It's easier when you aren't attached. She can stand back a bit and be practical." Jude smiled at her. "The rest of us carry quite a bit of baggage where Gran is concerned. Things haven't always been very good between her and us, have they?"

"No, she's always been a right old bat." Immediately she'd said it, Flora looked guilty. "There I go again! What I meant was . . ."

"What you meant was Gran hasn't been the sweetest-natured person in the world to get on with. I know," said Jude. She realised that she suddenly felt desperately tired. "I think I'll go and lie down for a little while. I might as well make the most of this time off work to try and get myself back together."

She had been given reluctant leave from the studios. Jude wondered if her absences would result in them getting fed up and firing her. At the moment, she didn't much care.

As her mother got up from the table, Flora saw how exhausted she looked.

"I'll do supper, Mum."

"Thanks. That would be really nice."

As Jude passed the phone in the hall, it rang. Tempted to leave it for Flora to answer, something made her pick it up.

"Hello?" she asked cautiously.

"Jude? Is that you?" asked a throaty voice on the other end of the line.

"Marguerite?"

"Got it in one! How are you, my dear?"

"Fine," said Jude with as much conviction as she could muster. "And you? Where are you?"

"I'm well and I'm in London. There was some sort of a crisis about venues for my next exhibition. So I had to drop everything and dash back." There was a slight hesitation and then she continued, "The reason I'm ringing is that I have some bad news, I'm afraid. Jude, Liam is dead."

Jude was aware of a vague buzzing sound in her ears. She cleared her throat.

"When? When did he die?"

"Over a week ago apparently. But I only found out today."

"But how? Why? Who told you?" Jude stammered.

"He was more sick than he let on. Liam decided that he'd had enough. He took an overdose, Jude. Manolis found him the next day when it was too late to do anything. He arranged the funeral. Liam was buried the day before yesterday. It seems Manolis didn't want any outside interference. He wanted to be the one to make all the arrangements. Then, when it was all over, he telephoned me to let me know." She gave a small sigh. "I suppose I should be grateful that he bothered to get in touch at all."

"But why would he want to take it on himself to arrange everything?" asked Jude, puzzled.

"You met the man! He was jealous of anyone who came

too near Liam. As soon as I left, I'm sure he was up there for as much of the time as Liam would allow him to be. Jude, I rang the solicitor and asked him about the Will."

"Yes," said Jude, only half-listening. Why had this news made her feel so shaken? Liam had made it plain that he wanted nothing to do with her or her family. A sudden silence made her realise that Marguerite must have asked her a question. "Sorry, what did you say?"

"The solicitor told me something Manolis had omitted to mention. He said that Liam remade his Will the day before he died. You should be hearing from him – the solicitor, not Manolis – sometime in the next few days . . . Jude?"

Jude was confused.

"In the next few days? How can his Will have anything to do with me? He didn't consider us to have any connection with him at all."

"My dear, I know this has given you a shock. I can tell by your voice. I am sorry. I just didn't want you to get a letter from Liam's solicitor out of the blue. You should know that Liam talked a lot about you after you'd left."

"He did?"

"Yes! You made quite an impression on him – even if the silly man didn't show it at the time! He told me that he thought you were an intelligent and extremely attractive woman. Listen, Jude. I must go now. I will keep in touch. I enjoyed meeting you. Perhaps we will be able to meet again soon."

"Yes, I'd like that," said Jude.

"Take care of yourself."

"You too."

Absent-mindedly, she replaced the receiver. She sat down with a bump on the bottom stair. Flora had switched on the radio in the kitchen and the sounds of Today FM pulsated through to the hall. She couldn't possibly have heard the phone ring, or the subsequent conversation.

Suddenly Jude had a vivid mental picture of Liam, sitting in the chair on the vine-clad terrace, a glass of wine in his hand. She remembered how she'd thought he hadn't looked all that well when she was there. When he'd told her that he was gay, it had crossed her mind that he might be HIV positive or even have AIDS. That might have explained his detachment – and his impatience to say what he felt had to be said before sending her on her way so unceremoniously. Whatever had been wrong: illness, feelings of being a failure as a writer, an uncertain future combined with depression, it had been terrible enough to make him decide to end his own life. Had he planned it beforehand or was it a spontaneous decision? It was, perhaps, too much of a coincidence that he had changed his Will the day before. Jude thought of him – a solitary figure – in the rented house on the hillside above the lovely bay. She imagined him tipping the pills into the palm of his hand, transferring them to his mouth and then raising the refilled wineglass to his lips. Had he looked back on his life and found it wanting in a way that was unbearable? Had he wished that he'd admitted his homosexuality years earlier, to have allowed himself the freedom to be himself? If he'd been given another chance, what would he have done differently?

She supposed those would be the kind of questions that would go through the mind of someone about to commit suicide. Or was he so lacking in sentimentality that to kill himself had seemed the only sensible option in the circumstances? Jude wondered about the women in his life; her mother, Patricia, his nameless second wife . . . and the unknown others. She thought of all the hurt and damage he had caused to them – not least to the small girl he'd rejected, the child who would have adored to have grown up with him as her father. Marguerite too had obviously cared a lot for him.

And the men? She wondered what they'd been like. She hoped that he had shared affection with men of a higher calibre than the awful Manolis. Would his life have been happier if he'd allowed himself to have a family, to have shared, to have given, to have been part of a normal, everyday, affectionate family? *"Like the one you belong to?"* asked the small voice inside her head.

Jude felt so full of despair, for a moment, she didn't know what to do with herself. She felt if she cried any more than she already had, she might never be able to stop.

"What's the matter, Mum?"

Flora's concerned voice broke into her thoughts.

"Nothing. I'm fine. Why?"

Her own voice sounded hoarse to her.

"No, you're not. You're crying."

"Am I?" said Jude in surprise.

"Is it Dad?"

Jude stood up slowly.

"Liam's dead."

For a moment, Flora looked blank.

Then she said, "Oh, you mean Liam Maybury, your . . . our . . ."

212

"Yes, him."

"But why are you so upset? You only met him for a few hours a little while ago. You said yourself you hadn't got any memories of him from when you were a child."

"I know," said Jude, giving an uncertain laugh. "Perhaps I'm upset because he was a link to my mother. Perhaps because he was a small part of my life when I was a very young child. Or maybe I feel sad because I think he was a troubled, lonely old man when he died. Flo, he committed suicide. Don't you think that's sad? To be so desperate, to feel that there is nothing worth living for, that that is the only thing left to you."

"Actually, Mum, I think it's stupid and selfish," said the suddenly pragmatic Flora. "I wonder why killing himself doesn't come as a surprise to me? He's made making other people miserable into an art form. You shouldn't get upset about it. You worry too much about people who don't deserve it. He did nothing for you, so why should you care?"

"Oh, *Flora!*" said Jude with a tired sigh. "You don't understand. You know next to nothing about him. It doesn't work like that."

Chapter Sixteen

It was getting late. Oscar and Flora hadn't got back from wherever they'd gone and Catriona had left several hours earlier. Jude was feeling tired. But this evening, there was something about her mother-in-law that made her decide that she should stay with her for a while longer, however weary she was feeling. The woman didn't appear to be in pain but she was unsettled. She seemed to be wandering in and out of a fitful sleep, occasionally muttering, her hands picking restlessly at the bedclothes.

Jude had been taken aback, when she helped Catriona change the bed earlier in the evening, by how feather-light Geoffrey's mother was now. Knowing how Patricia loathed her dependency on them and the elderly woman's disgust at her physical state, Jude had tried not to look at the wasted arms and legs as they lifted her up the bed and settled her on the re-arranged pillows before re-covering her. Even in her semi-conscious state, Mrs Larchet had continued to insist that her daughter-in-law leave the room if anything needed to be done to the colostomy bag. Although she would readily have helped, Jude was secretly grateful not to be included in this checking and changing. She was full of admiration at how un-phased Catriona was. The girl seemed to take everything in her stride. No matter what happened, she remained cheerfully patient throughout it all. Jude had even seen her make Mrs Larchet chuckle quietly once or twice.

She jerked awake in the chair beside the bed. Lifting her head slowly, she tried to ease the stiffness in her neck by massaging it with her fingers. Glancing at the clock on the bedside table, she saw that it was past eleven. She'd been asleep for the last half an hour. As she looped back strands of her hair, fumbling with the tortoiseshell comb, she looked down to see Mrs Larchet's eyes were open. Jude leaned over.

"Are you all right, Patricia?" she asked softly.

The woman gave her a small smile.

"Yes, thank you. I feel fine."

"Any pain?"

"No pain," said Mrs Larchet quietly. "Do you know, Judith, I've never really been ill before all of this happened and I never knew how good it is when you've been in a lot of pain and then it goes away. It makes you feel so . . . so grateful." There was no doubt about it, Gran was full of surprises these days. If Jude had been told beforehand that her mother-in-law would one day be bedridden with a terminal and unpleasant illness, the last thing she would have expected was that the woman would prove to be so undemanding and uncomplaining. "That Dr Kelly is very good," Mrs Larchet continued. "Do you know, he even washes his hands in hot water before he examines me so that they won't feel cold?"

Dr Kelly had indeed been a tower of strength, making almost daily visits to the house and always prepared to listen to anything the sick woman wanted to tell him, however trivial. Jude wasn't at all surprised that he had made a hit with her.

"Could you give me some water? My mouth's very dry," asked Mrs Larchet.

When she had taken three or four small sips, Jude lowered her mother-in-law's head gently back onto the pillows.

"Do you think you could manage a little soup?" she asked.

The woman shook her head.

"No. I don't feel I want anything more for the moment. Where's Plunkett?"

"Asleep in the sitting-room in front of the fire. Do you want me to bring him through for a while?"

But Mrs Larchet's eyes had flickered shut. Just as well, Jude thought. Plunkett would have tried to jump up on the bed. She admitted to herself that the poor animal had been rather neglected since his owner's return from hospital even though Flora and Oscar had taken it in turns to walk him down on the beach. He seemed to sense that all was not as it should be. He had recently got into the habit of sitting, leaning against the door from the kitchen into the extension, looking mournfully up at anyone who passed by with his sad, bloodshot eyes. Jude felt almost sorry for him. Her sympathy was somewhat qualified, due to his continual gnawing and chewing habits. Because of the almost continual rain, he had resorted to dismembering objects around the house rather than in the garden. Jude's bedroom slippers had been the latest casualties. She hadn't had the heart to be angry with him but had given him a severe look as she held the saliva-spattered remains in front of his nose and said 'No!' in a loud voice. That had only resulted in him wagging his tail and look longingly towards the front door.

Undecided, she stood beside the bed. Perhaps it would be a good idea to go to bed herself. Jude turned down the dimmer-switch so that the sleeping woman's features seemed to soften. She noticed how lightly she breathed, her chest hardly moving at all. Then, the eyes opened again.

"I want to say sorry, Judith."

Jude looked at her in surprise.

"Whatever for?"

"I think we both know that I haven't been completely honest with you about quite a few things. There's something I would like you to know. It might explain why I sometimes seemed to behave rather strangely." She stared up at Jude. "Will you stay with me for a little while longer?"

"Of course," said Jude, pulling the chair closer to the bed before sitting down.

That way, she could hear her better.

Mrs Larchet spoke quietly, every now and then breaking off, finding it difficult to summon up the strength to talk.

"When I was with Liam . . ." She broke off, looking anguished. Jude wasn't sure if she should say something to encourage her to continue or tell her that she shouldn't upset herself by speaking about things that would distress her. Mrs Larchet gave a small, shuddering sigh. "When I

217

was with Liam, as you know, I was already married to Robert." Jude nodded, her eyes fixed on the other's face. "Well, you see, I became pregnant. Geoffrey was a year old. Robert was so pleased. He thought the children would be good friends, being born so close to each other. But I had a miscarriage at seven months – just after Liam moved in with your mother." Her voice trailed away. Before Jude could say anything, Mrs Larchet made a visible effort to continue. "They told me that the baby . . . that it was a little girl."

"And Liam was her father?" asked Jude softly.

"Yes."

Her reply was barely audible.

She looked so frail and alone lying in the bed that Jude was filled with a longing to do everything, anything, in her power to try and comfort her. She just didn't know how. She supposed that the years of non-communication between them made it difficult for both of them. How different from the easy way she and her mother had been together! And how sad that it was only now, at the very end of her life, that Patricia Larchet felt able to confide in her. Tentatively, she put out a hand and lightly rested it on top of one of her mother-in-law's bony hands. There was no reaction, nor did the woman withdraw.

"And you wanted the baby?"

The blue eyes stared at her.

"Of course! More than anything in the world, I wanted Liam's child. I knew I couldn't keep Liam; I don't even know why he ever took up with me. I wasn't his type."

Did she know that he was gay? Jude wondered. And would that knowledge make his desertion easier to bear all these years later? No, she decided. It was too late to tell her now – it wouldn't do any good. She watched the woman's face attentively as she took a few shallow breaths before continuing.

"But I knew that, sooner or later, he would find someone else to turn his attentions to. It happened to be sooner than I'd thought – and that someone was your mother." She paused again for breath. "I thought that if I couldn't have him, I would have a little bit of him in my life that I could love and who would love me. And Robert need never know. Liam didn't want to get involved. He said that, as I was married to Robert, everyone would assume the child was Robert's. He said he wasn't prepared to make a fuss to prove paternity. The awful thing is, I think I would have left Geoffrey with Robert and gone to Liam if he'd asked me. But of course, he never wanted that." She gave Jude a self-deprecating smile. "Silly, isn't it? All the things we think we want? But I did want his child," she said regretfully. "But it wasn't to be. Liam went away and I lost the baby. He must have made your mother pregnant even before they got married. She had everything, him, his child . . . everything."

The desolation in her voice made it obvious to Jude that she had no choice but to confide in Patricia Larchet. She wasn't even sure why she hadn't told her when she'd got back from Ios.

"No, my mother *didn't* have everything. She only had Liam for a short time and I was not his daughter."

Mrs Larchet looked at her uncomprehendingly.

"What are you saying? You are not his child?"

Jude shook her head.

"No, my mother was pregnant before they were married. Liam never knew who the father was."

"Dear God!" Mrs Larchet looked appalled. She didn't say anything more for a few minutes. When she next spoke, it was with a painful slowness. "So all this time, I've been hating your mother, been jealous of you, thinking that you were the daughter I should have had . . ." Suddenly she said, "Did he tell you this when you went to find him in Ios?"

"Yes, he did. I didn't believe him at first. Or rather, I didn't want to believe him. But it was obvious he was telling the truth."

"You never told me, Judith."

"I had no idea it would be so important for you to know. I didn't want to tell you because I knew you and my mother had never got on and it just seemed that telling you would be . . . disloyal to her, that it was something private, something she was ashamed of. But I had no idea about all of this. I am so sorry. Sorry about everything. God! What a mess!"

Jude sat back in the chair and, for a moment, covered her face with her hands. It seemed that Liam Maybury had more to answer for than she had thought.

"Such a waste, such a terrible waste," said Patricia sadly.

Her daughter-in-law moved closer to the bed.

"Please don't let this upset you now. It's all in the past." She had been going to say, what matters is the future. But Patricia didn't have a future to look forward to. She took hold of both the woman's hands. "What matters is that you are in your own bed in your own place and we all care very much about you."

As she spoke those words of comfort, she wondered where Geoffrey was at that precise moment. He couldn't be with Sonia. Surely not. He knew how ill his mother was. Why wasn't he there beside her?

As if reading her mind, Patricia Larchet asked softly, "When's Geoffrey coming back?"

"I'm here, Mother."

Geoffrey was standing in the doorway. Jude was struck by how tired he looked as he moved across to the other side of the bed. Was she imagining it or was there just a slight hesitation before he bent over and kissed the woman's forehead? Was he, like his daughter, finding all the manifestations of his mother's illness distasteful? Did he too balk at the sour smell that lingered in the room? Well, she thought tiredly, too bad! It was time he did a little cherishing of his own.

Jude got up from the chair.

"Patricia, I'll leave Geoffrey to tuck you in. Just ring if you need me during the night, won't you?"

They had rigged up a buzzer that rang in their bedroom if there were any problems during the night but Patricia had made use of it only occasionally.

The blue eyes turned in her direction.

"Thank you, Judith. And I mean that. Thank you for everything."

For a moment, as they looked at each other, Jude felt a strange transference of emotion, a brief flash of something that was difficult to define or put into words. But in that moment, she felt that each had, for the first time, truly accepted the other. It was extraordinarily comforting.

* * *

It seemed that no sooner had she fallen asleep than Geoffrey was shaking her. Jude tried to pull herself up through smothering layers of exhaustion.

"For God's sake, wake up! Jude, wake up!"

She stared at him in the half-light from the landing.

"What's the matter?"

"Didn't you hear me ring the buzzer? It's Mother. I think . . ."

The panic in him galvanised her into action. Throwing back the duvet, Jude swung her legs over the side of the bed. She stumbled groggily to her feet and snatched up her dressing-gown from the end of the bed.

"What's wrong exactly?" she asked, trying to make out which way round the garment was in the dim light.

"I think you better just come down. Jude . . . I think she's dead."

He was pale, his dark hair tousled as though he too had slept for a while in his mother's room. There was no point in her trying to sound reassuring.

Barefoot, she went out onto the landing, noticing that Flora's door was still open. That meant she still wasn't back.

Silently, Geoffrey followed his wife down the stairs to Patricia's bedroom.

As soon as Jude got close to the bed, she knew that Geoffrey's mother was indeed dead. There was a complete absence of presence in the small body lying there, even though the pale blue eyes stared disconcertingly out into the room. Gingerly, Jude felt for a pulse on the already cool wrist. She knew there wouldn't be one but she felt she should go through the motions for her husband's sake if for no other reason. Geoffrey seemed to be glued to the floor at the far side of the room.

"Is she?" he asked in a low voice that shook slightly.

Jude looked over her shoulder at him.

"Yes, Geoffrey. She's dead." Carefully placing the woman's hand back onto the sheet, she went over and gently put her arms around him. "I'm so sorry, Geoff." She held him for a while without either of them moving. Then she asked, "What happened? Was it peaceful?"

For a moment he didn't answer, just stood with his head buried in her shoulder. Then, slowly, he pulled away. He half-turned as though he couldn't bear to look at his mother's face again.

"I didn't get that right either."

"What do you mean?"

"She drifted off to sleep just after you left and I thought I'd stay for a little while and make sure things were all right. I must have fallen asleep too because when I woke up she was dead. I didn't hear anything, really, Jude. I'm sure I would have woken if she'd been distressed or made any sound."

"Of course you would." He looked so miserable. She moved closer, wanting to hold him again. It had been so long since there had been any physical contact of any sort and she badly wanted to reassure him that it wasn't his fault and that his mother must have died in her sleep. "Look at her, Geoff! Look how peaceful her face is. She *can't* have suffered." Before she could say anything more, Geoffrey gently disengaged himself from her arms, stepping back from her. He glanced towards the door as though desperate to get away from the room, his mother, from her – from all of them perhaps. She didn't know. "Where are you going?"

223

"I'm sorry, I can't take any more of this," he said as he hurried out of the room.

She could hear his rapid footsteps in the passage and then the sound of the kitchen door closing. Almost immediately, a car engine started up in the driveway.

She couldn't, didn't want to think about what his departure might mean. Doing her best not to feel resentment that he had left her to cope on her own again – and deserted his mother, Jude moved back to the bed and gazed down at the dead woman. Not sure how it was done, she gently slid the woman's eyelids shut with her thumbs. She was only partially successful. The lids didn't close completely and after the first attempt, she didn't want to try again. Sitting down in the chair, she looked at the small, beaked face. The frown lines had been almost ironed out in death and the woman looked surprisingly ageless and tranquil. It was funny really, she thought. Tranquillity had never been one of Patricia Larchet's attributes in life.

The phrase so often used by old people when talking about the recent death of one of their number, 'It was a lovely death', came into Jude's mind. In the past she'd thought it quaintly amusing. Now, she hoped that her mother-in-law had indeed experienced a gentle death.

She knew that Dr Kelly should be told but what was the point in waking him at – she looked at the clock – three in the morning? Nothing would change what had happened now.

Jude didn't want to leave her mother-in-law lying alone. She tried to mutter some sort of a prayer. It was more a request than anything else. A request to any God who might exist to give the soul, the spirit, whatever it was that made up the essence of a person, to give it peace. If anything could be granted, Jude would have liked peaceful repose for Patricia Larchet after her troubled life. She couldn't begin to believe in, or ask for, anything more than that.

She suddenly remembered some one once telling her that there are people who believe that, when a person dies, the window should be opened to allow the soul to escape, unhindered from the body. Slowly she moved to the window and undid the cold, metal catch. She pushed it as wide open as she could. As it swung out, a ghostly reflection of the bed and its occupant, bathed in the soft light from the bedside lamp, slipped past her on the glass.

Instantly, the smell of sodden grass and wet earth filled the room. Somewhere in the still, dark garden, an owl hooted – a long ethereal sound that made her shiver suddenly. Jude knew with absolute certainty that she had never heard one in the Dalkey garden before.

* * *

Apart from herself, Oscar, Flora, Catriona and Ellen, there must have been a dozen or so people in the pews of the small Church of Ireland church for the short service the night before Patricia Larchet's funeral. Alan and Fidelma were away working or they would also have been there. She recognised Joan Ryan and some of her mother-in-law's bridge-playing friends. To Jude, they all looked pretty decrepit themselves. She thought how dismal it must be to have your small circle of friends eroded year by year; all the shared memories being enjoyed by a diminishing number as time ticked inexorably by.

Recently, Jude had told Fidelma that she loathed

funerals almost as much as weddings these days. The first made you feel vulnerable and the second was an occasion that only the gullible could really enjoy. They had laughed at the remark but only briefly. She knew that it was a pseudo-cynical attitude to take because, deep down, she still longed to be part of a working marriage – one that would come alive again. The idea of not being married to Geoffrey seemed bizarre. She also guessed that, quite probably, Fidelma herself wasn't averse to the idea of marriage with Alan. Would he get round to asking her? she wondered. Jude wasn't sure. It seemed that, these days, she wasn't sure about an awful lot of things.

She knelt and stood without taking in much of the ritual carrying on around her. *Was* there a future life for her with Geoffrey? He had run out on her yet again this evening, leaving Flora and Oscar anxiously doing their best to be supportive. At least they were there on either side of her. Jude had tried to explain his absence by reminding them that he found his mother's death difficult to handle.

Flora had given her a direct look.

"So?"

"So, try and imagine how he's feeling . . ." she had said, at the same time thinking that, however hard it was for him, he *should* have been there.

"It's no good you looking at me like that. I *have* to go to this union meeting," he'd insisted that morning. "You don't seem to realise, people are losing their jobs. Mine could be next for all I know."

Holding herself back, yet again, from saying all the things she wanted to say, Jude had done her best to sound reasonable.

"I just think that they would understand if you missed some of it. After all, you only have one mother and the time of a meeting can always be changed." She hadn't, however, been able to stop herself from asking, "You will be there at the cremation tomorrow, won't you?"

"Of course, Jude. Don't be silly," he retorted, looking uncomfortable. "I know you think I'm a heartless sod but I'm really not *that* bad."

Because he looked tired and drained and because she was determined to hang on to the idea that she still loved him, Jude had replied evenly, "Well, will you come straight home when the meeting's over?"

Unsmilingly, he had agreed.

She'd managed to stop Flora from having an argument with him but Jude knew that Oscar had confronted him as he left for work after breakfast. She'd watched from the upstairs window as they stood on either side of his car. She realised that Oscar had become more adult in the last while and she was struck by how alike they were, physically, with their dark hair and eyes and athletic build. Two very handsome men. Jude felt her heart constrict. Why did loving people have to hurt so much? And why was it all so bloody complicated?

She could see that Geoffrey wanted to leave. His car keys were clenched in his hand, resting on the roof of the car, and he looked impatient. Oscar had his back to her. He was speaking to his father, every now and then gesturing with both hands as though to emphasise what he was saying. Whatever he was saying was certainly being listened to by Geoffrey. His eyes never left Oscar's face. Not wanting her husband to notice her, she'd moved away from the window. She heard the sound of car door shutting and the engine starting a few minutes later. After a long delay, Jude was aware of Oscar's footsteps scrunching on the gravel as he approached the house. A few minutes later, he was on the phone to Ellen.

Denied a row with her father, Flora had taken it out on her brother when she heard that Ellen was coming to the service later in the day. Jude could hear her in the kitchen as she came downstairs.

"You can't be serious! You've invited that ditzy female to come along as well?"

Jude couldn't hear Oscar's response, just the parting shot her daughter made as she burst out into the hallway.

"Oh, well, that's all right then! Dad isn't coming but Barbie is! Great!" She stopped short in her tracks when she saw Jude. With a contrite, "Oh, fuck! Sorry, Mum," she disappeared up the stairs.

Jude noted that she managed to shut her door with a decided thump but she didn't actually slam it.

At the end of the church service, as she stood in the chilly porch shaking hands and accepting condolences from her mother-in-law's friends, Jude felt strangely detached. What an odd group we must appear to them, she mused, catching an elderly woman staring first at Flora's purple hair and then at Ellen's alarmingly short skirt. She was sure they were wondering where Geoffrey was, quite apart from their being critical on the appearance front. Joan Ryan was especially distant. She must have been remembering all the times Patricia Larchet had told her how badly treated she'd been by her son's family – although the woman had been noticeably absent when it had come to visiting her sick friend in the weeks before her death.

Jude hadn't been surprised that Oscar wanted to include Ellen in the proceedings. The girl had been extraordinarily sweet to Mrs Larchet and Oscar obviously found her kindness an added attraction – on top of the very evident physical ones she already possessed. Certainly, at the moment, in the good-manners stakes, his sister wasn't standing up to the comparison. In fact, in Flora's present mood, Jude reckoned that, for a lot of the time, her daughter was really just an uncontrolled liability.

She found herself, in the middle of shaking hands with the last of the sympathisers, wondering if Oscar had been to bed with Ellen. Perhaps, she thought. Probably, given the current attitude to sex among the young. The internal small voice that seemed so often like her daughter speaking, commented dryly, "*Ah, come on! Get real! What do you think they've been up to? Playing Monopoly? Of course, he has!*"

* * *

Any doubts Jude might have had about her son's state of chastity were dissipated a few days later. She'd come home early from the RTVI studios to find the bathroom door half open and a trail of soapy bubbles leading across the landing carpet to Jude and Geoffrey's bedroom. There was a strong smell of rose-scented bath oil. Girlish giggles and small squeaks came from inside the room. For an awful moment, the possibility that Geoffrey was entertaining Sonia in their bed made her feel faint. She found herself dizzily clinging onto the banister rail. Then she heard Oscar's voice. Relief flooded through her. She felt the colour come back into her face.

Jude hesitated, not wanting to play the heavy-handed

229

parent. Then she started to feel irritated. Damn it! If her son was getting up to sexual high-jinks, he could do it in his own bedroom, not hers. She pushed open the door and went in.

The sight that greeted her was unexpected to say the least. Two naked figures were kneeling on a bath towel that was spread out on the large double bed. At first, Jude wasn't sure which was the male and which was the female because of what looked like a generous covering of cream coating both bodies. Then she saw the canister of shaving-cream on the bedside table. Oscar appeared to be in the process of manufacturing Madonna-like turrets to Ellen's perfectly rounded breasts while she was engrossed in sculpting what looked like some sort of foamy codpiece around his far from dormant member. The sight was so amazing, she stood rooted to the spot. They turned and saw her at the same moment.

"Mum!"

"Jude . . . Mrs Larchet!"

Jude could feel laughter surging up inside her. The two figures looked as though they had been turned to stone – except Jude was pretty sure that she had never seen statues wearing such a look of stunned surprise. For a moment, she was in danger of bursting out laughing. Before her son's makeshift codpiece started to collapse entirely, she managed to pull herself together.

"This looks a lot of fun and I know you thought I wouldn't be home for a while so I appreciate your timing but it is *not* on to . . . do this in our bedroom. So, please just leave everything as you found it – and remember, Oz, that this is your father's and my room."

Oscar seemed suddenly to have come to his senses. He grabbed a corner of the towel to cover himself. Ellen collapsed into a sitting position with her arms crossed in a parody of respectability. With one last meaningful look in her son's direction, Jude left the room. She just made it into the kitchen before she started to shake with laughter. But it was laughter that left her suddenly feeling weak and unexpectedly close to tears.

Chapter Seventeen

There were to be two performances of *A Man For All Seasons* in ten days' time. Geoffrey said that he would be able to make it on the Saturday night. Jude had hoped to go on the previous evening but when it became plain that her husband couldn't or wouldn't change his plans, she said that she would go with him on the Saturday instead. Then she overheard a telephone conversation that made it obvious that, if she were planning to accompany him on the Saturday, he was going to change to the Friday performance. Apparently, he thought his wife was out of hearing range. She was pretty sure that the person he was talking to was Sonia.

Slipping into the sitting-room, she quietly closed the door behind her. Disbelief turned slowly to determination. What was it that she'd said to him when he had first admitted to having an affair with Sonia? Jude couldn't remember her exact words but it had been something along the lines of, 'I happen to think that this marriage is worth fighting for'. Well, if he thought he could turn up to his daughter's play in college, where he would be surrounded by people who knew him, with that – that creature on his arm, then he had another think coming.

They met in the hallway a few minutes later. Jude was looking pale. It was only with a lot of effort that she was able to stop her hands from shaking and keep her voice steady.

Geoffrey seemed anxious to avoid any sort of conversation. As soon as he saw her, he hastily scooped up his jacket from the back of the hall chair.

"I'm going to be late. I have to go."

"Another union meeting?" asked Jude, her face expressionless.

"No, actually. Not this time." He was immediately alerted by the guarded sound in her voice. He looked at her carefully. "Are you all right?"

"Why wouldn't I be?"

"I don't know. Your manner seems a little odd, that's all. I wondered if you weren't feeling well."

The voice in Jude's head screamed, *'I'm not well! I feel like puking all the time. I ache all over with the misery of what you are doing to us all. How can I be feeling well?* Instead, in a voice carefully devoid of any emotion, she replied, "It's difficult to talk to you these days. You're never around. Perhaps we can go out and have a meal together in the next few days and talk then. How about after the play on Saturday?" She looked at him questioningly. "I think you have to agree that we should try and spend some time together and talk?"

Geoffrey backed away, his hand on the front-door latch. "I really have to fly. We'll talk soon, Jude, I promise."

The door closed behind him before she had time to say anything more.

So, that was the way he was going to play it, was it? Sneaking off on the Friday with Sonia and then making some excuse or other on the Saturday, that he'd had a change of plans and had to unexpectedly fit in going to the play a day earlier. Obviously it would be unreasonable to want him to go a second time – with her.

Jude didn't know which upset her most; the fact that he was prepared to publicly air his relationship with the girl or that he hadn't the guts to tell her what he planned to do.

She had to talk to someone. Flora and Oscar had been upset enough all ready. She wasn't going to involve them any more than she had to. Trembling, Jude sat on the bottom step of the stairs and rang Fidelma.

"Hello, Fee?"

"Jude!"

"Have you got a moment? I need to talk."

"Of course. Hold on a moment while I just shut the door. Everyone's talking at the top of their voices in there." There was the sound of a door closing and the background conversation was suddenly snuffed out. "Are you OK?"

"No, not really! Do you remember my saying that I might have to fight to rescue my marriage and you asked if I had a plan of action?"

"Yes, I do. I thought that you were being incredibly brave. A lot of women in your shoes would be reaching for the smelling salts or throwing a wobbly – before rushing off to weep all over their solicitor's expensively suited shoulder. Why? *Have* you come up with a plan?"

"Not really. I've just been so occupied with trying to

keep my head above water, I haven't really had the time or the energy to sort myself out." Jude paused. "Fee, Geoffrey is planning to take Sonia to see Flora in *A Man For All Seasons* "

"He *what?*"

"You heard me. He seems to think that as everyone at work knows what's going on, then it's all right if the rest of the world finds out too."

"Bastard!" Fidelma's voice exploded with indignation.

"I'm trying hard not to think of him in those terms but I'm beginning to find it increasingly difficult. Once I'm reduced to calling him names, I may as well throw in the towel and admit he's a lost cause. And – I don't want to do that quite yet. Am I making any sense at all?"

Fidelma sounded more controlled when she next spoke.

"Of course, you do. I'm sorry! But you've had such a rotten time lately and I hate to think of him making you miserable. What are you going to do, Jude?"

"I'm not sure. I'm going round in circles. I had an idea that the best thing might be to go and track down Sonia. Have it out – face to face. But from what little I've seen of her, she's a tough nut and she'd just brazen it out and I'd be the one to end up with egg on my face. And there's something so pathetic about the hard-done-by wife begging her husband's mistress to please be nice and see sense and send him home again. I don't know what to do."

"Listen, Jude. Can we meet up? Give me a couple of days to have a think. Do you mind if I talk it over with Alan? He's rooting for you – as are half the male population in RTVI I might add – and he might come up with some good ideas."

"Thanks, Fidelma. I knew I could count on you," said Jude gratefully.

"Well, don't count your chickens but I reckon, between the three of us, we should be able to hatch something. Today's Wednesday . . . how about meeting up on Friday after work? That will give us a full week before the play starts."

Jude put the phone down with a slightly lighter heart. At least she didn't have to do it all on her own. She could count on Fidelma and Alan's support. She could count on Oscar and Flora too. She knew that. But she felt that the idea of enlisting their help in down-facing Sonia would only further undermine their relationship with their father. Jude knew that he was going to have to engage in extensive damage limitation as things stood. It would be wrong to embarrass him in front of them.

She had to face the fact that she and Geoffrey were the only people who could ultimately decide what happened to them all. 'Dear God, please give me the strength and sense to get through all this without anyone being irreparably damaged,' she found herself muttering quietly. She gave herself a small shake. That sounded like a prayer and she didn't believe in the efficacy of prayer. If she wasn't careful, she'd end up crouching in a pew, shrouded in a lace mantilla, praying to St Jude and lighting countless candles.

* * *

The day after Jude talked to Fidelma on the phone, two letters with Greek stamps on them arrived in the post. One was for Flora, the other, for Oscar. Unusually, Plunkett decided they were not interesting enough to chew so they lay unmolested and unnoticed on the hall floor for some time.

Jude didn't have to be in to work until later in the morning and Flora had taken an unofficial break in her studies so that her mother could hear her lines.

"I thought you were word-perfect weeks ago," she said as Flora handed her the dog-eared copy of the play with the part of Margaret Roper highlighted in bright yellow.

"I was! I am!" Flora snatched the part back to give it a last look. It was obvious to Jude that she was upset. Her complexion was blotchy and there were several angry-looking spots on her forehead and chin. "It's just that what with Gran dying and all the rest of it, I can't seem to get my head round anything properly at the moment." Flora flung herself down on the couch with an exaggerated sigh. Plunkett lifted his head and gave her a reproachful look. She gazed down helplessly at the book in her lap. "It's all going to be a complete disaster. The director's a total wally and King Henry's got halitosis and knobbly knees. People are going to take one look at him and start laughing. He's *supposed* to look all impressive. In fact he looks like Noddy with a hangover in tights that are three sizes too large for him. As for the eejit playing Cranmer!" But articulating a description of the sheer dreadfulness of the student chosen to attempt that part failed her.

Jude gave her daughter a hug. But Flora was too absorbed in how awful it all was to respond.

Her mother held out her hand. "Come on, Flo! Give me the book and let's get started or half the morning will have gone."

Flora thrust the book at her with a scowl. "Just don't get ratty if I fluff some of the lines."

"I promise," said Jude with what she hoped looked like an encouraging smile.

However, that proved more easily said than done. Flora, who two weeks earlier had been pretty well word-perfect, seemed now to be suffering from crippling amnesia. When an hour had gone by with the atmosphere in the room becoming more and more charged, she finally went on strike.

"That's it! I can't do it. I don't know why I went to the bloody audition in the first place. I'm going to forget the whole frigging thing and let everyone down – and they'll all hate me," she wailed, collapsing in a heap in one of the armchairs. "What's wrong with me, Mum?"

Jude laughed and went and sat on the arm of the chair. She put her hand on her daughter's shoulder.

"There's nothing wrong with you, Flo. You've just got all tense and worried. Try and relax a little and you won't have any trouble remembering your lines. They're all there in your mind. You'll be fine if you don't let yourself get into a state."

Flora looked up at her. "Look at me! I'm a complete freak! I'm covered in giant-sized zits and . . ."

"And what?"

"And I hate my sodding hair!"

A glimmer of hope surged through Jude's veins.

"We could see about having it dyed back to your own colour, if you wanted," she suggested in a matter-of-fact voice.

"Can't afford to. It cost an arm and a leg to have *this* done."

"Well, I'll treat you to a colour change."

Flora grabbed her mother's hand and gave it a quick squeeze. "Would you? Oh, thanks, Mum!"

Just then, Oscar came into the room, holding two envelopes.

Flora looked at him suspiciously. "Why are you looking like the cat who got the cream?"

"Because, sister dear, I think these have something to do with Grandfa . . . Liam's Will."

It was funny, Jude thought, the way none of them seemed to want to call the man by his name. It was as though, in spite of everything, he would always be related to them, however reluctantly.

Suddenly animated, Flora leaped to her feet and held out an impatient hand. "Well, don't just stand there looking dim! Which one's mine?"

Jude watched them as they tore open the crisp, white envelopes. There was a silence, during which she watched their expressions change from curiosity to surprised elation.

"I don't believe it!" Oscar held his letter out for Jude to see. "He decided to remember us after all!"

Reading quickly through it, Jude could see that Liam had left her son £5,000. It turned out that Flora was also richer by the same amount.

"I'll get a car!" announced Oscar.

"I'm going to Paris!" was Flora's offering.

Jude noticed that all her previous worries seemed to have magically evaporated. Her eyes shone. Spots, fluffed lines, hopeless director – all forgotten.

"Hang on a minute, you two! It takes some time for all the paperwork to be dealt with. You may not get the money for a year or more. So, no spending binges, *either* of you," she added, looking serious. "You mustn't spend one penny of it until the money is in your bank accounts and, hopefully, by then you'll have worked out a reasonably sensible list of priorities."

Their excitement dimmed visibly.

"Up to a year!" exclaimed Flora.

"Or more," said Jude, firmly.

"Jesus! Just as I thought my life was improving!"

"Flora, don't winge. Liam has left you some money. Just be glad that he didn't leave his fortune to the local library in Ios and that he wanted you and Oscar to have it. I would guess that he didn't have very much to leave to anyone."

Flora looked suitably chastened. "Sorry, Mum."

Jude knew her daughter was still recovering from the fact that her grandmother had left a ring Flora had always liked to Ellen and a pair of earrings she had also secretly coveted to Catriona. She hadn't said very much but it was obvious that these bequests rankled.

It was apparent to Jude that Patricia Larchet had tried to do her best. She had put various pieces of jewellery into separate, marked envelopes. When Jude asked Flora if she'd ever told her grandmother that she particularly liked the aquamarine ring and the opal earrings, her daughter admitted that she hadn't.

"Well, she wasn't clairvoyant, Flo! So how could she have been expected to know?" Jude had asked her, irritated that again Flora had found yet another thing to make a fuss about.

All of a sudden, an image of the over-attentive Manolis slid into her mind. She wondered what, if anything, Liam had left him. Even though she had found the man objectionable, she hoped that he'd not been neglected. If what Marguerite had told her about Liam's longing for a son was true, then he most probably had included him. Then, remembering that it was Manolis who had found the dead writer alone in the house, she realised it was quite probable that he would have helped himself to anything that took his fancy. After all, it was his house and, from what Jude had seen, there hadn't been anything much of value lying around. A thought occurred to her. What about Marguerite's paintings? Had she had time to go and rescue them after hearing of Liam's death? Jude hoped that she had. Although the Greek would be living dangerously if he imagined he could get away with trying to sell any of them. She reckoned that Marguerite wasn't the sort of woman you did that sort of thing to without living to regret it.

Having reread the letter, Oscar was doing his best not to look disappointed.

"Oh, well. It will be nice when it comes." He looked at his mother. "Did he tell you he was planning to leave us something?" he asked curiously.

Jude shook her head. "He never said anything at all about his Will. Conversation of any sort was quite difficult with him. I don't think he would have been too impressed if I'd grilled him about what he had put in his Will! It would have looked rather as though I had gone over there to do a bit of gold-digging, wouldn't it?"

"Well, I'm glad he *did* leave us something. It sort of makes up a little for when he was alive," commented Oscar, carefully folding the letter and replacing it in its envelope.

"Didn't he leave anything to you, Mum?" asked Flora suddenly.

"No, he didn't. And I'm glad because there was no need. He knew I had a good job and a nice home. It was much more sensible to leave some money to the two of you."

As Jude said it, she felt a chill in the pit of her stomach. She wondered for how much longer could she count on having a nice home. What if Geoffrey wanted to leave her to go and live with the elfin Sonia? They would have to sell the house and buy two smaller places. Perhaps it mattered more than she'd thought that she kept her job at RTVI.

* * *

Alan Carruth got to his feet as soon as he saw Jude making her way through the packed bar. As she approached, he noticed the blue circles under her eyes. Even though she still moved with the easy grace that was so attractive, what a difference there was compared to the light-hearted woman of six months ago who had seemed able to ride life's ups and downs smoothly, glowing with quiet self-confidence! What a fool her husband was! What man in his right mind would risk losing Jude in exchange for a fling with Sonia O'Dowd? As a producer, he'd often worked with super-focussed, determined females and Alan had come across many girls just like Sonia. He found them almost frightening in their single-mindedness. He knew their attractive outer selves hid steely, acquisitive natures. They wanted the Gucci attaché case, the Prada shoes, the Golf convertible, the apartment in Temple Bar, the suitable man – who would be dropped as soon as another more desirable escort appeared on the horizon. He wondered how long it would be before Sonia gave Geoffrey the cold shoulder.

He kissed Jude on the cheek and pulled back the table

so that she could sit beside Fidelma on the crowded bench seat.

"What can I get you, Jude?"

"A brandy and ginger ale with ice would be lovely, thanks, Alan." She turned to her friend. "Hi, there! How are things with you?"

"I'm fine," Fidelma replied smiling. "In spite of staying up till midnight with Alan, discussing ways to make Geoffrey come to his senses and drop that scheming little wagon he's involved with."

"And did you come up with anything?"

"Wait until Alan comes back and we'll run it past you."

Jude noticed there was an intriguing gleam in the other's eyes.

When they were all seated with their drinks, Fidelma said, "I want you to listen, without interruptions, until I have finished telling you what we think would be the best way to deal with the situation." She gave Jude a stern look.

"You're beginning to alarm me," said Jude, as she swirled the ice around in her drink before taking a large gulp.

"This is not going to be in the least bit alarming – just cunning! Firstly, it is obvious that Geoffrey can't be allowed to get away with taking that young one to Flora's play unchallenged. Secondly, it is also obvious that you have to be there and you have to upstage her."

"The way I'm feeling now, that might prove to be just a little difficult. I'd find it hard to upstage a teacup at the moment."

"We'll deal with that part in a minute," said Fidelma firmly. She swallowed some of her gin and tonic before continuing. "It is also patently obvious that you have to

243

have as much support as possible during that evening. So that means Alan and I will come with you and of course Oscar and his girlfriend."

Jude held up a hand. "No, hang on a minute! It would be better if Oscar and Ellen went on the other night. Why should they be put in an awkward position?"

"Because, dearest Jude, Oscar is *already* in an awkward position and he also adores you and would want to be there for you – and Ellen is besotted with him so she'll go along with whatever he wants." She looked at Jude's worried face. "I promise you. He will want to be there." She turned to Alan. "I am right, aren't I?"

"I really do think that Oscar should be there, Jude. I know you feel you want to protect him. But life is tough and he *is* nearly twenty. If he finds out that you are treating him like a child, he'll resent it. I know I would if I were in his shoes."

Jude still looked uncertain but she stayed silent while Fidelma took up the argument.

"After the play is over, you, Flora, Ellen, Oscar, Alan and I will go out for a delicious meal in *Da Vincenzo*. It's already booked, by the way! We will invite Geoffrey to join us."

"He won't come," said Jude with conviction. "I know he'll have something planned with Sonia."

"Maybe, maybe not. But it will be difficult to refuse with all the rest of us standing around while he makes up his mind. If he doesn't want to join us, we will have a splendid meal without him and make a fuss of Flora. If he does, then that will be an extra bonus – especially as Alan and I, as the dinner hosts, will make it very clear that Sonia is not invited."

"You can't do that. Geoffrey will be furious."

"Watch us!" Fidelma drained her glass. "One other thing. You are looking just a little battered at the moment. You are booked into the beauty clinic in Nassau Street for a complete overhaul next Thursday after work and you have a hair appointment with the utterly divine Michael in the Stephen's Green Shopping Centre on Friday afternoon. It's our treat and we will be mortally offended if you don't do as you're told. Isn't that right, Alan?"

Alan raised his hands in a gesture of happy capitulation. "Do it, darling – or my life will be hell!"

Whatever had happened to the understated, un-pushy Fidelma she thought she knew so well? wondered Jude.

"You're both really kind to go to all of this trouble. I'd only meant to ask you for a few ideas." Jude hesitated. "I can't help feeling a little iffy about all of this. It seems so calculated. You know, the way things are at the moment, Geoffrey won't care if I've had my eyebrows trimmed, my hair styled or whether I appear with my head under my arm. He's just not interested."

"Daft woman!" said Fidelma, poking her gently on the arm. "It's more for *her* benefit than his. You are going to be perfumed, groomed, calm and utterly on top of things – and won't she just *hate* that!"

Chapter Eighteen

Jude had to admit that she felt pretty good as she walked up the aisle of the college's small theatre. Because she regularly had to be heavily made up for television, she usually wore little, if any, for the rest of the time. But this evening her eyelids were dusted with eye shadow, her long lashes darkened with mascara and her lips lightly glossed. She was wearing her favourite dark-green trouser suit and jade earrings. Underneath the jacket, she wore the old gold watch-chain her mother had given her for her seventeenth birthday. Jude called it her lucky chain. It was what she had worn the night she'd first met Geoffrey as well as on the morning of her successful interview with RTVI. She had also been wearing it on the day he had proposed. Not wanting to tempt providence this evening, she wore it hidden, next to her skin.

She knew that the well-cut suit made her tall figure look slim. What she didn't know was that a lot of the women glancing at her, and then taking another closer look, would have given their eye-teeth to have had her long legs and casually elegant appearance. Michael had worked wonders. He had used a deep copper highlight that made her naturally red hair glint richly and he'd gathered together dozens of small French plaits and swept it all magically up into one coil on top of her head. As Fidelma had said she would, she did feel perfumed and groomed – if not quite on top of things. In fact, under the superficially calm exterior, she was horribly nervous. What if this all backfired and she ended up by making things worse?

"Wow! Mum, you look amazing!" Oscar exclaimed, when they all met up outside the college gates. He gave her one of his impulsive hugs, making her rock slightly on her high heels. "If Dad doesn't drool when he sees you, there's something seriously wrong with him."

"I couldn't agree more," said Alan, taking her arm. "What a woman!" He looked at her admiringly. Realising that Fidelma was observing him with raised eyebrows and a quizzical expression, he added, "Well, you can't blame me for being enthusiastic. Jude looks stunning." He half-heartedly attempted to straighten a rarely worn tie and tugged at the sleeves of his battered corduroy jacket. "And what is more, it's not often a tatty old gent like myself gets to accompany two sublimely gorgeous women to an event. I intend to make a grand entrance with a siren on each arm!"

Fidelma rolled her eyes and chuckled. "Would you listen to the man! It's going to be difficult to get from the entrance to our seats if you do that!" She too gave Jude an admiring glance. "You look *marvellous*." She turned to Oscar and Ellen. "Come on then, *mes enfants!* Onwards and upwards – or whatever the appropriate battle call is for the occasion!"

As she sat waiting for the play to start, Jude glanced anxiously around her. The place was packed. She recognised several faces and exchanged waves and smiles. After a while, she spotted Geoffrey and Sonia sitting a little further forward on the other side of the right hand aisle. It appeared they hadn't noticed her yet. The girl was wearing bright red. *How appropriate!* muttered the voice in Jude's head. *Scarlet for a scarlet woman!* How old-fashioned *that* sounded! It was the sort of comment Gran might have made! Sonia was looking up at Geoffrey intently, as though poised to catch any pearls that might fall from his lips. *She's looking rather like a stunned mullet,* whispered the Flora-like voice. But there was no doubt that the girl's close-cropped hair and enormous dark eyes gave her a very gamine, attractive look, Jude observed with a sinking feeling.

However, she couldn't help thinking that her handsome husband did look rather uncomfortable. Was he perhaps having second thoughts about the appropriateness of his being there with the girl? Or was he finding all the attention just a little over the top? She imagined that being the object of such intense interest might wear a little thin after a while. If they were still together in five years' time, she wondered what they would find to talk about.

Maybe, after years of marriage, couples took each other for granted but Jude had always enjoyed the way she and Geoffrey had been subconsciously aware of each other at social functions. Even if they were at opposite ends of a room, there had been a sort of secret connecting line of communication between them that meant they each knew when the other had had enough and wanted to go home or just wanted to be rescued from some bore who thought endless monologue was a satisfactory way to engage their victim in conversation.

Alan leaned over. "You OK, Jude?"

Jude smiled with a confidence she didn't feel. "Fine. Really!"

She didn't know how much Oscar had told Ellen, but the girl kept giving her shy smiles of encouragement. After the debauched scenes in the bedroom the week before, she had given Jude a wide berth for a few days until she realised that she seemed to have forgotten the incident. Jude felt comforted by Oscar and Ellen's presence – even if the evening did feel somewhat unreal. Aware that people in the row behind her were having a muttered conversation in which her name cropped up, she wished that the house lights would dim so that she could sink into anonymity.

But when Flora made her slightly unsteady entrance onto the stage, Jude forgot her surroundings. She watched her daughter as she gradually shed her nervousness and settled into the part. How extraordinary it was to see the transformation from fractious modern girl to this sixteenth-century creature who moved and spoke with such quiet dignity and presence. If Jude hadn't known Flora was playing the part of Margaret Roper, she doubted she would have recognised her.

Near the end of the play where Margaret visits her doomed father in prison and begs him to recant and save himself from the king's fury and his own execution, Jude suddenly realised that her vision was blurred by tears. Perhaps it was because her nerves were already raw but she found the scene unbearably poignant.

When the curtain rose for the cast to take their bows, Jude felt she would burst with pride. She joined in the enthusiastic applause, clapping until her hands buzzed.

Afterwards, as they made their way out, she wasn't sure where Geoffrey was or even if he had noticed that she was there. They waited for Flora to join them in the crowd of people milling around in the cramped courtyard in front of the theatre. Jude had asked Oscar not to say anything to his sister about the plans for the evening, other than the fact that Alan and Fidelma were treating them all to a meal after the play was over. Oscar had assured her that Flora didn't realise that her father was bringing Sonia.

Just as Jude was beginning to wonder where she'd got to, Flora emerged from a noisy group of fellow students. For once, she looked really happy. Gone were the brooding frown, the sullen mouth and the jerky tension of recent weeks. Instead Jude thought she looked almost radiant with relief and pleasure. There were still traces of stage make-up along her jaw and around her eyes. Her hair was standing on end as though she'd forgotten to comb it after taking off her costume and diving back into her street clothes.

Jude hugged her delightedly.

"You see! You didn't let anyone down. Quite the opposite. You were fantastic, Flo!"

Flora hugged her back, grinning broadly. "It was all right, wasn't it?"

"It sure was!" said Jude, smiling.

"Bloody great!" Oscar agreed as he thumped his sister energetically on the back. "You made Ellen cry!"

Flora turned and gave the other girl, what seemed to Jude, a genuine smile.

"I loved your clothes, costume. You looked really lovely . . . Flora," Ellen said with a tentative answering smile.

After everyone had finished congratulating the glowing Flora, whose gestures were becoming more expansive by the minute, Alan said, "At this rate, you're in danger of ending up as a star of stage and telly!" He looked over at Jude. "I'll have to have a word with some of the people in drama at RTVI about this young lady. You never know what might happen." Smiling at Flora, he added, "If you like, I'll help you record a voice-sample tape."

Flora looked surprised. Then she beamed.

"That would be fantastic! Thanks, Alan."

Jude suddenly had the feeling that she was being watched. She glanced behind her to find Geoffrey standing just outside the circle staring at her. It was hard to tell what he was thinking. What struck her most was an impression of his being just that: outside, looking in. She was relieved to see that, for the moment anyway, Sonia was not with him.

As soon as Geoffrey saw her watching him, he hastily turned his attention to Flora as he started to move towards them. Smiling, he went up to his daughter to congratulate her. For a moment, Jude was afraid that Flora was going to be distant. But after the smallest hesitation, she returned his kiss.

"Well, what did you think, Dad?"

"I thought you were most impressive and I was very proud of you. Really," he said, looking at her intently, "I wasn't sure in the past if you had that special something but, after this evening, I think that maybe you do. I was really impressed, Flo."

251

For a moment, it looked as though Flora was having difficulty speaking. When she next looked up at her father, it was evident to Jude that she was struggling to keep her composure.

"Thanks, Dad," she said in a quiet voice. Then, with a sudden, spontaneous gesture, she linked her arm through his and turned to Alan and Fidelma. "So! Why are we hanging around here? I'm absolutely *starving!* Did I hear someone mention that they were taking us out for some food?"

Surprised, Geoffrey looked over at Alan, who smiled briefly at him as he put his own arm around Fidelma.

"Our treat!" he said firmly. "Fidelma and I are taking all the Larchet family out for a celebratory meal."

Jude noticed that the 'all' was slightly emphasised.

"And Ellen," interjected Oscar.

"The Larchets – and Ellen completes the ensemble, of course," replied Alan, staring hard at Geoffrey.

All of a sudden, Geoffrey was aware that he was the focus of everyone's attention. He rubbed the side of his face with his fingertips, ill at ease again.

"Well, I . . ."

"Come *on*, Dad!" said Flora, giving his arm a small tug. "What did Gran Maybury used to say? Don't look a gift horse in the mouth – you might get bitten! I need food urgently. I don't know about you. And anyway, it'll be good for my image to be seen dining with *two* television producers at the same time. People will really start to think I'm going places!"

Jude waited tensely. Her daughter sounded so animated. Surely he wasn't going to let Flora down? Not now, in front of everybody. If he decided not to come with them, it would ruin an otherwise happy occasion. Jude didn't feel that she would be able to forgive her husband if he did that.

She saw him cast a furtive glance towards the entrance gates where Sonia now stood, leaning against one of the pillars, watching him closely, her arms wrapped around her in the cool night air. To Jude, the few seconds it took for him to make up his mind seemed endless. She knew that he was feeling trapped and she was sorry for that. It was, she realised, one of those defining moments in life that crop up unexpectedly from time to time. Whichever direction he decided on now, she knew that things would be irreparably changed. But perhaps his having to make a choice over letting Flora down or not might also encourage him into thinking seriously about his children and herself – and just what it was he wanted from the rest of his life.

"I have to drop someone home first and then I'll meet you at the restaurant. Which one is it?"

Jude was filled with relief, aware that she really hadn't known which way he would choose. She could imagine how angry young Sonia was going to be. She'd probably thought that she and Geoffrey were going off to have a nice cosy meal for two in some trendy Dublin restaurant where the management were so sure the clientele was well-heeled that there was no need to print the prices on the menu. *Good!* commented the voice in her head. *Go and eat with someone your own age*.

"*Da Vincenzo*." Alan gave Geoffrey a penetrating look. "See you there in fifteen minutes?"

Geoffrey gave a curt nod before turning and smiling once more at Flora. "See you in a few minutes, then."

Jude could see the effort he was making to give the impression that he was happy about the arrangement. It would be some time before he forgave Alan and Fidelma for their part in all of this, she thought. He would only see it as meddling in something that was none of their business. Flora was on too much of a high to worry about anything just now. Her usual critical self had foundered under all the heady compliments coming her way. The odd person was still coming up and tapping her on the shoulder, telling her how much they had enjoyed her performance.

Unnoticed by the others, Fidelma moved to Jude's side.

"You all right, chicken?" she asked in a low voice.

Jude gave an uncertain laugh.

"A bit weak at the knees but nothing that a glass or two of good wine won't cure. It was a bit of a sticky moment just then. I thought he wasn't going to come."

"You shouldn't have worried. At least he realised he mustn't spoil the evening for Flora."

By the time they reached their cars, Jude noticed thankfully that there was no sign of Sonia or Geoffrey.

* * *

"Do you want a drink, Oz?" asked Jude as she took off her jacket and dropped it onto the hall chair.

"No, thanks, Mum. I'm pooped. I think I'll follow Flo's example and hit the sack." He moved over to give her a kiss. "It went well, didn't it?" He peered into her face, trying to make out what she was feeling. "I don't just mean Flo being terrific in the play and all that but dinner after with Dad. That was all right, wasn't it?"

Jude gave him a reassuring kiss on the cheek.

"It was a lovely evening. Go to bed! You're looking a bit rough. I'll see you in the morning."

After he trudged up the stairs, Jude went into the kitchen and poured herself a glass of white wine from the opened bottle in the fridge. She took it through to the sitting-room, turning on a table-lamp and the fan-heater before sitting down on the couch. Yes, she supposed that dinner had been a success – superficially. She had caught Geoffrey staring at her several times, wearing an inscrutable expression, but whenever she'd tried to eyeball him, he'd quickly looked away. She hadn't been able to make out if it was because he was embarrassed or just irritated at their collective subterfuge. He'd always been the sort of man who liked to be in control of a situation. It must have been galling for him to find himself manoeuvred into a corner.

Throughout the meal he had been charming to Ellen and Fidelma, stonily polite to Alan and attentive to Flora. He had been pleasant enough to Jude and Oscar too but she had been aware of a slight wariness in his manner towards them. Was it because he felt there wasn't much point in pretending? Had he decided that, as far as they were concerned, he was guilty and there wasn't much he could do about it. Was that it? she wondered.

Although Jude had tried hard to enjoy the extremely good food, she found herself all the time monitoring her husband's behaviour, trying to read what was going on under the surface. The meal seemed to last forever. She was thankful when the final glass of liqueur and cup of coffee had been drunk and they finally stood up to leave.

They walked the short distance back to their respective

cars: Ellen and Oscar holding hands and chatting quietly between themselves, Alan and Fidelma following them along the footpath with Jude and Geoffrey bringing up the rear, linked by their still voluble daughter – although the decibel level had dropped slightly from earlier on in the restaurant. With an amused ache of affection, Jude thought that she had never seen Flora look so happy – or so pretty.

"We'll give Ellen a lift. It's on our way," said Alan, when they reached the cars.

He kissed Jude good night and then Fidelma and Jude exchanged embraces.

"Thank you both so much for this evening. I'll ring you," said Jude, adding in a louder voice, "I'll take Oz and Flo, then."

She was hoping that Geoffrey would offer to take one of them. But he had just nodded and climbed into his car, looking preoccupied.

"Can't I come with you, Dad?" asked Flora.

He shut the car door before answering. Then he rolled down his window.

"You look tired, Flo, and I've got to get some petrol. I'm nearly empty. You go back with Mum and I'll see you in the morning."

As Jude fumbled with her car keys, she thought angrily that his excuse had been a pretty pathetic one. Was he planning to go and tuck Sonia up, make up for letting her down earlier on? She hoped for all their sakes that he wasn't.

If Flora hadn't still been on a high, Jude was pretty sure that she would have insisted on her father taking her home but the mixture of afterglow from her performance and the onset of fatigue blunted her usual remarkable ability to be awkward. Oscar was too busy giving the departing Ellen lingering looks to have heard the exchange.

As soon as they got home, Flora flung her arms around Jude and hugged her in an unexpected show of enthusiasm.

"You looked fanbloodytastic tonight, Mum." She stepped back from her mother and stretched both arms out above her head. She gave an expansive yawn. "That was a *great* evening! That Alan's a lovely man. I'll have to get organised about what I'm going to use for the voice-sample tape," she said happily, before disappearing upstairs to bed.

It struck Jude as a pity that it hadn't apparently occurred to Geoffrey to make a tape for his daughter. But then, he'd had other things on his mind, hadn't he?

Now, as she sat, nursing her glass of wine, Jude waited and hoped. Maybe Geoffrey *would* just fill his car with petrol, buy some chocolate and come home. He never could go into a garage or newsagent's without emerging, clutching a Cadbury's cream bar or a Crunchie! They had laughed about this habit often enough. She looked at her watch. They'd only been back ten minutes themselves.

She woke an hour later, cold in spite of the heater. Her empty glass lay on the cushion beside her. Rubbing her eyes, Jude peered at her watch. Stiffly, she got up and moved the glass from the couch to the coffee table. He must have decided to visit Sonia after all. She felt as if all her energy seemed to have drained away as she picked up her shoes, switched off the heater and lamp and moved slowly towards the door. A feeling of mind-numbing hopelessness filled her. What was the point in going on with this charade any longer? She remembered her proud

statement to Fidelma so many weeks before – when she'd
said that she was going to fight to save her marriage. It
looked obvious that, after tonight, there was no marriage
left to save.

It took all Jude's strength to climb the stairs. She went
into their bedroom and shut the door behind her. Quietly,
she turned the key in the lock. She slipped off her shoes,
took off her earrings and the watch chain from around her
neck. For a moment she held it, coiled in the palm of her
hand like a snake. She looked down at it. Not such a lucky
ornament after all. Too exhausted to undress, she lay down
under the duvet, an old Indian shawl of her mother's
wrapped around her for comfort.

Chapter Nineteen

Geoffrey was sitting in the kitchen when Jude went downstairs next morning. She'd heard the car tyres on the gravel outside a few minutes earlier. So he'd been away all night! Locking the door had been a futile gesture. He hadn't come upstairs, just waited for her to appear.

Jude's head ached and there was a sour taste in her mouth. The fact that her clothes were crumpled and her mascara smudged was unimportant. As she walked into the kitchen, she thought wryly that if all the effort she'd made the previous evening had not stopped him from spending the night with Sonia then she sure as hell wasn't going to make any effort to look presentable for him now.

He looked up as she came into the room. This would be just about manageable if she kept her head, Jude reminded herself. With legs that felt like jelly, she walked over to the kettle and filled it with water, then plugged it in. She had the feeling that she was going to need strong coffee – and lots of it – to keep her going for the next while. The kitchen was cold. Her hands and feet felt icy. She went into the utility room and switched on the central heating. Then she went over to the kettle and stood, waiting for it to boil, her back to him.

"Do you want some coffee?" she asked, eventually, trying to sound as neutral as possible.

"No, thanks. I've had several cups all ready."

Sitting up in bed with the lovely Sonia, no doubt. Any attempt at neutral thoughts disappeared out of the window. She felt angry and bitter. Automatically, she spooned instant coffee granules into a large mug and reached for the sugar. Her hand shook as she took some, spilling it on the worktop. Neither of them spoke until, mug in hand, she sat down at the far end of the table from him.

For the first time, she observed him carefully. The early morning light from the window showed up his usually healthy complexion as grey. He hadn't shaved and his cheeks and chin were blue with stubble. There were bags under his eyes that made her, suddenly and unwillingly, see him as vulnerable. She noticed that his thick hair was more heavily streaked with grey than she'd realised. He looked as if he hadn't slept much either. Jude was surprised by her feelings of sympathy for him. She didn't want to feel anything just now, sympathetic or otherwise.

"I know what you're thinking," said Geoffrey.

"Tell me. What am I thinking?"

"You think that I spent the night with Sonia. I didn't. I went to a hotel."

"Well, I reckon it was a reasonable assumption to make, considering that you took her to the play last night and presumably were prepared to take her out to dinner afterwards – if you hadn't been put on the spot."

"I'm glad that you agree that I *was* put on the spot."

Jude gripped the mug handle tightly. "There should have been no need for your having to be put on the spot if you hadn't behaved so badly." Angrily she asked, "What on earth possessed you to take your . . . that girl . . . to our daughter's play? Do you seriously think that that was the right thing to do? How do you think I felt, seeing you there with her? It was as though you were trying to humiliate me in front of as many people as possible."

Geoffrey was silent for a moment. When he next spoke, he sounded as though he were having difficulty forcing the words out.

"God! Jude, I didn't mean to humiliate you. It sounds ridiculous, I know, but I think I was attempting to make some kind of public statement." He suddenly banged the table with his hand. The unexpected noise made her flinch. "I can't go on with this pretence any more, Jude! I know you have been unbelievably patient and good and I'll never forget how kind you were to my mother but . . ."

"But you've had enough. Is that it?"

"Yes. I'm sorry but yes, it is."

"And you want to walk away from our marriage?"

"I can't pretend that I think it would be a good idea for me to stay and that it will all work out in the end – when I know it won't."

"So, you're going to just disappear from our lives. What about Flora and Oscar?" She could hear her voice cracking as she spoke. "What about them?"

"I have no intention, whatsoever, of abandoning them.

I'm still there for both of them, whenever they need me."

"So, let me get this straight. Technically, you aren't walking out on your children, just your wife." She looked him in the eyes. "Aren't I right? It's me you've had enough of, isn't it? *I'm* the one you're walking out on."

He stared back at her silently. With the half of her mind that wasn't paralysed with anger and horror at what was happening, Jude could see that he was suffering as much as she. She buried her head in her hands for a moment. When she looked up again, he quickly lowered his eyes, so that he didn't have to see the look of anguish on her face.

"Do you love her?"

"If you mean in the sort of way I loved you, then, no. I don't think so."

"Hang on a minute," Jude said in a puzzled voice. "If you don't love her, then why are you leaving me for her? Why are you hell-bent on causing so much misery?"

Suddenly, Geoffrey stood up from the table, his face grim.

"Didn't you hear what I just said? You and I are *over*. I can't say it any more plainly than that. I care for you enormously, Jude but that's all. I know that Sonia is probably just a gold-digging, manipulative girl but she's woken me up to the fact that I had stopped expecting any excitement or fun in my life. There was just work, more work and that was all." Seeing the look of hurt on Jude's face, he moved around the table towards her. "I'm so sorry . . ."

She held up her hand, stopping him from coming any closer.

"She was just a bit of excitement, was she? And she showed you how boring marriage with me had become.

Well, I'm sure she's more adventurous in bed than I could possibly be. Poor Geoffrey!"

He looked surprised. "What do you mean?"

Jude stood up so quickly that she felt the blood drain away from her face. She steadied herself against the side of the table. She could smell his sweat, see the look of puzzlement in his tired eyes. It was important that she remained in control of herself. Whatever happened, she mustn't faint.

"I mean just that. If you can't see how sad it is that you don't want or aren't able to work to make our marriage into something good again, then I do feel sorry for you." She looked at him with an unflinching stare. "You are a fool, Geoffrey. Perhaps in the future, you'll come to realise that; realise that today you lost the right to my love – and my respect."

He took a step back from her. He didn't like that, she thought. *Good! The truth usually hurts.*

He gave a small cough before speaking again. Jude could see that he was going to try and pretend that he wasn't put out by her unkind remark.

"I have arranged to stay with a friend until I can find somewhere to live. I hope we can get through all the practical side of this without things getting out of proportion and you becoming bitter."

A small sound escaped Jude that was more like a croak than a laugh.

"Why should I feel bitter, Geoff? After all, your leaving means that I can be myself again."

* * *

263

"Mum, the side gate's open and I can't find Plunkett." An out-of-breath Oscar appeared at the back door. Seeing him with his hair flopping untidily into his eyes like that made Jude's heart lurch. He looked so like Geoffrey when she'd first met him. "I've hunted all over the garden and in Gran's flat and he's not there. He must have slipped out when he found the gate open."

Oh, God! thought Jude. The poor animal had been so neglected these past few months, he's probably chosen to commit suicide on the busy road outside rather than continue living in a house where everyone was either out or too preoccupied to make a fuss of him. From the time Patricia Larchet died, Jude had allowed him to sleep in the kitchen. When Geoffrey left, two months later, he had somehow inveigled himself onto the old armchair in Jude's bedroom. Although at first she'd made a feeble attempt to stop him from following her up to bed, she'd found his company pleasantly comforting. She'd sometimes be woken in the night by excited yelps as he chased a rabbit, nose and all four feet twitching frantically as he dreamed. Every now and then his feathery tail would thump against the arm of the chair.

"I'll come and look for him. You go down towards the shop and I'll go towards the Dart station."

Jude hurried into the hall and grabbed her coat. It was early December and bitterly cold. She opened the front door and was met by a blast of wind that made the skin on her face feel immediately taut and icy. It was nearly four o'clock and already beginning to get dark. Most of the cars had their headlights on. As she reached the gate, she looked to the left and saw her son's tall figure a couple of

264

gardens away. He was peering hopefully through someone's hedge.

Plunkett's probably miles away, if he's not lying dead at the side of the road, Jude thought, guiltily. He was a bloody nuisance but it was hardly his fault that he'd ended up living with a basically un-doggy family. The large 'For Sale' sign, that had been roughly nailed onto the gatepost outside their house, rattled in the wind. She set off, walking briskly in the direction of the railway line. Pieces of newspaper shredded themselves against a garden hedge and a Coke can rolled noisily backwards and forwards in the muddy gutter. As she searched, Jude realised that not only did she feel cold physically but there was an inner chill that didn't seem to succumb to the warmth of layers of clothing or blazing fires. These days, she only seemed able to forget how miserable she felt when she was at work. When she was at the studios, a kind of grim determination to do her best and prove how good she was at what she did took over and fuelled her during the working day. Everyone said that she was doing a marvellous job. The last programme in the series had gone out the week before to great acclaim. *The Irish Times* said it was by far the best current affairs programme that RTVI had put on for years. *The Examiner* thought she had an unusual gift of going straight to the heart of a problem without ever making the interviewee feel bullied or antagonised. The reviewer claimed that she never patronised the people she interviewed, unlike some of her male counterparts. This was all very pleasant, but by the time she got home in the evenings, Jude was increasingly exhausted.

As she drew level with the half a dozen caravans in the

rubbish-littered laneway beside the railway line, Jude wondered if she might not find herself living in one if a buyer, prepared to offer a reasonable sum for the house, didn't turn up soon. Ever since Geoffrey's departure, the life of the house seemed to be draining away. First Mrs Larchet, followed by her son and then last week Flora had moved into a flat in the centre of Dublin with two friends from College. Now, even Plunkett appeared to have deserted her in disgust.

"How can you afford to stay in a flat?" Jude had remonstrated.

"Dad's given me enough for the first month's rent and deposit and I've got some voice-overs lined up, Mum. I'll be rolling in dosh so you don't have to worry. Really!"

Jude hadn't argued.

Through Alan's contacts, Flora had gone to a couple of auditions and been successful, which, as her mother knew, was phenomenal good luck when she was still a student. It appeared that Flora was well on the way to doing what she'd always wanted. Jude had done her best to give a good impression of not minding her daughter leaving home.

"Well, if you're sure. That's really exciting news, Flo. Well done!"

"I'll be back regularly," Flora promised. "And you can come and visit me and I'll even cook you a meal."

"I look forward to that," said Jude, thinking of her daughter's various past attempts at producing meals in which a bizarre combination of ingredients were barely adequately cooked and the result far from edible.

She still vividly remembered the food poisoning she and Oscar had suffered after Flora's brief flirtation with sea trout.

"And with you having to move and all, it will be easier all round, won't it?" Flora had added cheerfully.

"I suppose it will."

Feeling strangely bereft, Jude nodded in agreement while all the while wondering how long it would be before Oscar too wanted to fly the nest.

She tapped on the door of the nearest caravan. There was a light in one of its windows and she could hear a baby crying inside. A young lurcher puppy emerged from under one of the other caravans. It slunk up behind Jude and sniffed at her suspiciously. She bent down and held out her hand but it cowered at her sudden movement and retreated back to its hiding-place. After a delay, the door swung open and the tired young woman Jude had often seen around stood on the top step, framed by light. When she saw who the visitor was, she looked surprised, even wary.

"Yeah?"

"Sorry to bother you, but I'm looking for our dog. He went missing some time this afternoon."

"The red dopey yoke in the big collar?"

Jude laughed. That was as good a description of Plunkett as any.

"Yes, that's the one! The Irish setter. You've seen me walking him around here sometimes, I think."

The baby in the woman's arms, having recovered from its own surprise at Jude's appearance, started to cry more persistently, angrily beating small fists against its mother's chest.

"Yeah," the woman said, yanking a soother out of her jeans pocket and plugging it firmly into the infant's mouth. "I know the fella."

"Have you seen him today?" persisted Jude.

"No."

Jude smiled at her and then started to turn away. "Right! Thanks anyway. Sorry to disturb you."

Just as she began to walk away the woman called out. "If I see him, I'll let you know. Number 58. Right?"

"Right! Thanks!"

Jude turned and raised her hand to wave but the woman was already closing the door against the freezing evening air.

It was nearly an hour later when she and Oscar, their breath making small grey clouds in the lamplight, met on the pavement in front of the gate. No one appeared to have seen Plunkett. It was as though he'd disappeared into thin air.

They went inside and made mugs of hot chocolate, carrying them through to the sitting-room fire where they warmed their hands around the hot drinks.

"I'm sure he'll come back. He's just gone off for a bit. You know how he loves going down to the beach to gallop around and bark at the waves. He'll come home when he's run out of bark," Oscar reassured her.

"But I went down to the beach and there was no sign of him. The traffic's awful and you know what a fool he is."

"Mum, you worry too much. He'll be fine. You wait and see!"

Jude used to think of herself as being quite the opposite of a worrier. She didn't like the thought of being the sort of person who sat and mulled over all her troubles with an anxious expression. It was a depressing image.

"Do you think I'm turning into a miserable, middle-aged woman?"

"Of *course* not!" He lowered his mug and looked at her, amused. "You're great, Mum. You really are – for your age!"

"Thanks a lot!"

"If you want to know, Flo and I were talking about it the other day. We both agreed that, after meeting some of our friend's mothers, we're quite happy to put up with you."

Jude pulled a face at him. "You say the sweetest things."

"Ah, well!" replied Oscar, lazily pushing back some of the hair that had fallen over his forehead. "I'm a lovely lad, really."

Jude looked at him and smiled. "You are – quite often!"

Another search after supper yielded no sign of the missing dog. Jude went to bed hoping that he wasn't lying hurt somewhere. As she lay under the duvet, the heat from the electric blanket soaked into her. She'd bought it a few weeks earlier. Before, she'd always snuggled up to her husband on cold nights. Be positive! she told herself, closing her eyes. The bed is lovely and warm. *And you can stretch in any direction without damaging yourself on another person, put the light on and read at midnight if you feel like it and watch your favourite programmes until dawn when the mood takes you. You can even eat cream crackers in bed. Sounds like bliss!* said the Flora-voice. Right! Jude told herself firmly. Things could be worse.

She opened her eyes again. Unfortunately, that wasn't really true. There had been little direct contact with Geoffrey since the start of October. She'd seen him in RTVI but they had both gone out of their way to avoid each other. Apart from Flora and Oscar and visits from Fidelma, Jude really hadn't seen anyone outside work.

She and Geoffrey had managed one fairly cordial

meeting in which they had agreed that no solicitor was going to get his or her hands on any of their hard-earned money if they could possibly help it. They would sell the house, each taking half of everything. Geoffrey said that if they could deal with it all equitably, there would be no need for a bloody solicitor. Now they were just waiting to find a bloody buyer.

The estate agent had been enthusiastic when he first looked around the house.

"This is perfect. A real 'walk in and hang up your hat' job!" the, in Jude's eyes, incredibly young-looking man smilingly announced after a high-speed tour around the rooms. As he climbed back into his Alfa Romeo, taking care not to crease his expensive-looking suit as he put on his seat belt, he said, "This will be snapped up very quickly, I'm sure."

"What about the decline of the Celtic Tiger?" Jude asked. "I thought that the house market had been badly hit."

The car's engine purred into life. With his slim-line mobile phone nesting in his lap and one hand on the steering wheel, he waved the other nonchalantly in the air.

"Don't you worry, Mrs Larchet. Leave us to do the worrying. When the punters see the brochure we are going to bring out for your house, they'll be arriving in droves. And," he added, "by the way, I think you are just terrific on the telly!"

Another wanker! observed the Flora-voice. As he'd roared up the road, Jude turned back to the house, wondering if she should have Catriona on more or less permanent stand-by to keep everything in pristine condition for the expected hordes.

That had been over six weeks ago. Since then, two lots of what could be considered serious house-hunters had been to take a look. Countless bored weekend jaunters with ghastly, lollipop-licking children running loose all over the place had arrived in large numbers.

Catriona had become expert at sussing them out.

"No, you go off to work, Jude. I'll deal with them. I don't have four younger brothers of me own for nothin'. One of me hard stares has them kids turned into jelly. They don't know if I'm planning on eating them or just shoving them down the stairs. Mind you, some of the parents are worse than the kids! Lookin' in drawers and cupboards like they was on some class of a treasure hunt!"

Even the suave young estate agent was at great pains not to upset Catriona.

"If he thinks I'm making him cups of tea while he hangs around waitin' for that lot, he'll be waitin' a long time," she told Jude in determined tones.

Jude had long ago come to the conclusion that Catriona was a force to be reckoned with in many different ways. She hoped the young man didn't tempt providence by stepping out of line and requesting something as controversial as a cup of tea.

She couldn't help noticing that he wasn't able to hide the fact that his initial optimism over them getting a quick sale had diminished a little.

Chapter Twenty

The young estate agent was looking ruffled.

"I do hope you don't mind but she's *insisting* on taking a look at the place," he said with an apologetic smile. "I told her the asking price and she didn't bat an eyelid. Said she'd more than enough to cover it, thank you very much. In fact, she got quite annoyed. Said I should mind my own business and that I wasn't to waste her time asking stupid questions. It's all very awkward."

Jude couldn't understand why he was so concerned.

"If she's serious in looking at it, we can hardly turn her away, can we? It's not as though we've had any offers yet."

"No," he admitted grudgingly. Not wanting to appear negative, he hastily added, "Although the office is still getting enquiries."

Maybe, thought Jude. But the enquiries never seemed to turn into anything concrete. She was curious to know what he held against the latest would-be viewer.

"Why are you so reluctant to let her come and take a look?" she asked.

"Well," he stopped, embarrassed, "you've probably noticed her around the area. Short lady – in Doc Martens? She wears a green woollen hat a lot of the time, well, most of the time."

Jude looked at him in surprise. "You mean our local bag lady?"

He nodded, mutely.

Jude digested this extraordinary piece of information.

"What's this lady's name?"

"Doris. Doris Leach. She's English and, as you've probably already noticed, fairly eccentric." The estate agent looked as though he were in the middle of having a bad dream. Any moment now he would wake up and start showing the property to respectable clients who'd arrived in respectable cars. "In fact," he continued thoughtfully, "I think she's probably quite mad."

Jude had often noticed the woman down on the beach, collecting sticks and had wondered where she lived, or indeed, if she had a place of her own. She thought that the name sounded like something out of a *Carry On* film or the London music hall of eighty years ago. Jude was starting to feel quite sorry for the uncomfortable-looking man. He was usually so sure of himself.

To put him out of his misery, she smiled and said in a business-like manner, "Well, a prospective buyer is just that. When does she want to come?"

He cleared his throat.

"Actually, in about fifteen minutes. If that's all right. It's just that I have an appointment I really can't miss and she *wouldn't* change the time. It *had* to be today at ten."

"No problem! I don't have to go out for another hour so I'll be around. Catriona's here as well. Don't worry! You go off to your appointment and I'll let you know if there are any developments," Jude reassured him cheerfully.

"There won't be, I'm afraid. She's not the type that results in developments," he replied morosely.

"We'll just have to wait and see, won't we?"

Jude shut the front door and leaned against it for a moment. How odd! The local bag lady might be the next owner of the house. Well, why not? She was starting to think that nothing much would surprise her these days.

When Jude told Catriona about the expected visitor, the girl was in the middle of polishing the large dining-room table. She straightened up and stared at Jude in disbelief, the duster hanging from her hand like a limp yellow flag.

"You mean yer one with the shopping bags and the green woolly hat?"

"The very same," said Jude.

"Jesus!"

For once, Catriona appeared to be lost for words.

At ten o'clock exactly, there was a sustained ring on the doorbell. It wasn't the sort of ring that you could say you hadn't heard. Catriona looked at Jude and raised her eyebrows expressively. The bell rang again.

"Shall I let yer woman in?"

"We can't leave her standing on the doorstep. Quite apart from anything, she'll bust the bell if she goes on ringing it like that," said Jude, with a laugh.

As soon as Catriona opened the door, a black-booted foot plonked itself down on the mat, speedily followed by a second. Their owner was wearing a long plaid skirt that reached the top of the boots, a thick navy blue jacket with pockets that bulged – and a bright green woollen hat with a darker green pompom. A few wispy strands of grey hair stuck out from under the hat. She looked about five feet high, her head just about level with Jude's shoulder. Jude reckoned that the woman's figure would best be described as egg-shaped. Her face and hands were weatherbeaten. She had never seen so many folds, lines and crinkles on one person's face before. It was a 'lived-in' kind of face. The woman's eyes were small and bright blue. As they swivelled in their sockets, they seemed to be taking in every detail of the hall before fixing on Jude, who was aware that she was being carefully scrutinised as she stepped forward, holding out her hand.

"Hello, Mrs Leach. I'm Jude Larchet."

"Miss – not Mrs. Never Mrs," replied the woman firmly.

There was definitely a touch of London in her accent. London and something else that wasn't easily definable. She spoke very emphatically. There was a hint of phlegm in her voice; possibly the remnants of some chest infection.

"I'm sorry I . . ." Jude began.

"I suppose that silly young man in the ridiculous car didn't fill you in properly," interrupted the woman, stuffing both wind-chapped hands into her jacket pockets. "I thought not! Flash car, big ideas but not enough up here." She jabbed a finger in the direction of her head.

"Would you like to start upstairs?" Jude asked her, trying to keep a straight face.

"That's what I'm here for."

Before anyone had time to say anything more, Miss

Leach started to climb the stairs, her boots clattering loudly on the wooden steps. Jude followed the small figure's bulky backside, thinking that she looked a little like a female version of Humpy-Dumpty. Except if this Humpty-Dumpty ever fell off a wall, she doubted there would be much damage done. She was wearing far too many layers of clothes.

It took ten minutes for Doris Leach to be shown the entire house. One lingering stare was accorded to each room. Only once did she stop for any length of time. It was in Oscar's bedroom, where she strode towards the window and looked out over the back garden.

"I'm afraid the garden's not at its best at the moment," said Jude.

"It's winter, ain't it? What do you expect at this time of year?" The woman turned back to the view. "Trees. Good! I like trees," she said approvingly, screwing up her eyes and gazing at the tall beech trees standing at the end of the garden. "Silver, copper and gold!" she added softly to herself.

"Silver, copper and gold?"

"Silver trunks. Copper and gold leaves in autumn." She stepped suddenly back from the window, almost knocking into Jude. "Right! We done upstairs then?"

"Yes."

"There's no need to take me outside. Outside's fine. Right! Show me the rest."

Obediently, Jude led her downstairs.

When every room had been inspected and they were standing in the hall again, Doris Leach, feet planted well apart, hands deep in her overloaded pockets, looked up at Jude.

"I like it. I'll give you what you're asking."

Out of the corner of her eye, Jude was aware of Catriona stopping her energetic dusting of the banisters. She seemed to freeze in mid-action, gaping down at the two women below.

"Are you sure?" asked the astonished Jude. "I mean, wouldn't you like to go away and think about it? Perhaps come back some other day and have another look?"

"I don't need to go away and think. I know what I think right now." Miss Leach yanked her woollen hat down more securely over her ears. "You can ring that Jonathan Whatshisname from the estate agency place and tell him. I'll come back tomorra morning. Same time. Tell him to meet me here." Before Jude could open the door for her, Doris Leach had done it herself and steam-rollered her stout body out onto the front step. Turning round, she gave Jude a quick nod. "Nice place. I wouldn't leave it if I was you but then, I'm not you. Though there must be a good reason for you wanting to move." She suddenly leaned forward, suspicious. "It's not yer drains, is it?"

"No," said Jude. "The drains are just fine. Mains drains, you know?"

"That's all right, then. Right! See you tomorra, Jude."

Without pausing, she set off towards the gate, her Doc Martens scrunching across the gravel. Jude noticed that today was the first time she'd seen the bag lady without her bags. She wondered where she'd left them.

When she'd closed the front door, she saw that Catriona was still halfway up the stairs, still clutching her duster, only now, she was sitting on one of the steps, looking stunned.

"I just don't believe it!" she said in an awed voice. "That one wants to buy this house?"

Jude sank down onto the bottom step and looked up at her.

"Apparently she does!"

"Holy Cow!" There was a silence before the girl said, "Ah, the poor old thing must be mad or polluted with the drink. That one has never got the cash for a place like this."

"There was no smell of drink on her and I don't think she's mad. Far from it! She's coming back tomorrow morning."

"I heard," said Catriona dryly. She got up slowly. "Wait and me ma hears about this! She'll have forty canaries!"

Jude also got to her feet.

"I'd better go and ring Jonathan Whatshisname at the Estate Agent's!"

* * *

"You've sold the house?"

Oscar looked at her in surprise.

"Well, I'm in the process of selling the house. It *is* for sale, you know," said Jude.

"But you haven't got anywhere to go to. Dad's found somewhere to stay but you haven't even started house-hunting."

She looked guilty.

"I know. I've been so busy at work and I suppose, if I'm truthful, I hadn't really accepted that we *were* going to have to move." She gave an uncertain laugh. "I shall have to get my skates on now, won't I?"

"When did all this happen?"

278

"This morning. Miss Leach told the estate agent in no uncertain terms that she wanted to move in as soon as possible. No surveyor or anything like that. Apparently she's paying for the whole thing when she signs on the dotted line. No mortgage or having to borrow the money."

"The full price?"

"The full price. Although I had words with the 'silly young man', as she will call Jonathan Porter-Hughes. He wanted to try and bump up the price by pretending that carpets and curtains were not included and if she wanted them it would add a couple of thousand on."

"What happened?"

"He suggested it. I glared at him and told him that, on the contrary, it was he who had made the mistake and that they were included. She said, 'Right!' – which seems to be her favourite expression. And that was it – more or less!" Jude chuckled at the memory. "She almost smiled at me. I think she saw the glare. I suspect that not much goes unnoticed by our Miss Leach!"

"And she's the woman who . . ."

"The bag lady. Yes."

"Bloody hell!" said Oscar, slumping back in his chair. "I always thought bag ladies weren't the sort of people who owned houses."

Then he leaned forward, resting his elbows on his thighs. After a few moments he sat back again. Running his fingers through his hair, he gave his mother a cautious look. Jude knew that look. It meant he wanted to say something but wasn't sure if now was the right time.

"Spit it out, Oz!"

"What?"

"Come on! I think I know you well enough to recognise when you're bottling something up. What is it?"

He stared down at his feet, looking uncomfortable.

"I feel a bit mean bringing this up now, just after Flo's moved out."

He looked over to where she sat beside the fire, the paper on her lap.

"For goodness' sake, what is it?"

"Ellen's going over to London for a while."

"And?"

"And . . . I thought I might go over too. Just for a bit," he added quickly.

Not you as well, Jude groaned to herself. She gazed down at the paper unseeingly.

Oscar continued, "It's great because we can stay at her sister's in Hackney while I look around for some work."

"But Oz, Dad and I were hoping that you'd do some sort of third-level course, go to university, something more – so that you've got a better chance of getting a reasonable job." Jude tried to keep the pleading note out of her voice. "What on earth are you going to do in London that you can't do here?"

He gave her a broad smile. "Not much! But Ellen's going to be over there, not here." He moved closer to her and squatted down on the rug beside her. "Mum, I'd have to wait until the next academic year if I *did* want to go to college. I won't go to London until you find somewhere you'd like to live and I'll be here to help you move. I'm not running out on you. Honestly!"

But that was just what it felt like to Jude. She absent-mindedly twisted the wedding ring on her finger. She hadn't been able to bring herself to take it off quite yet. It was hardly her son's fault that the timing was unfortunate. She looked down at him. Putting her hand out, she held the back of his neck for a brief moment. For some reason, she suddenly remembered the first time she had taken him to have his hair cut when he was small and he had cried when he saw the scissors. She smoothed the thick dark hair down with her fingers. Seeing the anxious expression in his eyes, she gave it a gentle tug before taking away her hand.

"Well, if you want to go to London, I suppose you should go. Have you told your father?"

"Yes. He wasn't too thrilled but he said if I only went for a short time and had a serious think about what I wanted to do afterwards, he supposed it was all right."

"You were *supposed* to be having a serious think about what it was you wanted to do for the past year and a half, Oz," said Jude in a quiet voice.

The phone rang in the hall.

"I'll get it!" said Oscar, scrambling to his feet.

Saved by the bell, thought Jude.

He was gone for a few minutes. She could hear one end of what seemed to be an animated conversation. When he reappeared, he was beaming. "Guess what!"

"What?"

"Flo's only gone and got herself a real live theatrical agent!"

"I don't believe it!"

"She has! She wants to speak to you, Mum."

Out in the hall, Jude picked up the phone.

"Hello, there! What's all this about a theatrical agent? I

thought it was difficult for actors to find an agent even when they'd finished at drama college."

"He saw my Margaret Roper and liked it. Oh, Mum, things are really taking off. What with the voice-overs and now this! It's unbelievable!"

Jude couldn't help smiling. Flora's excitement was infectious.

"Congratulations! It's terrific news. What happens now?"

"He's sending me off to a couple of auditions next week. So I've got to find some pieces to do. I'll have to really work hard in the next few days to get them right." Flora paused. When she next spoke, her voice was more subdued. "You all right, Mum? Only Oz said the *bag lady*'s going to buy the house. Or has he got it all wrong as per usual?"

"No, he's right. She is going to buy it."

"How come? I mean, she's hardly rolling in it. Like, she's worn the same hat ever since I can remember."

"I've no idea. But she's even managed to persuade the estate agent that she's serious. He told me after she'd left this morning that, apparently, she banks at the Anglo-Irish Bank in Stephen's Green and is a client of one of the biggest solicitors in Dublin."

"You're joking! That's amazing! Well, I suppose if she has the money, that's great news then, isn't it?"

"Yes," said Jude, forcing herself to sound cheerful. "I suppose it is."

"I'll have to go now, Mum. It's getting late and tomorrow's going to be mad-busy. I'll ring you soon. Take care! Love you!"

"Love you too! Bye, Flo."

As she put the phone down, Jude reflected that her

daughter was moving on, leaving her behind. Well, it was what happened and what one should want for one's children – for them to sprout wings and leave the family nest. Still, in spite of all the rows and banged doors, she realised that she was missing Flora more than she'd thought possible.

* * *

Plunkett didn't come home the next day, or the following one. Oscar put a notice up in the local shop and Jude rang the gardaí, who suggested she got in touch with the nearest animal welfare centre. The thought of Plunkett languishing behind bars was so awful, that she and Oscar decided to go there rather than just phone. They searched among the dozens of barking, bewildered dogs. He wasn't there.

The days seemed to slide into each other, packed with work and hunting for somewhere to live. Miss Leach was adamant that she wanted to move in by Christmas. That gave Jude four weeks to find a place for herself.

A new series of the current affairs programme was in the pipeline. It was to have a slightly different format from the previous one but the station confirmed that they definitely wanted Jude as its main presenter. So impressed were they by her performance on the programme over the autumn, there had even been talk of her being given an award at the RTVI award dinner just before Christmas.

"So, bang goes any hope of me getting my old job back," she lamented to Fidelma, when they met in a corridor at work one day.

"Well, I was going to ring you. I've got some good news that should cheer you up."

"I could do with some good news for a change," Jude replied with a wry smile. "There's still no sign of Plunkett, Geoffrey runs a mile if he sees me on the horizon and Flo seems to have disappeared off the face of the earth. I know she's busy but I'm lucky if I get a weird, abbreviated text message these days!"

"I think we've found you somewhere to live," Fidelma said, looking pleased with herself.

"You haven't! Where?"

"The American woman in the flat below Alan has decided to decamp to the South of France. She's had enough of our soft Irish climate apparently! Anyway, Alan had a word with her yesterday and asked her if you could come and see the place. She hasn't even put it on the market yet and if you liked it, she'd be willing to take a bit off the price because she wouldn't have to be paying estate agent's fees."

Jude had always liked where Alan, and now Fidelma as well, lived. The block of apartments was in the heart of Donnybrook in south Dublin with an underground carpark. The windows looked out over well-kept gardens with tall trees that blocked out most of the surrounding houses. She had often been struck by how remarkably quiet and sunny the place was. It would be perfect for work too. She would be able to walk to the studios when the weather got better.

For the first time in months, Jude felt a twinge of anticipation. It would be a lovely place in which to live and it would be good to be near Alan and Fidelma. Up until now, her moving house was because circumstances were forcing her to leave the home in which she and Geoffrey had lived for nearly twenty years. Now it suddenly seemed like a good idea.

"When can I see it?"

"After work today, if you want. She's a writer, so she's there most of the time. I'll give her a ring and warn her." Fidelma put an arm around Jude. "You wait and see! If my life can turn around in the way it has, then so can yours, Jude. Things are going to get better and better for you. I promise!"

* * *

It seemed that her friend's prognosis for the future was proving accurate. The morning after looking over the Donnybrook apartment and saying a loud and definite 'yes' to buying it, Jude got a phone call from someone high up in RTVI. She was to receive an award for her work on the current affairs programme.

After she'd hung up, she stood in the hall, arms crossed, hands on her shoulders, trying to take it all in. She would be forty-seven in one month's time. She listed the minuses: no husband, daughter gone, son going, dog missing. The pluses: a beautiful new home that she could just about afford, good friends, an apparently successful career, even if she did prefer her old one and . . .Well, she reckoned she'd concentrate on those three for the moment.

Jude had got better at not constantly thinking about Geoffrey. She still missed him at odd times. It would come at her out of the blue, unexpectedly – a sudden pang of remorse that was a physical pain that almost made her catch her breath. Every now and then, she asked herself if there hadn't been something more she could have done to save her marriage.

When she'd mentioned this to Fidelma, her friend had laughed scornfully.

"Don't be daft, Jude! Geoffrey had made his mind up that it wasn't going to work. There wasn't anything you or anyone else could have done to change things. Just be glad that you're out of it." She'd given her a mischievous look. "You might surprise yourself. Now that you're a liberated woman again, you could just fall in love with some one new. There *are* a few honourable men still out there, you know!"

The idea filled Jude with horror. She wasn't going to put herself at risk in that way ever again.

She was, however, determined not to wallow in self-pity. She'd seen it happen with other women. She still wept occasionally for the loss of her husband, although she knew that what she had said to him, in the kitchen, weeks earlier, was painfully true. His actions meant that he had lost her respect as well as her love.

Jude was glad to see that although there had been harsh words spoken between them, Geoffrey had made a point of keeping in touch with Flora and Oscar.

Flora, with her newfound self-confidence had remarked to her mother over the phone a few days earlier.

"I told Dad I thought what he'd done to you was rubbish but I said I still loved him – although things weren't ever going to be quite the same again."

"What did your dad say?" Jude asked cautiously.

"He agreed – more or less – and he said he loved me too."

Thank God for that! Jude was more relieved than she let on. Why should the children have that bond broken between them and their father just because everything had gone pear-shaped between their parents?

Oscar said very little but Jude knew from things he let slip that he was seeing his father in the house near the studios where Geoffrey was temporarily living with an old schoolfriend.

When her son realised that she knew he was visiting him, he went to great pains to explain that he wouldn't have gone there if Sonia had been around.

"It's quite all right, Oz. I'm glad you're seeing each other," Jude reassured him.

She knew her husband well enough to know that he was probably suffering more than she was. Guilt did not make an easy bedfellow. She also guessed that Geoffrey would be at pains not to say anything critical or hurtful about her to them – not that Oscar or Flora would have let him get away with it if he'd tried. However hurt or angry she herself had felt, Jude had been adamant that she would not belittle him in any way in front of them. There had been times though when she'd been grateful for the safety valve of Fidelma's friendship. You could say anything to her and she'd understand and never repeat the unrepeatable bits to anyone else. Her ability to patiently listen, to sympathise and then to gently prod Jude in the right direction made her worth her weight in gold.

In fact, thought Jude, as she stood alone in the hallway of the quiet house, it was quite possible that Fidelma was right. Perhaps the pinprick of light at the other end of the tunnel wasn't the light of an oncoming train after all!

The following morning, she arrived at work, more positive than she'd felt for months.

She made her way through the security doors and up the flight of stairs to where Alan was usually to be found first thing in the morning in the large open-plan office. As she entered the room, she saw that, not only was he not as his desk, but everything was eerily quiet. Usually there was a constant background noise of people chatting before settling down to the day's work, conversations on phones and the intermittent tapping of keyboards.

A small group were huddled around one of the desks near Alan's. Jude thought how pale they looked in the harsh light from the strip lighting on the ceiling. Several faces turned to look at her as she approached.

"Everything's very quiet in here today," she remarked cheerfully. "What's the matter? Has someone died?"

A producer from the drama department came over, hands tightly clasped in front of her. It struck Jude that her face looked unusually careworn.

In a voice that was almost a whisper the woman said, "Fidelma Joyce died last night. Alan went home late and found her lying on the bedroom floor." She swallowed hard. "He phoned for an ambulance immediately but she died before it got there."

Chapter Twenty-one

Afterwards, Jude couldn't remember much about packing up the house and getting ready to move into the new apartment. Fidelma's death and Alan's desolate dignity, both during and after the funeral, left her feeling more saddened than ever. Whenever she saw him, she floundered around, trying to come up with something to say that might give some small measure of consolation and comfort.

For Jude, the gap Fidelma left was a source of almost constant grief. She could barely imagine what Alan was feeling. He seemed to be on automatic pilot, refusing to take time away from the studios, burying himself in his work.

After beginning to feel more optimistic, Jude now felt that she was drifting in treacherous waters, far from anything solid to which she could anchor herself. There seemed to be no safe haven any more. With all the pictures taken down and most things in boxes, the house had lost its feeling of homeliness. Now, it was just a roof and four walls – a temporary staging-post where she snatched a few hours' broken sleep before moving on.

At other times, it was as if life had become rather like some deadly game of chess in which, one by one, the pieces were being removed by an invisible opponent. It had started with the loss of her mother, then the father who disowned her, her husband, her home, the departure of her children – Oscar was leaving after Christmas – and then this final taking away of someone whom she'd known since childhood – a dear friend, whom she realised now, she had loved and, sometimes, taken for granted. The thought of never seeing Fidelma again was unimaginable.

Jude had left the studios to look for Alan as soon as she heard the news. Realising that she couldn't afford to begin to think about the implications of Fidelma's death just then – if she did that, Jude knew that she would go to pieces – she also knew that she had to find the man who had, in Fidelma's own words, 'turned her life around' and, in the process, had his own life transformed.

Alan's mobile rang out, as did the phone in his apartment. When she got back to the apartments, his car was parked in the underground carpark, so she knew that he must be somewhere near.

In the end, she found him sitting, hunched into his coat, in the nearby park. There had been a hard frost the night before and the ground was still white where the low winter sun hadn't yet reached. He seemed to Jude to have aged in one night. His usually relaxed face and air of wry amusement, as he regarded the world around him, now looked as though it had been used as a punch-ball. When she saw the heavy bags under his eyes and the furrows on his forehead and on either side of his mouth, Jude wasn't sure if she should approach him. But his face was pinched from the cold and he looked as though he might well have been sitting there for some time. She was beginning to feel frozen herself, her hands and feet starting to feel numb. She couldn't just turn away and leave him there. Jude walked over to the seat, the frozen grass crackling under her feet.

The sound of her footsteps roused him. He raised his head slowly. It took a few seconds before he seemed to be able to focus and recognise her standing in front of him. He gave her a tired smile.

"You never think this sort of unthinkable thing will happen, do you?"

Jude sat down beside him and took hold of one of his icy hands.

"Alan, I'm so, so sorry."

He turned towards her and Jude saw that his eyes looked almost as though they were bleeding, they were so red and raw.

"God! Jude, so am I! I would have done anything in my power to protect her. There was no sign of anything being wrong. I don't understand . . . she looked so well – and so happy."

"She *was* happy. Fidelma told me just a few days ago that she'd never imagined she could be so happy. Alan, *what* happened?"

"They told me at the hospital that they were pretty sure she'd had an aneurism that suddenly burst in her brain." He put a hand up to his swollen eyes and said in a choked voice, "Because she hadn't been unwell before she died, they're going to have to do a post mortem." He looked at Jude, his face strangely contorted. "They're going to cut her open and . . . the whole thing is just ghastly. I can't bear the thought of what they'll do to her." He gave a shuddering sigh and put his other hand, which looked ivory-coloured from the cold, on top of hers. "I'm sorry, Jude. You and she were very close and here's me wailing into the darkness, full of self-pity. Forgive me."

"There's nothing to forgive, dearest Alan." Jude gave his hand a squeeze. "Please come inside and get warm."

He shook his head. "I *can't* go back to the apartment. Not yet. I stopped thinking of it as mine almost as soon as she moved in. Her imprint is everywhere. I know that everywhere I turn, she'll be there."

Jude thought of how much pleasure Fidelma had had in making the place less like an untidy bachelor pad; whether it was choosing a beautiful vase for the living-room or a rug for their bedroom or just buying flowers to brighten a corner of the apartment.

"Then come home with me. Most things are in boxes ready for the move but there are still chairs to sit on and I can light the fire and switch on the central heating." Jude gripped his hand more tightly. "Please, Alan. It's freezing and you're in shock. You need to be somewhere warm."

For a moment he stayed where he was, head bowed. Then he made a slight movement of acquiescence with his hand, too exhausted to say anything more or to argue with her.

Slowly, as though every part of him ached, he stood and walked stiffly back to her car with her. Even though they walked side by side, it seemed to Jude that he was moving within a separate space of his own that isolated him from her and the other figures hurrying along the pavement around them. She guessed that the same feeling of unreality she was experiencing affected the way he saw the world around him. If he was capable of seeing anything at all at the moment.

* * *

As much as he could, Oscar had helped his almost silent mother to continue packing up the house. He had never seen her so distracted. It was as though the real Jude were no longer present – just her body going through the motions, doing what was necessary and no more. He saw that she was hardly eating and it often took several attempts to catch her attention. When he asked a question, it would have to be repeated at least once before she replied. He gave up asking what she wanted put into the various boxes. He did his best to guess how she would like it done and hoped he had more or less got things right. Flora too appeared, contrite that she hadn't been to the house for so long. Even Geoffrey rang Jude and told her how sorry he was to hear about Fidelma and if there was anything he could do . . . But she didn't want his help or his sympathy. Not now.

Half the furniture had been put into storage for when he moved into his own apartment during the following month. She hadn't asked and wasn't interested in knowing if Sonia was joining him there. Jude was glad for him to take his favourite pictures, ornaments and what he wanted from the bookshelves. As far as she was concerned, the more he took the better. There would be less for her to pack up. The house had become too full of objects – things that they'd acquired over years of marriage, things that held memories of them together, as a couple. Now, she knew she neither wanted them nor would miss them. She was certain that, in the future, what she needed was less clutter in her life.

* * *

Alan stayed with Jude and Oscar until after Fidelma's cremation. At first, he had been a quiet presence in the house, barely speaking – it was almost like having a gentle ghost wandering around the place. Slowly, he began to talk when Oscar was out and he and Jude were alone. He had always been the sort of man who was more interested in other people than in himself. Even now, he turned his attention on Jude. She could see that by trying to cheer her up, he hoped to avoid dwelling on his own grief.

"Will you do something for me?" he asked her a few days after the cremation. "It's something I really can't face myself. I know it's a lot to ask, Jude, but would you deal with Fidelma's clothes?"

Much as she dreaded the task, Jude agreed. She spent a miserable morning alone in his apartment, packing away her friend's clothes into bags, helping to erase this part of Alan's life, hoping to minimise what could only be another source of pain for him.

The next day, he asked her if she would go with him to Glendalough to scatter Fidelma's ashes on the lake.

They drove out into the Wicklow Mountains in Jude's car, Alan sitting beside her, carefully holding the small grey urn between his large hands. It had been raining heavily and the waters of the lake were a steely grey under the thick low clouds. Walking to the end of the small wooden jetty, they stood looking out over the lake to the head of the valley that was shrouded in skeins of drifting mist. All around them there was the sound of water running, dripping from the trees, gurgling around the half-hidden rocks in the small river to their left. On this cold December day, where the only colours seemed to be grey and brown, there was no one else around. Even the sheep that usually grazed near the lake had disappeared.

Lifting the urn over the water, he tipped the contents out. A sudden gust of wind lifted the ashes into the air so that, for a moment, they swirled, suspended in front of them before another flurry of air caught them and they disappeared, swallowed up by sky and lake.

For a few minutes they stood, side by side, in silence. Though in tears, Jude tried hard to make it a moment of affirmation, of celebration of her friend's too short life. She was suddenly aware of Alan's hand on her arm.

"Fidelma would have liked that ending, I think."

She gave him a watery smile and nodded dumbly.

After giving one last lingering look at the lake, he led her back towards the pine-needle-strewn path above them. "Come on, we'll go and have a drink in her honour in the hotel in the village and then you can take me back to the apartment. It's time I stopped behaving like a coward and faced the future," he said in a tired voice.

Jude could not think of anyone less cowardly than this tall, gentle man with the craggy face. She was well aware of how he was fighting to maintain his composure as he stood beside her, his grey hair blowing untidily in the wind.

She couldn't help noticing how he avoided too much eye contact with her. By doing that, she wouldn't be able to see the pain in them. Jude knew that the last thing he wanted was her pity.

* * *

The day before she and Oscar moved out of the house, Jude had an unexpected visitor. When the doorbell rang, it was already dark. She had only just got in. She was tired and certainly not feeling in the mood for visitors. But as she was standing in the hall with the light on, she could hardly pretend not to be home. Unwillingly, she opened the front door. The wrinkled face of Doris Leach peered in at her, reminding Jude of an apple that had been stored for too long, all elasticity shrunk from its skin. Blinking a little in the light from the hall and without waiting to be invited, she stepped inside.

"Thought I'd come and see that things was all going ahead," she announced breathily. "No problems then?"

Jude shut the door.

"No problems. We will be out by lunch-time tomorrow, as agreed."

"Right! That's good." Miss Leach pulled off her woollen gloves and unwound the scarf from her neck. Jude watched, fascinated. The scarf seemed to go on forever. Obviously the woman was planning to stay for a while.

"I was just going to have something to eat," Jude said tentatively, hoping that might encourage the other to say what it was she wanted to say and to then go and leave her to take off her shoes and have her supper in front of the fire in peace.

"That sounds just the ticket!" said Miss Leach with enthusiasm. "Thanks. I could do with a bite to eat."

Some situations are not worth battling against. Sometimes it is easier to give in gracefully. Jude decided that this was one of those times. She led Doris Leach into the kitchen and installed her in a chair by the radiator.

The woman held her hands out over it appreciatively. "Wonderful thing – central heating, ain't it?"

"It is," agreed Jude, putting a covered dish into the microwave. "I'm having some stew and couscous. Does that suit you?"

"Yeah, I'm partial to a bit of couscous."

Jude was surprised. Still, if bag ladies could buy houses, why couldn't they also enjoy a wide range of cuisine?

She glanced over to where the woman sat, gazing raptly at the radiator, tapping its sides, testing to see just how hot it was with her fingertips. She had unbuttoned her jacket to reveal a bulging stomach. But the woolly hat was still firmly in place. Jude wondered if she ever took it off to wash. Perhaps she wore it in bed. The woman looked over to where Jude stood, boiling a kettle of water for the couscous.

"Ate it when I was in Africa, didn't I?" she said suddenly.

"You were in Africa?" Jude tried not to sound surprised by this piece of information.

"Africa, America, Tibet – all sorts of places. Couscous is nothing to get excited about, compared to wot I've had dished up to me in some of the places I've been. Mind you, there's nothing quite so nasty as yak milk. That give me the runs for days, that did."

Jude was longing to ask how someone who had ended up apparently living the life of a bag lady in a Dublin suburb had also managed to be a world traveller but she didn't want to either patronise or offend her guest.

"You come from England, don't you?"

"That's right! London. Born just down the road from Billingsgate fish market, I was." She gave Jude a speculative look. "S'pect you're wondering how come I got the money to buy this house, ain't yer?" Jude wasn't sure what to say. The woman continued. "When you had a dad like mine, wot spent half his time in jug and the other half living it up, you learned to put a bit of money by for a rainy day. Mind you," she said with a small chuckle, "we never knew he was going to win the football pools on top of all his other little – business dealings, did we? *That* came as a bit of a surprise, I can tell you. Me mum never really got over the shock." She gazed up at the ceiling with an amused look on her face. It was as though the warmth of the room and the promise of food had a relaxing effect and made her more inclined to talk. "Put it all in the bank, he did, while he thought about what he wanted to do with it. Before he had the chance to do anything, didn't he get run over by a bus?" The microwave pinged inappropriately. Jude opened the door and took out the stew and placed the couscous inside. So, Doris Leach's dad had made a killing on the pools! She wondered how his daughter had managed to get her hands on any of it. "Me mum died of a broken heart they said," continued the woman, "but I think it was too much Guinness. I didn't have no brothers an' sisters. So there I was, alone at twenty and all the money in the world."

"And you decided to see the world?"

"I thought, Doris me girl, now's the time to do a bit of travellin' before yer luck runs out and you're skint again." She glanced at Jude. "When you live in the East End of London, you don't take good luck for granted. It's best not to count on it lasting."

"But you obviously didn't use all the money up," ventured Jude.

Doris Leach gave her a mischievous look. "I didn't, did I?" There was a silence in the room. As though taking pity on Jude, she added, "Invested, didn't I? Got good advice and made one or two little investments. You see, the thing was, I knew I wouldn't be twenty all me life. I knew one day I'd want to stop movin' around and be warm and comfortable." She gave a little laugh, as though appreciating her forethought. "There comes a time when the cold starts to get into yer bones. Oh, I reckon I owe meself a bit of comfort before I pop me clogs." She gave a small nod, as if in agreement with herself.

Jude couldn't stop herself from asking, "So you never married?"

The only response she got for being so inquisitive was a snort of annoyance, followed by a sharp glare from the bright blue eyes.

Feeling accused of asking an obscene question, Jude carried their supper into the sitting-room where they sat down on either side of the fire. The woman hardly spoke while she ate, concentrating on the food, shovelling it in with apparent relish. When she had wiped her plate clean with a piece of bread, she put it down carefully on the carpet beside her and gave a small burp of satisfaction. Leaning back against the cushion, she folded her hands across her stomach and looked over at Jude.

"I heard you lost yer dog."

Jude thought guiltily that she had almost forgotten about Plunkett's absence. So much else had happened since he disappeared.

"Yes, I'm afraid we did. He seems to have vanished into thin air."

"Doesn't sound very likely to me," commented the other woman, dryly. "Things the size of him don't vanish, in my experience."

"You haven't seen him or heard anything about where he might be?"

"He could still turn up," replied Miss Leach in a vague voice. She suddenly got to her feet. "Right! Thanks for the food. Very nice it was too. I must be off now."

Curiosity welled up in Jude.

"Can I give you a lift to . . . wherever you're going?"

Again that slight, crooked smile of amusement as though the woman knew exactly what Jude was thinking. "Nah, I don't need no lift. Thanks all the same."

When she stood on the doorstep, buttoned, gloved and scarf re-wound around her almost non-existent neck, the woman said, "Right! See yer tomorra, then. Goodnight!" and strode off into the darkness.

* * *

On the following morning, when the doorbell gave a sustained peal, Catriona looked at Jude and Oscar and laughed.

"That must be herself. No one else with manners on them would ring like that one!"

When she opened the door, an unexpected sight greeted them.

A slightly out-of-breath Doris Leach was holding onto a length of rope. Attached to the other end was a very thin and bedraggled red setter, its ribs clearly visible through its tangled coat.

"Plunkett!" they all exclaimed in unison.

The woman and dog stepped into the hall.

"Wherever did you find him, Miss Leach?" asked Jude in amazement.

"I got friends. I asked around. Had a hunch where he was."

"Where was he?" said Oscar.

"Less said the better," replied the woman, giving him a sideways glance. She looked down at the dog, who wagged his tail at her. Since his arrival, he'd shown no interest in any of the Larchets. Doris Leach turned to Jude. "This place you're movin' to – fancy flat, is it?"

"I'm moving into an apartment, yes."

"Will they let you keep a dog?"

Oscar and Flora looked at their mother, who was standing with jaw dropped and hand up to her mouth in disbelief at her stupidity.

"I never even thought of that. I'm such an idiot!" She turned to the others. "What on *earth* are we going to do?"

They stared blankly at each other. When nobody seemed able to come up with any sensible suggestions, Miss Leach cleared her throat.

"Seems to me that you shouldn't have a dog if you forget about him that easy." Once again, they looked at each

301

other, uncomfortable at the truth of what she'd said. "I'll take him. I like dogs. They're a darn sight nicer than humans, that's for sure. Right!" Decision made, she threw a sharp look in Catriona's direction. "You, girl!" Jude could see the 'girl' bridling. Miss Leach continued. "I'll need someone to do a bit of cleaning up. I got plans for this place."

Oscar was fascinated. "What sort of plans, Miss Leach?"

She gave him a quick look and then, because he looked genuinely interested, she said, "I got friends who aren't as lucky as wot I am. So, some of them are moving in with me. And that means," she said, fixing Catriona again with a beady eye, "that means I'll not say no to a bit of help from time to time. Cat got yer tongue?" Catriona was looking more spaced-out than Jude had ever seen her. "I'll give yer ten pounds an hour. Take it or leave it."

Ten pounds an hour was nearly twice what Jude Larchet paid Catriona.

"You won't want to be catching buses into the flat in Donnybrook," Jude reminded her gently.

"I'll take it, so," said Catriona in a weak voice. "But just for a trial run, like – until we are sure it's working out OK," she added hastily.

"Right! That's settled then."

When they left, Catriona was in the kitchen brewing up tea with Miss Leach, moving around her warily as though a little nervous of what the woman was going to say next. It was obvious to Jude that she wasn't quite sure she'd made the right decision.

Before shutting the front door for the last time, she

heard Doris Leach telling Catriona to turn up the central heating.

"Me an' the dog need a bit more heat, we do."

She had an idea that Plunkett was going to live very happily indeed in the new set-up.

"Will Catriona be all right with her?" asked Flora as they climbed into the car, squeezing into the gaps among the last of the smaller boxes and table lamps.

"I think they'll both be just fine," said Jude, smiling. "I'd love to be a fly on the wall while they're getting to know each other, though."

Flora looked at her mother. "Do you mind that she's going to turn it into a drop-in centre for . . ."

"For bag ladies?" said Jude, as she switched on the engine. "No, I don't. In fact, I think it's a great idea. She'd be the perfect woman for the job. I can't see her putting up with any nonsense from anyone."

Flora broke into a broad grin. "Can you *imagine* what Gran would say?"

They all looked at each other and laughed.

"You never know! The new and improved version mightn't mind too much," suggested Jude.

"Somehow, Ma, I *don't* think so!" said Flora with a giggle. She had a sudden picture of her grandmother's bewildered ghost, dodging around an untidy collection of tramps and hobos and wailing in a plaintive voice, 'I don't want to complain – but . . .'

* * *

"Nice place," remarked the removal man as he dumped the

last of the boxes on top of an already alarmingly high stack of containers and tea chests that balanced precariously on top of what would, one day, revert to being Jude's dining-room table.

"This is a really deadly apartment, Mum."

Flora leaned over various objects to get a better view out of the window at the gardens one storey below.

The midday sun streamed in through the large living-room windows. It was one of the things Jude had immediately fallen in love with, the way the apartment always seemed to be so full of light. Even in the Irish winter, the walls appeared to be luminous with its reflected rays. The sheen on the light oak floors and absence of any curtains added to the feeling of airy spaciousness.

Like on her first visit there with Alan and Fidelma, Jude felt a little jolt of pleasure. Even though Oscar would be leaving after Christmas, she allowed herself to hope that it would soon seem like a real home – the refuge that had been missing since her marriage fell apart.

Term had finished and Flora promised that she would be there over Christmas with Oscar and Jude.

"We'll make it into a special one," she said, at the same time wondering if her mother was ill or not. She looked so very pale these days. "We could ask Alan to come down for Christmas Day."

"I don't know if that's such a good idea, Flo. He's got elderly parents over in Mayo. He'll probably want to spend Christmas with them.

"But we *will* make it a nice Christmas," insisted her daughter. "You wait and see! Oz and me are going to shell out for the tree. The decorations must be somewhere around," she said, looking doubtfully at the mountains of boxes piled up against the walls.

Jude gave her a reassuring smile.

"It will be lovely. Don't worry!"

Although she was determined to look and sound positive, secretly, she found herself wishing that Christmas would just go away.

Chapter Twenty-two

"You will have to hire a dinner jacket for it," Jude warned her son over hot chocolate and croissants with apricot jam.

They were having what the Larchets had always called 'one of their French breakfasts'. They all remembered, with great affection, a family holiday they'd spent in a *gîte* in the Languedoc when Flora and Oscar were small. Every morning, a battered van would pull up in the narrow road outside the house and sound its klaxon – a noise that sounded remarkably like a cow in labour. The children would rush outside and buy fresh croissants from the smiling van driver. As marmalade was unheard of in the little village, apricot jam was then spread liberally over the warm mouthfuls of croissant instead.

They still carried on the tradition, relishing it as an occasional Saturday morning treat.

"I don't mind. I'm sure Dad will lend me a black tie."

"Dad will be using his. Don't forget, he's getting an award too."

"Oh, would you mind buying one for me, Mum? It's just that I spent more than I meant to on Ellen's Christmas present." He looked at her pleadingly over the top of his hot chocolate. "I'll pay you back. Promise!"

"But, of course," said his mother, gravely. "I'd better give you the money today. After all, the award dinner is only a week away."

She knew perfectly well that he meant what he said at that moment of promising to pay her back, but from past experience, it was unlikely that he would remember. His part-time job at the local garage didn't pay all that well and although Ellen was the most undemanding girlfriend he'd ever had, she knew he'd gone way over the top with the silver pendant he had bought for her. He would make someone a very generous husband one day, she decided, watching him as he downed the last of his chocolate. Jude was amused by her thoughts. *I'm starting to sound middle-aged to myself. Is that how other people see me?* she wondered.

Oscar leaned over and gave Jude a kiss on the cheek. Then he sat back in his chair and surveyed the room with pride. He had done nearly all the arranging of the furniture, with the odd suggestion from his mother. The old brown couch had transferred itself to the new accommodation fairly gracefully and the pale apricot and coffee rugs looked good on the oak floor. They had bought new ivory-coloured lampshades for the table lamps and new cream and apricot cushions that perfectly matched the recently hung curtains.

"The place looks great, doesn't it?"

Jude glanced at the stack of bulging cardboard boxes of

books that still stood along one of the walls. She hadn't had the time or the energy to sort them out, even though the shelves were dusted and waiting on either side of the gas fire with its imitation coals. That was the only thing she hadn't liked about the apartment. She missed the sound of the blazing fires they used to sit around in the old house when Geoff was . . . *Stop!* commanded the voice. *That's all in the past. You have to move on. The place looks terrific.* I know. I'm doing my best, she assured it.

"Mum?"

Jude looked at him blankly. "What?"

"I said the place looked great," Oscar repeated, patiently.

"Yes, Oz. It does. It's looking really nice. I'll pull myself together and make a start on the books this afternoon. Flo has threatened to come round and help – plus new boyfriend."

"Poor sod!"

"Oz!"

"Well, I suppose anyone who can keep my sister happy is to be congratulated. Though, from the way she usually treats them, he's got his work cut out for him. I wonder how long he'll last."

"Just because you and Ellen are love's young dream doesn't mean that you can't be happy for her."

He grinned. "Don't worry, Mum! I'll be kind! Charity is my middle name." He swallowed the last mouthful of croissant and stood up. "Anyway, me and Ellen are off to the races this afternoon – so I won't be around to say the wrong thing."

"I hope you won't be putting on any enormous bets."

"Just a very small one – or two," he said, teasing her.

"You never know, I might have a win and then I can refund you for the tie!"

After he had disappeared back to his room, Jude remained sitting at the table. She gazed out of the window at the leafless lime trees and wondered what Alan was doing in the apartment above.

It was now three weeks since Fidelma's death. Although everyone at work still tried to be careful about what they said when he was around, inevitably her name cropped up or there was a mention of the programme she'd been working on as a researcher. When this happened, Jude noticed that, superficially, he handled it well, carrying on with whatever he was doing without showing any emotion. But she knew that he spent long hours on his own in the apartment he had shared with Fidelma, listening to music or working at his computer. He repeatedly refused people's well-meant invitations to go for a drink or a meal. Jude had tried to persuade him to go with her to the cinema to see a film by one of his favourite French directors. He had shaken his head and kissed her lightly on the cheek.

"Be patient with me, Jude. I need more time to gather myself together again. I'm not quite there yet."

"As long as you *promise* you'll come down whenever you do want to talk, share a bottle of wine or eat – or just sit companionably while I arrange flowers. Whatever!" she'd said.

"I promise," he replied with a smile. "But you know how it is. In the same way that you can't force yourself to love someone just because they need your love, neither can you make yourself let go of the person you love because people tell you that's the only sensible thing to do. How can I?

The first thing I think of when I wake in the morning is Fidelma. She's with me throughout the day and she's the last thing I think about before I sleep. When I manage to get to sleep, she's there in my dreams." He grimaced unconsciously. "She'll always be there until I can somehow learn to let go." He put his hand up to his eyes, rubbing them wearily. "Only I'm not sure that I *want* to let go, Jude. There won't ever be another woman like her. I don't want to forget any tiny detail of how she was or what we had together."

She'd found herself mouthing the usual platitudes about having to move on, that Fidelma would want him to be happy, that there was a life out there that still had to be lived. However, her encouragement had a hollow ring to it, for a lot of the time Jude was finding it difficult to follow her own advice.

He hadn't come down and, apart from snatched glimpses of him during the working day, Jude hadn't spent any time alone with Alan since their visit to Glendalough at the start of December.

Now, sitting at the table, she half-heard Oscar in his room, talking on his mobile, making final arrangements with Ellen for the afternoon. It was good that they were so fond of each other. Hopefully, Flora's new man would be good for her too. Experience of previous encounters with her daughter's boyfriends had made Jude learn not to expect anything too run-of-the-mill or normal. Up until now, 'normal' in men had been classed as deadly boring and strictly to be avoided by Flora. So it was quite possible that she would appear with a tattooed, bracelet-wearing guy in tow, who wore rings in strange and painful places and who quite possibly didn't even speak English. Jude remembered the charming but silent Chinese student who used to follow Flora around in a state of almost constant bewilderment and the pot-smoking Rastafarian who smelled as though he needed less dope and more time spent giving himself a good scrub in a bath.

Licking her finger and dabbing at crumbs of croissant on her plate, Jude turned her thoughts to the award dinner on the following Friday. She was touched that Oscar appeared genuinely pleased at being asked to escort her. She sucked the end of her finger thoughtfully. There had been unsubtle hints dropped by various people at the studios about several possible candidates for the job but she felt more comfortable at the thought of going with her son. She supposed she could have asked Alan but Jude was pretty sure, even if he'd accepted, it would have been to please her, not because he wanted to be there.

It was funny, she thought, that both she and Geoffrey were to receive awards on the same evening, at the same event. The documentary before last that he had made about homeless children had caused a big stir, and some controversy.

As he'd said at the time of the screening for the cast and crew, "The more controversial the better. They might remember it for longer than just the usual five minutes."

'They' had been a reference to, not just the public or the politicians, but the powers that be in RTVI.

She wondered if he would be taking Sonia to the award dinner. Inevitably, that made Jude start to think about what she should wear. Unlike the evening when she had gone to see Flora's play, this time, she would be dressing to please herself, not her husband – or his mistress. She looked down at her wedding ring. Why was she still wearing it? Protection from lurking males who didn't know that she was separated? Habit? Nostalgia? She tested it to see how easily it would come off. Forgetting that she had lost weight over the past few months, she was surprised at the speed with which it slid along her finger. It was so unexpected that she dropped the ring on the floor. Jude watched as it spun for a moment before finally tilting over and falling flat beside one of the rugs. For several minutes, she left it there. Suddenly she bent down and scooped it up into her hand. Walking quickly out into the small hallway, Jude went into her bedroom. She opened a drawer and, without looking, dropped the ring in among the clutter of scarves and belts, then she shut the drawer with a bang.

Another defining moment, she thought to herself, glancing down at her left hand. The ring-finger seemed thinner where the wedding ring had once been. The skin was definitely paler too. It felt strange not to be wearing it. She realised that it was the first time she had removed it since she and Geoffrey had married in the sombre chapel in Trinity College all those years ago.

She glanced at her reflection in the mirror. Did she feel any different? Sadder, wiser, more liberated? Ambivalent seemed to be the most suitable word to pop into her mind. She leaned forward and took a closer look at herself. God! What a mess! Make-up would mask some of the shadow under her eyes. She turned sideways, realising that she hadn't looked at herself properly for months. Her breasts that had always been small now seemed to be non-existent. Jude turned and faced the mirror straight on. As she looked at herself, the thought struck her that she was possibly the most unsexy, unfeminine, unappealing woman she'd seen around in a long time.

Feeling suddenly weepy, she wrenched a paper handkerchief out of the box and blew her nose hard. Well, tough! She'd got enough on her plate without getting all tired and emotional about her appearance. She was about to leave the room when, on a sudden impulse, Jude turned back to the mirror. Slowly, she let down her hair and for the first time in a long while, brushed it until it was smooth and untangled. When she'd finished, she put it up again carefully. Then she rubbed moisturiser into her skin and put on a small amount of eye-shadow and mascara. She peered at herself again. That would have to bloody well do for now! But as she left the room, Jude had to admit to herself that she felt a little better.

* * *

At the start of the following week, violent storms rolled in from the Altantic. From Galway to Dublin and Waterford up to Belfast the news was full of stories about flooded fields and houses, stranded cars, trees uprooted and roofs blown away. On the Tuesday night, Jude got back from the studios to find that there was no electricity. The apartment was cold and dark. She couldn't remember where she'd put the candles or even if there were any.

She stood, undecided, in the middle of the living-room. She supposed she could always go and search for a restaurant that hadn't been affected by the power cut but she wasn't feeling hungry.

Every now and then, car lights on the nearby road

flashed past, lighting up the bare branches in the gardens outside and making brief, moving shadows on the wall beside her. Oscar was away in Dublin for the night, staying with a friend. Jude wondered if she should go up to the flat above. She didn't want to disturb Alan but at least she might be able to borrow a torch or a candle.

There was no answer to her first knock. There was the sound of a door closing inside the apartment so she knew that he was there. She tried again and waited. When there was still no response, she turned and started to make her way back towards the stairs in the eerie glow of the emergency lighting. She didn't hear the door opening. Just as she reached the top step, Alan called out to her.

"Can I help you, Jude?"

He stood with the door half-open, a candle in one hand. As she walked towards him, she saw that he was looking haggard. The shadows cast by the flickering light accentuated the grooves in his face.

Without thinking, she exclaimed, "Alan! You look dreadful!" When he didn't reply, Jude asked, "May I come in, just for a moment? I was hoping to scrounge a candle off you."

He opened the door wider and let her in. Once inside, he led her into the living-room and put the candle down on the table. He indicated a collection of candles in various containers. Their combined light was surprisingly bright. Jude could see that the room was untidy, with books and scripts strewn around the place. Articles of clothing lay over the back of the couch and wineglasses and plates and mugs littered the floor and covered the smaller table by the window.

"Help yourself. As you can see, there are plenty to choose from."

Jude immediately remembered how Fidelma had loved candlelight and how she and Alan often used to eat in the gentle glow of several candles.

"I've even managed to introduce Alan to the idea of having a bath with me, surrounded by scented candles," she'd told Jude gleefully a few weeks before her death. "He thought I was off my trolley at first but I think he's quite come round to the idea!"

"I'm sorry to intrude, Alan," Jude said gently. Something about him made her feel that perhaps it was a good thing she had. She had never seen him looking so desolate. "Is there *anything* I can do?"

For a moment he stared at her, then he suddenly seemed to collapse against the wall. It looked to her as though the fight had gone out of him, as though all his reserves had been used up.

"I don't know if I can go on like this," he said in a voice that was devoid of emotion.

She moved quickly over to him, putting her arms around him. Holding him tightly, Jude rested her cheek against his shoulder.

"Don't give up! Please, don't do that," she whispered.

With his eyes closed, he said, "I always thought of myself as self-sufficient before I met Fidelma. At first, I considered our relationship to be a joyous, unexpected bonus in my life – something that would probably not last forever but I was just content to be with her and let the future take care of itself. Now, when it's too late, I know that she was the one person with whom I wanted to spend

315

the rest of my life – with whom I *could* have spent the rest of my life. I'm not the same person I was before I met her. I'm sure she didn't mean to – but loving her has changed me – so that now I feel that I'm not capable of being independent and self-reliant any more. It's pathetic, I know but I just feel appalled at the thought of all the days stretching ahead of me, on and on, into the future without her."

Jude didn't know how to comfort him. It was painful to see him reduced to this state. Silently, she continued to hold him.

All of a sudden, he lifted his head and said, "Would you come to bed with me?" Feeling her suddenly tense against him, he added quickly, "Not to make love, dear Jude. Would you hold me? It's just I need us to lie together and be close." He looked at her intently and, for the first time, gave a small smile. "And I'm so bloody cold – it might warm me up a little!"

So they had undressed and lain together in the bed that he had shared with Fidelma. After a while, they both fell asleep, waking in the middle of the night. For a long time, Jude listened while Alan talked. He spoke about the plans he and Fidelma had made for the future, of the fun they'd had on the few precious weekends they had spent together, away from Dublin and work. Finally, he spoke of his love for the dead woman. And then he wept – terrible, wild, shuddering sobs that seemed to shake his whole body. Jude held him in her arms until, exhausted, he fell asleep, with no tears left to shed.

* * *

On the day of the award dinner, Jude woke early, thinking about the evening to come. Today she would receive a token of recognition from her peers. She realised that being given the award was an achievement. So why was she feeling so unenthusiastic about the whole thing? It couldn't be just because everyone would be seeing her husband with another woman on his arm – whereas she would be on Oscar's. Could it? Well, it was certainly a part of it. The ceremony was being televised, which meant that the whole of Ireland, if it was interested, would see that the clever one from that slick current affairs programme wasn't so clever after all. Sure, she couldn't even manage to hang onto her husband – and him with his bit on the side there at his side in full view of everyone with not a bother on her! No shame at all! Not the sort of thing that goes down well with the older generation in rural Ireland – even if it was the year 2000.

She knew that already there had been a mention in the Social and Personal column in one of the national papers about Geoffrey escorting Sonia to some book launch or other. A reporter had rung Jude when she was at work. He'd asked her if it was true that her marriage had broken up.

Realising that it was pointless to lie, she said it had.

"Do you mind telling me what went wrong?"

"Yes, I do mind. It's none of your damned business," she snapped.

"There's no need to get aggressive," complained the man at the other end of the line.

"I disagree. How would you feel if your marriage broke up and someone rang you and wanted a cosy chat about the all the gory details?"

"Well, don't give me the gory details, just general ones," he suggested brightly.

"Not a hope in hell," replied Jude, slamming the phone down.

Their unsatisfactory conversation had been clumsily summarised and printed on an inside page of the sort of paper Jude hoped her friends didn't bother to read.

In the end, she hadn't bought anything new to wear. She decided that she would opt for her favourite black dress. It had a high neck, long sleeves, narrow waist and graceful long skirt and was woven in the softest alpaca. Long silver earrings and silver bracelet, black high heels and the Indian wrap her mother had worn on special occasions, completed the ensemble. She took some time over her make-up and when she'd finished, Jude applied a few squirts of *Givenchy*.

She'd seen Alan only once since she had slipped out of his apartment while it was still dark on the morning after the storm. They'd bumped into each other in the carpark at work. She was relieved to see that he was looking a little better. He had given her a hug.

"Thank you, darling Jude. I feel blessed to have you as a friend. I hope you don't feel that I abused that friendship the other night?"

"Of course I don't! Are you all right?" she'd asked, anxiously.

"More than I have been." He smiled at her. "All that weeping and wailing must have been quite cathartic. Don't worry! I'll survive. We both will."

He had agreed to come down and have a drink with her, Oscar and Flora before Jude and Oscar left for the dinner. Ellen and Flora's boyfriend had also been invited.

Jude liked Dave. Flora had managed to surprise her mother yet again when he had been introduced for the first time at the book-unpacking. Expecting the unusual, the new young man in her daughter's life was spectacularly conventional. His hair was short and shiny. He wore a shirt, sweater and jeans. He didn't drink very much, didn't smoke and didn't do drugs, Flora assured her. He was artistic and worked for an advertising agency in Leeson Street. The thing that Jude most liked about him was the way his rather serious face would break into a broad smile if something amused him. She also liked his zany sense of humour. He seemed to have the ability to look at things from a slightly different angle to everyone else. This alternative approach resulted in a gently ironic view of life that was refreshingly different.

Jude hoped there wasn't a catch. He was almost too good to be true! The most amazing thing of all was that Flora was mad about him. She didn't seem to want to give him the runaround that her previous boyfriends had suffered. For the first time in her life, her daughter appeared to be thinking before she reacted to something said or done, instead of lashing out and acting impulsively.

Oscar was as stunned as Jude by this new sister of his.

"There's hope for us all!" he exclaimed when Flora had given way over an argument in which she'd taken an impossible stand. Before the advent of Dave, she would have lost her temper, shouted and sworn loudly. "I think we should use the new calendar. Forget BC and AD. It's now BD and AD. Before Dave and After Dave!"

"Toe-rag!" his sister had muttered under her breath as she heaved a cushion in his direction.

Jude was glad to see that some things hadn't changed.

Oscar appeared in her bedroom in his hired dinner jacket, a black ribbon dangling from one hand

"Help! Can you do this for me, Mum?"

As Jude tied the bow tie for him, she thought again how like his father Oscar sometimes was. Geoffrey had never mastered the art of tying a bow tie properly either.

When she'd finished, she walked around him, looking him up and down.

"You look *marvellous!* No other word for it."

"So do you!" Oscar watched her as she moved away from him to pick up her evening bag from the dressing-table. He said in a quiet voice, "I'm so proud of you, Mum."

When Alan appeared, he too looked at Jude with pleasure.

"God, Jude! You're an amazing woman." He came over to her and kissed her. Then he turned to Oscar. "You're very lucky to have the chance to be her escort. I hope you realise just how lucky you are."

Oscar laughed. "I'm beginning to feel rather nervous about this evening. It could be dangerous – being seen out with such a glamorous celebrity. They'll all be wondering if you've gone and found yourself a toy boy, Mum!"

"I won't dignify that remark with an answer!" replied his mother.

* * *

The hotel's large banqueting hall was packed with dinner-jacketed men and women in a wide range of, what each of them considered to be, appropriate evening wear. The light from the dozen or so large chandeliers sparkled on sequined dresses and elaborate jewellery.

"Nice to know I'm rubbing shoulders with Dublin's glitterati!" observed Oscar, looking around him, extremely unfazed by it all.

They sat down at their table and Jude introduced her son to the other guests. There seemed to be a mix of award winners, their spouses or partners, journalists and the sort of people who were regularly to be seen in the press attending launches and gala dinners.

Jude watched Oscar as he chatted amiably to a handsome blonde woman on one side of him. She thought how much he'd grown up in the last few months and how handsome he looked. She casually scanned the room for signs of Geoffrey. She soon spotted him sitting at a table, not far from their own, with Sonia at his side. From what Jude could see, the girl had chosen the minimal look for the evening. Her shoulders were bare and her dress had a plunging neckline that showed her long, slim neck off beautifully. Jude wondered if she was wearing any underclothes. The material shimmered as though it were made out of some sort of metallic thread and clung to her body as though moulded to her. They were both engaged in animated conversation with the other people at their table.

Suddenly, as if she sensed that she was being watched, Sonia turned her head, her eyes meeting Jude's. For a brief moment they held each other's gaze. Before the girl turned away again, she gave a small smile of satisfaction. To Jude, it looked as though Sonia wanted to convey the message that Geoffrey was there with her – not Jude – and victory was hers.

The man on Jude's left said something to her and as she turned towards him, she realised that Sonia hadn't succeeded in making her angry. On the contrary. It was the sort of behaviour that she would have expected from the girl and if Geoffrey wanted to be seen in such a very public way in her company, then he fell even lower in her estimation.

Jude smiled at her fellow diner. "Sorry! What did you say?"

When the award ceremony got underway, Geoffrey was one of the first recipients. He stood in the bright television lights and made the sort of short standard speech that everyone approved of – unemotional, factual and amusing. When they thought that he'd finished, he gave a slight inclination of his head towards the table where Jude and Oscar were sitting.

Shielding his eyes from the glare, he said, looking in their direction, "I would just like to add that, without the support and understanding of my wife and family, this project would have been very much more difficult and Jude's suggestions on how to approach some of the more awkward interviews were invaluable." He smiled. "Thank you, Jude."

He walked off the stage amid applause.

Jude could see several heads craning to get a better look at her, wanting to catch a glimpse of her reaction to her ex-husband's unexpected remarks.

"The silly cow won't like *that!*" remarked one of the women sitting on the other side of Jude's table. With eyebrows raised in amusement, she made a gesture towards the far table where Sonia was doing her best not to react to Geoffrey's accolade to his wife. Jude recognised the woman as a production assistant who had worked closely with Alan and Fidelma in the past and also with Sonia.

"Serve her right!" Jude heard someone else mutter.

Oscar touched her arm, looking at her questioningly. "All right, Mum?"

Jude smiled. "I feel fine," she assured him.

And, she realised, she was telling the truth. It was nice that Geoffrey had gone to the trouble of saying what he had. Especially as it must have been difficult when he knew quite a few of those present considered Jude to be the injured party. But also because he must have known that his remarks would cause friction between himself and Sonia.

However, that was his problem, she told herself firmly.

And when she stood up to walk the short distance to the stage, Jude felt an extraordinary sensation of walking on air – as though a whole host of worries had fallen from her shoulders. As she took the elegant glass trophy from the smiling Director General, she felt that something fundamental had changed. Perhaps Oscar was right when he'd said that they should be measuring time in Life After Dave. Or should it be, 'Life After Geoffrey'?

Suddenly, she realised that she *was* capable of putting the past behind her. This was the first day of that new life. Jude didn't doubt that it would be difficult but, just now, standing in the light with the enthusiastic applause rolling around her, she really didn't mind.

The End

Also published by Poolbeg

Diving Through Clouds

NICOLA LINDSAY

Kate Fitzgerald's spirit hovers above her hospital bed,
looking down on her body lying still now.

In the days following her death she finds herself far from
extinguished but in some sort of limbo with unfinished
business to attend to before she can go on to the next stage
of her non-being.

Still bound to the world by some invisible umbilical cord, she
travels freely back and forth into the lives of those she left
behind, her cold unloving husband, William, their estranged
daughter Celia, her best friend Veronica and her gentle lover,
Milo. With her new found powers of insight she tries to
understand the past and shape their future.

ISBN 1-84223-099-9

Also published by Poolbeg

A Place for Unicorns

NICOLA LINDSAY

Anna wakes sweating and terrified. Over the past few weeks her dreams have become more vividly alarming – the sense of being lost is so real.

Eight-year-old Anna arrives in Pisa with her mother, the beautiful but selfish Rosalind, for an Italian holiday. While Rosalind seems happy and carefree, Anna is homesick for her father David who has been left behind in disgrace. He drinks too much and Rosalind knows he is unfaithful.

Their Italian idyll is shattered by a fatal car crash that leaves Rosalind in a wheelchair and forces their return to England where David must take care of his embittered and angry wife and his unhappy daughter.

Further devastating events bring Anna to the wild but beautiful Ballynacarraig in the west of Ireland to live with her eccentric Aunt Pog.

As she grows into a young woman, Anna continues her search for the love and affection she was so starved of in her youth. Is Anna always to be unlucky in love or can her faith be restored by the handsome Benny?

ISBN 1-84223-100-6

Also published by Poolbeg

Eden Fading
NICOLA LINDSAY

'Rachel reread the five scrawled lines on the back of the postcard. There was no mistake. She was being offered a house in Tuscany for a whole month . . . perhaps life was going to improve after all...'

Beautiful young widow Rachel has been struggling with life since the tragic death of her much-loved husband Simon.

Six months on, she is still troubled by the card left with some simple white flowers by his grave. It read: *'For my brother – from his sister, D.'*

But Simon was an only child.

Perhaps a month in the sun would help her to come to terms with his death and rid her mind of the niggling doubts the card had evoked.

Ensconced in her close friends' beautiful villa, strange happenings disturb the tranquil beauty and begin to unnerve Rachel. As events become more threatening, Rachel begins to rely on the dark and handsome gardener Francesco. She is attracted to him but why is he reluctant to show his passion for her?

In the fading Tuscan summer, Rachel wonders if she has been followed to Italy by someone linked to Simon's death and to a past in which she played no part.

ISBN 1-84223-101-4